D0065086

A SISTER'S SURVIVAL

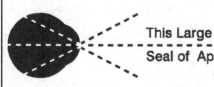

This Large Print Book carries the
Seal of Approval of N.A.V.H.

THE REEVES SISTERS

A SISTER'S SURVIVAL

CYDNEY RAX

THORNDIKE PRESS

A part of Gale, a Cengage Company

Farmington Hills, Mich • San Francisco • New York • Waterville, Maine
Meriden, Conn • Mason, Ohio • Chicago

LIBRARY OF CONGRESS CIP DATA ON FILE.
CATALOGUING IN PUBLICATION FOR THIS BOOK
IS AVAILABLE FROM THE LIBRARY OF CONGRESS

ISBN-13: 978-1-4328-6094-3 (hardcover)

Published in 2019 by arrangement with Dafina Books, an imprint of Kensington Publishing Corp.

Printed in the United States of America
1 2 3 4 5 6 7 23 22 21 20 19

"All I'm trying to do is survive and make good out of the dirty, nasty, unbelievable lifestyle that they gave me."

— Tupac Shakur

"To live is to suffer, to survive is to find some meaning in the suffering."

— Friedrich Nietzsche

CHAPTER 1
SURVIVAL

It was the early part of January. Gamba Okorie and Elyse Reeves were in the parking lot of an AutoZone on the west side of Houston. Elyse was quietly stationed in front of Gamba's Chevy pickup. She peered through the lightly tinted windshield and watched as Gamba pulled on a handle underneath the dashboard. Then he exited his truck and stood beside her.

After months of running into each other while she was working at her sister's restaurant, the two had become close. Gamba had become someone Elyse could rely on as she dealt with the mess of her family.

"Go ahead, Elyse," he said.

"Reach down over here. And when you feel underneath it, you will come across a skinny metal part. Push it to the right, then lift it up. Do it." He patiently waited.

Elyse hesitated but desperately wanted to follow Gamba's precise instructions. However, compared to her petite frame, the steel hood appeared enormous. What if she wasn't strong enough to lift the hood and it slammed on her delicate hand? She knew it would hurt and she'd look like a fool. But she nodded at Gamba and struggled to do as he said. Gamba smiled at her effort and meekly assisted her till the hood was all the way up and secured.

"Great job," he said with an encouraging wink. Elyse's knees felt like a bowl full of jelly.

Twenty-six-year-old Gamba was tall and dark with thick, purplish lips topped by a mustache. His wide nostrils hinted of his Zimbabwean roots, with broad shoulders that swelled with thick muscles that warned his enemies to never ignite his fury.

"Now tell me, Elyse. Do you know what you're looking at?"

She stared at her mentor with lustful eyes. *Do you know how perfect you are,* she asked on the inside. But she pulled herself together and tried her best to appear as if she were deeply interested in an assortment of engine parts.

"Nah," she finally admitted. "Not really."

"No problem," he told her. "I will teach you. I'd be happy to do it."

The second that Gamba began to talk and

point, an erotic sizzle swirled around in Elyse's belly. Elyse simply wanted to close her eyes and fully enjoy listening to the authority and strength that he always conveyed.

"No problem. You won't ever have to worry about that as long as I'm around, but just in case I'm not here, you ought to know these things."

"Mmm hmmm." Elyse would turn twenty years old in April. And up until that point, she hadn't experienced a romantic relationship with a man. She'd never known how it felt to make love. She'd only known brutality and coldness. Sex that was never consensual. She remembered how horrible it felt to be violated by Nathaniel Taylor, her older sister Burgundy's husband. The abusive experience she endured at the hands of Nate nearly caused her to lose her mind.

She stared at Gamba, hoping that if they ever got together, he'd be different from her brother-in-law — prayed that he'd never hurt her.

When Elyse realized that Gamba could quiz her at any moment, she tried her best to concentrate.

"This, Elyse, is where the transmission fluid is kept. And that's the receptacle for your windshield wiper fluid."

Gamba reached inside and grabbed a yellow plastic handle.

He removed the dipstick, glanced at the tip, then thrust it back inside of the long tube. "This, Elyse, is very important. The best type of engine is a well-oiled one. And you must learn to check and see how much oil is remaining, for you never want it to run out."

"Why not?" she politely asked, silently wishing she had a fan with which to cool herself off.

"Good question. The oil is a lubricant, and all the parts need it to keep the engine functioning and moving. It's like humans needing oxygen to breathe or else we will die."

Elyse felt her mind wandering again, and she nearly let out a moan until she realized what she'd been doing. Her cheeks flamed red, and she felt ashamed. Would her emotions for a man ever be normal? Could she ever enjoy a true relationship?

She and Gamba had been hanging out since last December when he decided to take her under his wing. He'd never shown any romantic interest. She figured it was because she used to act and look too much like a tomboy with her long-sleeved shirts, golf hats, and baggy slacks that covered her figure. These days she wore shirts that clung to her breasts, paired with hip-hugging jeans, and occasionally she'd throw on some booty shorts or a dress.

But even with the cute little outfits, it seemed as if Gamba barely noticed.

What if she was wasting her time? What if she had no real future with this man or any other man?

"And so, if the oil runs out," Gamba went on to say, "the engine will start to grind. It will make loud, screeching noises then, God forbid, it will lock completely up. Basically, the parts grind together, engine gets over-heated, and the car parts get hotter and hotter."

Feeling overheated herself, Elyse waved her fingers across her face and enjoyed the little bit of cool air. She hoped Gamba didn't think she was weird, like everyone else — people, especially her family, thought she was an oddball, awkward young woman.

But Gamba was deep into his lecture, not aware of how Elyse fanned herself and the cute way she licked her bottom lip.

"Elyse, I'm going to teach you how to change your own oil. You understand?"

"Yeah," she firmly told him. "I understand."

"And by the time we're done, you will

know how to change your own tire."

Her brown eyes widened in distress. At nearly seventy-four inches, Gamba's pickup stood much taller than Elyse, who was only five feet one.

The tires were so huge it seemed like they could easily crush her to pieces. She was thin and willowy and hadn't been active in a gymnasium since she'd graduated from high school.

She glanced at her bony arms. "You see this?"

"Yeah." He nodded. "So?"

"I'm not strong enough."

"Shhhh," he told her and pressed his finger against her soft lips. As his finger lingered for a moment Elyse tried to keep herself from whipping out her tongue. She wanted to suck his finger, suck on other parts of Gamba's sexy body. But she told herself that he wasn't thinking about her, her lips, or her shameful lust. He saw her like a sister, nothing like a lover. And Elyse hated that all Gamba wanted to do with her was to teach how to change a damned tire.

"Gamba," she said, her voice quivering with anger. "No! I can't do this."

"You, young lady, are much stronger than you realize. I believe that."

"But I just don't think I can —"

"Have you tried, Elyse? Have you?"

She stared once more at the gigantic truck that towered above her. It looked like it could kill her without even trying. Elyse shivered and whined. "Gamba, me? Change a tire? I-I can't do that. I just can't."

"Yes, you can, sweetheart. Don't be scared of anything that looks too hard, Elyse."

"Don't be scared?" she asked.

"Right, never be scared of anything or anybody because you —"

"But, Gamba," she said in a rare interruption, "my sista Alita told me . . . She said if someone wants me to do something . . . and they say, 'Don't be scared,' then that's a bad man. He's trying to do a bad thing. He's lying his ass off and he can't be trusted."

"And you believe everything your man-hating sister tells you?"

She nodded. She could agree that Alita did have nasty opinions about most men, but what if it was the truth? At that moment, Gamba seemed anti-Alita. And to Elyse's ears it sounded like he doubted her just because she trusted in the one family member who had cared enough to rescue her.

"I'm not trying to be disrespectful," he gently replied. "But what if your sister is wrong? Because instead of thinking negative, what if you throw away all that fear and end up doing great things . . . things you never dreamed you could do?"

"I-I dunno. I have to ask my sista about it first, then I'll let you know what she says."

Even though he was tempted to, Gamba could not be genuinely upset at Elyse. Nor could he blame her paranoid, overprotective sister. All he could do was gain her trust by assuring her that he understood.

"Your brother-in-law, Nate . . . well, yeah. *He* is a bad man. He wanted you to do bad things. He should be in jail, but that's another story altogether. But this right here . . . learning how to drive defensively, being able to do simple car maintenance, it's not wrong. And I'm not, either. I just don't want you to be afraid, and that in itself doesn't make me the bad guy. You get it?"

He took a moment, wanting to explain things in a way that would make her feel safe.

"Elyse, what if you're out on the road driving. And I'm with you but I'm tired as hell and I couldn't help but doze off." He laughed to himself. "That's what happens to a hardworking man sometimes," he said. "We hardly ever get enough sleep. So anyway, you and I are in my truck and you're behind the wheel, and we happen to drive on a road where some stupid person left some nails in the street. And you drive over the nails and we get a flat. What would you do?"

She thought for a second. "I wake you up."

"Good one, Elyse." He chuckled. "But seriously, sweetheart, everything that I am teaching you will empower you. I'm only here to help."

Elyse hated when he said that he was "only here to help." At the same time, she felt ashamed for being ungrateful to someone who begged her to believe in herself. But in Elyse's world, trust was a slow-moving golf cart, not an Aston Martin.

When she failed to reply, Gamba proceeded to tell her the exact type of oil that the engine required, how much the tires needed to be inflated, and used a portable air compressor to show her the proper way to pump air into them.

"Got it?" he asked when he was done demonstrating.

"Yeah," she lied. "I got it." He'd been instructing her for a good thirty minutes. At this point, information overload made her feel dizzy with exhaustion.

In observing the stressed look on her

tender face, Gamba was concerned. He never wanted to overwhelm her. But he was on a strict mission to give her the strength that she would need to make it in this cold, cruel world.

"Don't be upset, Elyse," Gamba gently told her. "You're doing fine, really well so far. I believe in you, and I know that you'll be able to handle everything that I teach you."

"But why teach me?"

"What do you mean?"

"I lived with my sista Burgundy for a long time. You've taught me more in weeks . . . than she taught me in years. She let her husband do me wrong. She's a bad sista, a terrible woman."

Elyse's heartfelt confession made Gamba feel sad for her, yet he remained unfazed. "I don't know the answer to why your sister neglected to school you on the things that a woman should know. Maybe she had her own issues that she was dealing with. But all I can say right now, Elyse, is that you act like a wallflower, but you are a rose. A dozen roses. So, hold your head up high. I want you to forget about the people that hurt you."

At his positive words, Elyse felt her chin and head lift. And she slowly forced herself to trust in Gamba and in herself. At least for today.

In that wonderful way of his, Gamba continued speaking calmly yet firmly to her. She fought hard not to stare into his dark eyes; she wanted to compose herself whenever he smiled, for it was true that each time Gamba broke out into that wonderful laugh of his, Elyse wanted to laugh, and melt, and throw herself in the safety net of his arms.

Even if the topic bored her to death, right then Elyse decided she could listen to him talk all night. He seemed so strong and self-assured.

After another five minutes, Gamba wrapped up his lecture then slammed the hood of the truck.

"Come on, let's go," he said to her. He reached for his keys while she jogged to the passenger side so she could climb in the seat, sit back, and allow her mind to rest after harboring many sexy thoughts. Before she could get in, Gamba stopped her.

"No, don't sit there. Elyse, I think you're ready. You can drive."

"No, Gamba," she complained. "I don't like big trucks."

"I know you don't. But it's only because you're scared. You don't have to be."

She shook her head in defiance.

"Even though you don't feel comfortable, Elyse, do me a big favor and try anyway. Just get in. We can go down this block till we reach the corner; we can drive a few miles on the next street, then turn around and come back. Easy!"

"Gamba!" She folded her arms across her chest and stood firm.

He smiled at Elyse until she couldn't help but smile back. When he tossed the keys at her, she ran around to the driver's side and got in.

She'd do anything to please him. Gamba had been so tender with her, had expressed such confidence in her, that it would not hurt her to try and make him feel happy for a change.

Expelling a deep breath, Elyse adjusted the seat and mirrors, started the ignition, then they chugged along.

"Relax," he instructed her. "You're gripping that wheel and driving like you're eighty."

She laughed and sat back. It felt odd to be up so high above the ground. But thankfully it was an easy Sunday afternoon, and the streets were not very busy.

"Okay, I think you can go a little faster," Gamba encouraged her. "We're leaving this residential street and we're turning onto a main street. Do like thirty-five to forty-five miles an hour."

"Ohh," she said with a shudder. She could see there were a few more cars now zipping along up and down the road.

"I-I'm scared," she finally admitted.

"Nothing's going to happen, Elyse. When will you believe that I got you?"

"You got me?"

"I'm here for you."

Elyse nodded. "Okay," she whispered. And she pressed her foot on the accelerator. The truck lurched forward hard enough to jostle them in their seats.

"Oh uh," Gamba said. "That's too much gas. Just give it a little bit of a push. Do it again."

Before she could respond, a late-model luxury car swerved into the truck's path. Alarmed, Elyse slammed hard on the brakes. She and Gamba jerked forward. The tires screeched. Shocked and afraid, Elyse raised both her hands and placed them over her eyes, but she accidentally lifted her foot off the brakes and hit the accelerator.

The truck sped up, hopped over a high median, and violently rocked several times before landing on the grass. The truck kept moving, rolled down the median, back onto the street and began heading in the wrong direction.

She opened her eyes. "Gamba!" she screamed. A blue SUV narrowly missed them.

Gamba sprang into action. He maneuvered his body against Elyse and grabbed the wheel. He forced the truck to swerve. They almost hit another oncoming car; Gamba slowed the truck down. It scraped against a utility pole and came to a stop.

Elyse screamed then sat stiffly in her seat.

"You all right?" Gamba asked, more worried about her than the truck.

She nodded.

Just then the driver's side door got yanked open.

Elyse stared into the eyes of her brother-in-law. The harsh expression on Nathaniel Taylor's face said it all.

"What are you doing, Elyse?" he asked. "Why are you driving this truck? Why haven't you reported to work this past week?" Nate and Burgundy owned Morning Glory, the restaurant where Elyse was employed.

"Did you lie to us again by calling in sick when you are out here messing around with this man? Answer me, Elyse!"

The accusations flew out of Nate Taylor's mouth. Suddenly Elyse felt like a piece of

20

property, a runaway slave being confronted by her master. She shrank back.

Gamba rounded the truck and was now facing Nathaniel. Elyse slowly got out of the truck and watched.

"What were you trying to do back there?" Gamba asked Nate. "You intentionally tried to run us off the road! Why do that, man? You crazy?"

"I wasn't talking to you. I'm talking to my family." He turned to Elyse once more. "Did you hear what I asked you? Did you make up a lie about being sick just so you can hang out with some man you just met off the street?"

"You don't know who or what I am," Gamba said.

"I know exactly who you are," Nate told him. "You're just one of my customers. But I'm her kin. Plus, I'm her boss. I have a right to ask her anything I want."

"You shouldn't even be within a hundred feet of Elyse, you spineless piece of shit," Gamba told Nate.

"What did you say to me? I will wipe the floor with your ass."

Gamba's voice was steely. "I wish you would lay a hand on me or her."

The tension grew so thick that Elyse prayed to be invisible. She couldn't believe

21

that two grown men were fighting over her.

When Gamba drew back his fist and aimed it at Nate's jaw, she grabbed his arm and yanked.

"No, Gamba, don't. Please!" she cried out.

Gamba lowered his hand. Though he longed to rip the skin off of Nate, he knew he could not lose it in front of the woman who'd just begun to trust him.

"All right," Gamba said backing off. "You're her boss. Fine. All I can say is, she'll return to work when she's ready."

"And who are you to be answering for Elyse? You her man?"

Gamba wanted to say yes. Elyse wanted him to say it too.

"I'm *a* man, that's what I am. And way more of a man that you could ever be," Gamba replied. "So get back in your car and go on about your business. She's with me right now." He gently wrapped his arm around her shoulder.

"You don't belong, young thug," Nate said as he watched them. "You are permanently banned from my restaurant, and you need to stay out of my family's business."

"Man, don't use the family card. If you really cared about *family,* you wouldn't have done what you did. You sick fuck!"

"W-what," Nate sputtered. "Who told you

22

that? What did they say I did?"

"You know exactly what you did. Sick-ass old man."

Elyse felt comforted by Gamba's hug, but at the same time she envisioned Nate's cold, hard fingers probing every part of her body . . . She remembered how he'd masturbate in front of her and then smile as he watched her reaction . . . She could not forget the wild, distant look in his eyes as her tried to coerce her to have sex with him.

As the two men continued to argue, Elyse noticed that the car keys were in the ignition. The engine was still running.

Elyse broke away from Gamba and got back in the truck. She shifted the gear to reverse.

Gamba looked up, startled. "Elyse, don't," he said and ran toward the truck. She ignored him and put the gear shift in drive.

All she could remember was Nate's awful penis being shoved inside her. His cold, hard lips pressing clumsily against her mouth, forcing her to kiss him until she wanted to throw up. His gazing at her body like he owned it and she was nothing but a piece of meat.

Elyse pressed her foot against the accelerator.

Nate's eyes widened in horror. The truck

moved steadily toward him. Nate yelled, but Gamba jumped at the man, crashing against his body and pushing him out of the way. Gamba fell on top of Nate, who covered his head with both of his hands.

They lay against each other for a few seconds breathing wildly.

Gamba got up and pulled Nate to his feet. He saw to it that Nate was all right and made him vow not to make any more trouble with Elyse.

"Leave her alone, you hear me, man? You understand?"

Nate only nodded, thinking about what would have happened if he'd gotten hit by the truck. He had come very close to losing his life, and he never wanted that to happen again.

"She can take all the time she needs to get herself together. I know she goes to a psychotherapist," he told Gamba. "She's a sick girl and needs help, all the help she can get."

Gamba decided to let that remark slide.

Soon Gamba returned to his truck, opened the door, and reached in to grab Elyse. She reeled back, afraid that he was about to hit her. But he simply hugged her tight.

"It's okay, Elyse. He'll never bother you again."

"You sure?"

"I'm positive."

She looked past his head and noticed that Nate had driven off. It felt like a miracle to witness a man as tall and as noticeable as her brother-in-law grow smaller and tinier until she could no longer see him. Yet a nagging feeling told her Gamba was wrong, and Nate would be back.

Right then it felt like the horrible things that had happened to her would continue, as if bad times couldn't help themselves and she was powerless to stop them.

"Gamba, I don't know about this. I don't know if I can make it."

"Look at me. Look me straight in my eyes, Elyse."

She did.

"You're young but you've been through a lot."

"Yeah."

"And I have too."

Her timid ways reminded him of when he was overseas, fighting a war that he did not start but one that American troops were expected to finish.

And coming across this vulnerable woman transported Gamba Okorie right back to the war zone. He remembered the dangers of combat, the uncertainty of whether or not he'd live to see another day. Was he going to kill someone or was someone going to kill him? He had barely trusted anyone, and that helped him to understand the young woman.

He opened his mouth, took a big gamble, and told her, "We all have been through a lot. But we're as strong as the things we have survived. You and I have much in common. We've had our troubles but what's more important is that we overcome them. And if our people survived being stolen from their own turf, being shackled to the bottom of a sea liner and living among their own feces, if they can survive being sold to a white man for less than the cost of a horse. Survive being stripped of their clothes and beaten till their skin cracked open and blood seeped from their swollen backs. If our ancestors were denied the right to read, got obstructed from attending school and getting an education, to one day earning a doctorate degree. If people can make it after being kicked to the ground, sprayed with a water hose, called a stupid nigger and treated inhumanely, to one day being sworn in as the president of the United States and the leader of the free world . . . you and me, both of us, any one of us, have every-thing it takes to rise up and make it in this evil, fucked-up world."

Gamba's words caused hope to surge inside of Elyse's heart and soul; this vision of what survival looked like. What survival could become.

CHAPTER 2
LICENSE TO MARRY

Gamba and Elyse traded places. Now he was driving them away from the boulevard. The more they drove, the more she wished to distance herself from Nate, from the near car wreck, from everything. But it was tough. The day had been quite overwhelming. When she thought about how she could have actually mowed down her brother-in-law with a big truck, run over him the way a stream roller is used to level a crooked surface, Elyse slouched back in defeat. She dabbed at her eyes with the backs of her hands. She craved peace, normality, and refuge from her disastrous world.

"Elyse, you all right?" Gamba asked. "Why are you crying?"

"I'm not crying," she claimed. She quickly patted her tears dry. Feeling self-conscious, Elyse coughed and cleared her throat. "Nate was right. I think I may be sick. I'm coming down with a cold or something," she lied as she sat stiffly in her seat.

"Elyse, we need a break. I think it's time that we go see your people."

"See them? Like who? No!"

"Definitely not Burgundy. But what if I take you back home?"

"No, Gamba! Not Lita. If she knew Nate followed us, she could get him killed."

"Looks like *you* were the one trying to kill Nate."

"No," she stated, again not wanting to imagine that a murderer could live inside of her. Murderers were bad. "I wasn't trying . . . I-I just can't drive big trucks. Told you dat. You didn't believe me."

Gamba couldn't help but smile. "Yeah, you did try to warn me. I'm sorry I pushed you too hard, Elyse. Just trying to help."

"I know," she replied. "It's all right."

"But what happened back there is a cause for concern," he continued. "We don't want this guy to continue harassing you. And I think Alita would want to know about this," Gamba insisted as they traveled down the road. "In fact, I know she would," he said with a laugh.

"No, no Lita. We can go to my other sister's. Coco's. Let's go there." Elyse promptly gave Gamba orders, telling him where Coco lived.

Gamba secretly watched Elyse from the corner of his eye. She had wiped away her tears. Her jaw was rigid with determination. He liked what he saw, the beginning signs of strength.

Soon they pulled up to the house where Coco lived with her kids Cadee, Chloe, and Chance. She was a big woman with a protruding belly, due to give birth in a couple of months.

"Say what?" Coco said as soon as she opened her front door and saw Gamba with Elyse. "Y'all two been thick as thieves for a minute now. What's up with that?"

"Nothing." Elyse was tight-lipped.

"Oh, don't give me that. The family ain't seen you hang out with a man like this in what? The fifth of never."

"Well, you better be glad she's hanging with this man," Gamba said and pointed to himself as they all stood outside the house. "Because that other man that we got her away from is steadily trying to provoke her."

Coco eyed him warily. "Who you talkin' 'bout?"

"Who else?" Gamba asked.

Coco frowned in distaste. "My brother-in-law is such a fool. Horny ass . . . that man is married. Why's he hounding Elyse? She don't want him, do you, Sis?"

Elyse looked appalled. "You ask me that? Really?"

"Yes, really. No one in their right mind would want a man like him. But Burgundy lets all his coins blind her. She knows he's up to no good, and she still ain't filed on him. I know you can't stand her ass either, right? If you still have love for that woman, you're out your mind too. Hell to the naw, naw."

At that, Coco waddled away with one hand lodged against her hip. She was a sassy, beautiful woman. At nearly twenty-nine years old, her main goal in life was to keep tabs on her baby daddy, Calhoun Humphries.

"Y'all come on in before Nate does a drive-by and finds you at my spot. I'm not trying to deal with his drama 'cause Lord knows I got enough of my own right now. I'm about to drop my last baby, and after that it's a wrap. No more scallywags for Coco!"

Gamba and Elyse entered the dining room and were met by the strong aroma of food sitting in pots on the stovetop. Coco's house shoes slapped against the tile floor as she walked.

"I cooked if y'all want something to eat. Pork ribs smothered in my own barbecue sauce, mustards and turnips with ham hocks, mac and cheese, fried corn, and a bowl of fresh salad is in the fridge. Anyway, wash your hands first. I don't play that nasty hands shit. You smell like old motor oil, both you and Elyse. What kind of freaky shit y'all be into?"

Gamba grinned at her in appreciation. "You got jokes, huh? How about you, Elyse? You want me to fix you a plate? Coco, let me tell you, we're tired and hungry. Been through a lot this afternoon."

Gamba washed his hands and had Elyse do the same. Then he prepared Elyse a plate and fixed one for himself. Everyone sat together at the dining room table while Gamba filled Coco in on the recent drama with Nate.

"And now," Gamba said, "things are popping off to the point of being seriously dangerous."

"He's lost his damn mind," Coco said with a frown. "He shouldn't have to know every time my sister punches in or out at Morning Glory."

"I think Elyse should quit her job," Gamba concluded.

"Oh, you don't have to worry about Nate trying anything at his restaurant. Burgundy and her hubby try to act like they're aristocrats, but they really just some damned scammers. They're not stupid enough to do anything to mess up their two-bit hustles."

"I don't like him," Elyse muttered as she ate. "He scares me."

"As long as you're with me, you'll be safe," Gamba assured her. "But if *I* run, *you* run."

Coco laughed aloud, happy that Gamba was concerned enough about Elyse to protect her. Lord knows she did not have time to run behind her baby sister.

"Elyse, don't be scared of him. You don't need to run from anybody," she replied. "Knowing Nate, that man is all talk."

"Can *you* guarantee your sister's safety, though?" Gamba asked.

"I sure can. Nate's a whack job but he ain't a total crackpot. The most he can get away with is lusting after my baby sis like the perv he is." She paused. "Did he ever expose himself to you? Whip out his dick like it was a prize?"

Elyse stared quizzically at Coco.

"I'm just saying, that's what men like him do. Get their kicks off the fact that they got money and a penis. Or muscles and testosterone. I call it MPT. Muscles, penis, and testosterone. And he's the type of man who thinks he can rule women just because he's got all that."

"That's it," Gamba said in anger. "She shouldn't be subjected to that type of behavior. She should quit on him with no advance notice."

"But see, like I said before, you don't have to worry about any of that. My sister Alita always has her eye on Nate. She'll pop in that restaurant every chance she gets when she knows Elyse is working. On top of that, from what I heard, Burgundy never lets Elyse work at Morning Glory when she's not there."

Gamba eyed her wearily. "Burgundy! The one that knows what's happening but hasn't done much about it?"

"Yep, that's B. I don't know what she sees in him. But like I said before, Burgundy acts sophisticated, but she's a fool like the rest of us. We are a family of fools, except for Dru," Coco said with a warm chuckle. "Any other woman would have left Nate's dirty ass by now."

"You talking?" Elyse said, finally interrupting. "Way you put up with Calhoun but you still with him?"

Her clapping back like that was such a rare occurrence that Coco couldn't help but be shocked.

"Lord, have mercy. Good one, Elyse. I see

34

this Gamba got you all gassed up. *You* cracking on *me*? This is a side of you I ain't never seen before. Hell, you need to pop off at Alita when she gives you all kinds of hell over nothing. Keep me and my man out your mouth. We doing just fine."

Elyse shrugged as if Coco's business with Calhoun really did not concern her.

"So, if you two are doing that well," Gamba said as he wolfed down his food. "Does that mean we're about to get a wedding invite?" Alita had told him all the family business, including how stuck Coco was on Calhoun.

"I dunno," Coco replied. "Maybe you ought to see Calhoun about that. Because I sure as hell won't be asking no man to marry me." She paused. "Plus I've asked him a dozen times already." Coco gave a boisterous laugh in spite of herself. She rose up from the table and waddled over to check on a cake she'd been baking.

Right then seven-year-old Cadee and four-year-old Chloe raced into the room. Chance, who was two and a half, stumbled in behind them. Cadee and Chloe were Calhoun's kids, but Chance was her "in-between" baby whom she gave birth to during a brief breakup. She never wanted anyone to know the identity of Chance's biological father.

"Sit your little asses down," Coco yelled at the kids. Her children were adorable, but a handful. Chance refused to take his seat, and Coco ended up chasing behind her son, who enjoyed running in circles till his mom was out of breath.

"You better listen to you mama."

"No," Chance yelled and ran some more. Then he came to an abrupt stop. He wobbled around on his feet then slumped to the floor. His eyes rolled to the back of his head.

"Stop playing and get up, boy. I'm not in the mood for your silliness."

But Chance just lay there; his skin looked ashy and yellowish like he hadn't washed up in a good while. "Why you look all pale? I know I gave you a bath last night and you this filthy already?"

Gamba set down his fork and went to see about Chance. Within seconds the little boy seemed to recover. Gamba asked Elyse to bring Coco's son a glass of water. He stayed next to Chance and watched him drink until he knew he felt better.

"You'll be all right, little man. Hang in there," Gamba said.

Watching Gamba with Chance, Coco thought about the words she'd spoken to her son. She had recently been reprimanded by her sister Dru, who told her she needed to stop yelling at her kids so much. Dru told her that children were a gift from above and that she needed to shower them with love, not annoyance.

Feeling guilty, Coco stared at all of her kids then opened her arms wide. The girls raced into her bosom. But when Chance stood up, instead of running to his mother, he tried to climb in Elyse's lap.

Forgetting just that quickly, Coco snapped at him. "Leave her alone, little man. She's tired and don't want you hanging off her like that. She ain't like me. She's free and single."

"You single too," Elyse said. "Just like me."

"No ma'am, Pam," Coco disagreed in a huff. "We may be sisters, but I'm nothing like you. I'll bet my life on that."

Coco then turned around and continued offering her kids some much-needed love and attention. She generously gave to others what she hungered for herself.

January came and went. And now it was several days before Valentine's Day. Calhoun Humphries took his time getting home to Coco's that Friday night.

Coco was waiting for her man the second he walked through the front door.

He said hello to her then proceeded to the kitchen.

When he looked around, he saw the gas stovetop bore no pots or skillets. No pilot lights were on. Calhoun frowned and peeped through the window of the oven. Seeing nothing, he dramatically sniffed the air as he gave Coco a hardened look.

"What?" she snapped at him. "You trying to tell me something?"

"What the fuck, Ma," he said. "You know I've been working hard all day —"

"Like hell I do! I don't know what you been doing, Calhoun."

"Don't even try it. I texted you a copy of my schedule this morning. You know I had to do fifteen deliveries today. Do you understand how long it takes to go back and forth all across town driving my truck and dealing with this Houston traffic just so I can get these sodas to these grocery stores?"

"Poor baby. If your job is that hard, then quit."

"What?"

"You don't need to be working there anyway," she said in a soothing voice. "Instead of risking your life driving on these dangerous roads, you can just stay home with me and the kids."

"Yep, you're a fool." He sighed. Sometimes he felt like Coco did not know him well. Calhoun was young, just in his mid-twenties. He had a lot of male friends who had bagged sugar mamas who gladly offered to foot all the bills. These women would buy the men clothes, let them drive around in their cars, they'd pay for it all. But Calhoun wasn't that type of guy. He had big plans and even bigger dreams.

"Babe," Coco reminded him, "I get Social Security checks."

"That little bit of pocket change ain't enough to take care of three kids plus another one that's on the way." Just the thought of him having all these kids at such a young age made the veins in his head pulsate.

"I know that the kids and lack of money must be stressing you out." She squirmed. "But maybe I can get my sister Burgundy to start paying me under the table. Hell, I've been doing a lot of her errands. Running back and forth to the post office and picking up things for the barbershop. I'm like an employee, and she needs to start paying me instead of telling me 'family first.' That nonsense pays none of my bills."

"You damn right it don't. As much money they got, they ought to be putting you on payroll. But you think they'd be down for that?" Calhoun asked. He knew that Burgundy and Nate Taylor were well off and always acted like candidates for a *Black Enterprise* feature. But Calhoun also knew how much of a tightwad Nate could be. Calhoun hated rich people who had clenched fists. Why have all that money if it wasn't going to be spent?

"I swear to God, if I had money like your people, I'd be balling out big time." Calhoun's eyes glistened. Luckily, he'd had a tiny taste of how it felt to have money due to his winning cash from a couple of lottery tickets.

Ever since then, he'd been hooked. And Calhoun wanted more.

"All I know is I'm sick of working hard like a dog and barely making any funds, Ma," he complained. "Seems like I work just to take care of the kids."

"Well, what else is there?" she asked.

"I'm not complaining," he replied, not wanting her to grow suspicious. "I love the kids to death, but I also gotta have a life."

"What you mean by that, Calhoun?"

"Nothing." He shook his head. "Nothing." He sighed. "Looks like I got to go out and spend some money again for some dinner since you didn't love me enough to cook for me. I don't get why you been neglecting

40

your man. That ain't like you, Ma." Calhoun made a quick move toward the front door.

"Wait a second, hold up," Coco pleaded as she tried to reach him before he left. "I'm down for you, baby, you know I am."

"Then what's the problem?"

She pointed at her belly. "This pregnancy is wearing me out!"

"No one told you to have that child."

"*What?* I don't believe you said that. How could you say that, Calhoun? We're talking about your seed." She rubbed her round belly and talked to her unborn child. "Your daddy did not mean that at all. He's just stressed. We all are, but we do love you, baby."

Instantly Calhoun felt foolish and had a change of heart. He extended hands in apology, and he hugged her. "Damn. If you had a gun and wanted to shoot my ass, I would not blame you one bit. I'm sorry for saying what I said. You forgive me, Ma?"

"You know I do."

Relieved, he kissed Coco's forehead. She let him. Then her pouty lips found his mouth, and she forced him to kiss her as she sucked his tongue. God, why did she have to be so in love with this man? They were like most other couples. Some days it seemed they just weren't working, and noth-

41

ing fit together. Other times, when he held a nice after-work drink in his hand and had a decent meal in his belly, he'd be gentle, peaceful, and kind, just the way she wanted him to be.

As Coco released Calhoun from her lips, she could not help herself.

"I think," she whispered, "the only way to make this thing work the way love is supposed to work is to make things —"

He stiffened. She felt it.

"Why you freeze up?" she asked.

"Ma, don't flip. I'm tired."

"I'm tired too. And the way to get things right, to get my mind in a better, normal state is to just go on down to the courthouse."

He said nothing. But she couldn't stop talking. "See, baby, you know that there ain't no other man in this world for me." She felt her heart beat wildly against her chest.

"Is that right?"

"Shut up, fool. I ain't checking for no man but you, and you know it. Crazy as it sounds. Plus, we ain't getting any younger. And if we can just put on our grown-up drawers, and go get that marriage certificate —"

"A piece of paper? Really, Coco? What

good will that do?"

"Huh? You got something against marriage?"

"Nah, Ma."

"Then what?"

"Why you been hounding me about becoming a wife?"

"See, it's like this. I've been talking and
telling you what I want for what, two years
now? Talk is cheap. And I don't want to give
you no ultimatum. But I will get you to take
us to the county clerk's office, and we could
take that first step. Because real couples
don't just talk about it. Real couples that's
real, they be about it."

He nodded, eyes glazed. "Go on."

Excited, Coco continued. "And see, all
you gotta do is bring them that seventy-two
dollars. Bring your driver's license. You
don't have to have a witness or anything
like that. It would be just us. I could get
Dru to watch the kids. It won't even take
that long either if we go first thing in the
morning. And we can just get that paperwork out the way, you see what I'm saying?"

"Hmmm."

"We're already together all the time when
you're not working or in the streets. Plus I
love you and I know you love me or you
wouldn't be sticking around this long."

"Hmmm."

"Stop answering with 'hmmm.' Calhoun, tell me what you think?"

"Once we get that license, then what happens?"

"Then," Coco happily explained, "we got ninety days to get married or else it expires."

"How long can you get married after you get the license?"

"Pretty fast. Within three days. So, it could happen quickly, or we could take a little time and wait a few weeks." Just the thought of finally getting hitched made Coco want to shriek with happiness. So far she'd felt her life had been tough. Having kid after kid wasn't easy. She yearned to catch a break, to be in a legitimate marriage and not just be a baby mama.

"Calhoun, baby, if you can just do that one little thing for me. Go on down to the county clerk's office with me, that way I'll know you mean business."

"I see," he told her.

" 'I see'? Is that all you got to say?" He did not respond. "Why you so quiet, Calhoun? What you thinking about?"

"Nothing."

"Yeah, right, Calhoun. I know you."

"If you really knew me, Ma, you would never have to ask that question."

Coco heard what her man said, but why didn't her heart agree with his words? She secretly and sometimes openly envied Alita. The girl was a man hater, but at least she knew how it felt to have been married at one time. And then there was Burgundy! Coco was tired of watching other women live their married lives.

Although one time Alita had warned her that things changed once a couple gets married.

"How so?" she asked.

"The fighting gets more brutal, even violent," Alita had said. "So, you better think long and hard about if you believe you two can make it for the long haul. 'Cause if you decide you don't want him anymore and try to leave him, he may try to kill you. And the kids. Don't think it hasn't happened. Look at the news."

Coco knew she could not argue, and it gave her something serious to consider.

"Yeah, Sis, take it from me, once shit gets legal there is more at stake, more to lose. Just thinking about that makes some people act the fool. 'Cause in the game of love, it's all about winning. Nobody likes losing, Coco."

Even if everything that Alita claimed were true, Coco prayed that her situation would turn out different.

"Baby," she finally replied to Calhoun after thinking things through, "we've been tight for so long, had a few ups and downs, but we still got back together. So I want to think that I *do* know you pretty well."

"Okay then, if you know me like you think you do, then you know I ain't about you staying on my ass like a fucking pit bull. Got enough pressure as it is."

"I know, baby. I know. I can't forget that you're under tons of stress because of your job and maybe even due to the kids. I can be a better woman to you when it comes to that. I honestly don't want to add to your problems."

"Then why do it?"

She was silent. The truth was too much of an embarrassment. Could there ever be such a thing as loving someone too much?

"Are you gone answer me, Ma?"

"That's just me. When I get stressed you gone be stressed too. I share my shit. You know how I do." She shrugged as if that small gesture would explain her feelings.

"Whatever you do, it always makes things worse, so just stop it, all right?" Calhoun's voice cracked, a rare thing coming from him.

When he got like this, Coco's first instinct

was to correct the issue and smooth things over. She was tempted to say more, but she was afraid. She knew she had to play her cards right. She had to handle this "love" thing with utmost care because she couldn't imagine facing the world alone.

Coco knew that to have her man's kids, but not have him, would truly devastate her.

CHAPTER 3
LOVE HURTS

By the time Valentine's Day arrived, even though it was cloudy and overcast outside, Coco was jovial and more cheerful. Calhoun had surprised her three days earlier when he let her drive him to the county clerk's office. They signed up for a marriage license, and he slid a modest ring on her finger. Ever since then she'd been singing around the house and treating her kids with love and patience.

And now it was early evening on the most romantic holiday of the year.

Coco was home speaking with Calhoun on the phone.

"So, what's the latest about our dinner date?" she asked.

"Say, Ma, I gotta work overtime. But I promise to take you out tomorrow."

"Tomorrow? The day after Valentine's Day is side chick day. I am *not* a side chick."

"Look, plenty of good men can't take their

women out on the actual holiday. So be a sweet woman and wait till tomorrow, Ma."

"I want to eat out today. What time you think you'll be getting off?"

"Uh," he hedged. "Ain't no telling. Because of the bad weather we got way backed up. We kind of busy. I gotta go." He made kissing noises, which made Coco feel only slightly better. She hung up the phone, a mournful look etched on her face.

"Oh, well. I guess this is what I signed up for when I said I wanted to be with a truck driver. Better get used to it," Coco told herself.

She gathered Chloe, Cadee, and Chance, and they all assisted her with baking a few dozen cupcakes topped with white icing and red hearts. But an hour and a half later, once they had finished decorating the dessert, Coco received a phone call.

"Hey, Lita," she answered as she took a tiny bite from a cupcake.

"You sound like you eating again, huh?" Alita said.

"Yep, I am. But what you want? Aren't you out with your boo?" Alita was still dating Shade Wilkins, a churchgoing man whom she'd met last year. Coco was surprised her sister hadn't scared the guy off.

"Yeah, um, we are together at a restaurant.

I'm sitting here watching all the other couples in love."

"Must be nice."

"Humph! I wouldn't say all that."

"What you mean by that, Lita? Which restaurant are you at?"

"First of all, you sitting down?"

"No, I'm not. Now answer the question. What restaurant are y'all at?"

"The same one that Calhoun Humphries is at. And he is with another woman. And no, it's not his mama or his sister."

"What you say?"

Alita proceeded to give Coco the address of the restaurant where she and Shade had been posted up during the past hour. The joint was super crowded with all sorts of couples scattered throughout the place.

"Yeah, Sis," Alita continued. "He's looking mighty comfy too. Like he is booed the hell up."

"What the fuck?" Coco began to gather her children and her purse and scooped up her car keys. "What is he doing exactly?"

"Chile, I don't even wanna tell you, you being pregnant and all. I don't want you to be upset and affect the baby." Alita paused. "But whatever, you need to come up here and see this clown for yourself. I need to prove it to you that you never should have messed around with Calhoun the Loser. In fact, I feel like going over there and —"

"No, Lita. Don't. Let me handle this." Coco racked her brain trying to find a good excuse for why her man would be out in public on Valentine's Day with another woman. "For all we know it's his cousin. You know he comes from a big family."

"Nah, Sis."

"Or it might just be a coworker."

"Really? Mmm hmm. Coco, you're a big fool. Don't be so blind and stupid over a man. You better than this."

"I know I am, Lita. I don't want to be anybody's fool. But I have to consider the source. You hate my man first of all, and nothing he does will ever be right or look right in your opinion."

"Well, you need to see what I'm seeing, and then we can talk! Bye-bye, dumbass."

"Wait, don't hang up," she pleaded. "I want you to stay on the phone."

Coco got settled in the car and pressed her foot all the way on the gas pedal. It seemed like every light was turning red by the time she got to them. She imagined all kinds of scenarios for Calhoun's dilemma.

At one point, she even told Alita to hold on while she dialed Calhoun, but the call when straight into voice mail.

The closer she got to the restaurant, the worse she felt. Her voice trembled. "Lita, I don't know if I want to see this. I mean, I do, yet I don't."

"Why not, Sis? You need to see his lying, no-good ass with your own two eyes."

"How could he do this to me? He told me he had to work."

"He working all right. Working hard to make another bitch happy."

"But, Lita, how is it that Calhoun can't see you . . . or hear you?"

"Because I have on some of those biker glasses with the rearview mirror on them."

"No, you do not. Girl, are you crazy?"

"Look, check this out. Shade and I made it to the restaurant and got us a booth, right? And we got seated, and were sipping on our drinks, having a good time laughing and talking."

"I don't want to hear all, Lita. Get to the point!"

"Okay. So, Shade, you know he loves to ride motorcycles, and so he showed me these new biker glasses he got, and I asked if I could try them on. He said okay. So, I put them on and I stand up and try to test them. And I look in the rearview glasses, and that's when I saw your man. I could not believe what I was seeing. And I was

52

like, 'Shade, you sure these things working right because I see my sister's boyfriend with another woman.' "

"I just can't believe this shit. Anyway, I'm pulling up now. I need to find a parking place, though. It's gonna be a minute."

"Okay, do that and come on in and go to the left side of the restaurant. That's where your so-called man is posted," Alita told her.

"When I walk in, am I going to see his face or the back of his head?"

"You will see his face. You know how bitch-ass Negroes do. Always sitting facing the entrance so they can see who's coming in the spot. All right, Sis. I'm about to hang up. I'll be watching."

And moments later, unbeknownst to him, Calhoun's baby mama stood in the middle of an aisle staring at him. The kids stood quietly beside her. It felt like someone had kicked Coco in her belly. The pain was so severe she wanted to cry and scream. Love hurt. And betrayal from a man whom you loved and thought loved you was one of the worst feelings in the world.

Seated across from Calhoun was a woman who looked nothing like Coco. Whereas Coco was big, round, and wore Afro puffs, this woman had a long, thin neck with silky black hair that hung past her shoulders.

Two servers carrying trays filled with food almost collided with Coco; her very pregnant body practically blocked the aisle where she'd been watching her man.

"Excuse me, miss," the hostess finally said as she walked over to Coco. "We only accept reservations here, and if you don't have one, it's going to be a long wait. Plus, your standing here is a major distraction. I'm afraid you're making the other customers nervous."

"Are you fucking kidding me?"

"No, I'm not." The woman was aghast. "In fact, don't even try and wait for a table. We can refuse service to anybody. We honestly won't have any available tables. I suggest that you leave and next time make a reservation."

Coco was furious. She ignored the waitress, who stood there waiting for her to leave. Coco took a few steps forward and continued watching Calhoun smile and converse with the woman whose face and body she could not see.

Coco glanced down at her protruding belly. If she had to do it all over again, she wished she hadn't started getting pregnant and having child after child for an uncommitted man. Why did she have to be so stupid in love?

Calhoun's eyes sparkled, and in the dim lights made for romance, Coco knew that she could not allow her man to freely offer his love to another woman. Especially on Valentine's night.

In Coco's mind, Calhoun was like Trey Songz, the good-looking bad boy that many women wanted, but Coco was the lucky chick that he picked to come up on stage with him.

She craved him . . . the sexy curled lip, the way he threw back his head when he laughed. The swag. Coco wanted him still.

But how?

Right then Calhoun lifted the woman's hands and drew them to his lips. Coco watched Calhoun kiss hands that weren't attached to her own body. Her heart sunk when she saw him continuously smile like he was in love. Coco drew her hand to her heart and clutched invisible pearls that she wished were real.

He leaned across the table and kissed the chick on the lips.

Coco couldn't take it anymore. She was just about to walk over to Calhoun's table. But an armed security officer asked her to leave.

She glanced at his gun and said, "Okay, sir. I'll leave now. Don't want no trouble."

Coco nodded at the officer, glared at the hostess, then walked out with the kids following behind her.

At his table, Calhoun filled his date's glass with wine. Samira Idris was an Eritrean from East Africa and had relocated to Louisiana with her family several years ago.

Calhoun was infatuated with Samira's beauty, elegance, and sophistication. He completely dismissed thoughts of Coco while he was chatting with the woman. But he couldn't forget her for long. He was nervous and needed to break some difficult news to Samira.

He picked up his glass and told her, "To the most beautiful woman in the world." He knew he sounded corny, but unexpectedly falling in love could make a man do things he never thought he'd do.

"Anyway, I wanted to talk to you, Miss Lady, and tell you some of what's been going on with me." He coughed and cleared his throat. "You know I got a girl. I already peeped you on that situation."

"Yes, you did," Samira said in anguish. "And you know how uneasy your situation makes me feel. I don't want to be associated with a man that already has a woman. And I'd never want any woman to do that to me either."

"That's understandable. And that's why we're here," he said. "I know I told you awhile back I would be breaking up with Coco."

Samira stopped herself from outright laughing. She thought that his girlfriend's legal first name sounded so ridiculous and unsophisticated. "Yes, you did."

"And, um, I also wanted to tell you that she went and got a marriage license for us."

Samira's eyes grew dark with concern.

"She did? Why?"

"What you mean?"

"She can't do that without your permission. You two must have made that decision together." Samira felt miserable and sickly. Suddenly she was no longer hungry.

"I'm just saying, my girl . . . I mean, Coco is real pushy when she wanna be."

"A woman can't force a grown man to do anything."

"That's the thing," Calhoun told her. "Sometimes I don't know what I want."

"I see. And if what you're saying is true, then that means you must love her more than you claim that you do."

Samira's assessment made Calhoun feel conflicted. He didn't want to lie to Samira, but he didn't want to tell her the truth either. Yet something had to give.

"That's why I wanted to keep it one hundred with you," he said.

"What?"

"I need to let you know that . . . I owe it to Coco to do right by her."

Samira's facial expression was void of emotion.

"And so I-I will marry her. We have like ninety days to do it."

Samira pushed back from the table and stood up. She quietly grabbed her evening bag and wrapped her shawl around her shoulders.

"Sit down, please."

"Why, Calhoun?" she asked in a quiet, even tone. "So you may further humiliate me? This is like a breakup dinner."

"But you and me, we weren't really together, right?"

That did it. Samira neatly folded the white cloth napkin that had just been covering her lap. She looked beautiful. The multicolored dress she was wearing was an outfit that she'd designed and made herself. In fact, Calhoun had been giving her money since he'd met her, to help her dream of becoming a fashion designer come true.

"I want to thank you, Calhoun, for helping me out all this time and being supportive when you could. It was nice know-

ing you. And good luck on your marriage."

"Samira!"

But she walked away. She tried to keep herself from running as she traveled through the crowded restaurant in a slow manner so as not to bring attention to herself. She did not want anyone to know she'd just been dumped by a guy whom she would have never given a second glance to, but who'd captured her heart nonetheless.

Samira looked down to reach inside her handbag to grab her keys; in doing so she nearly bumped into a pregnant woman who was rushing past her. Three young kids ran behind the lady.

Samira wondered if she'd ever be fortunate enough to have a man who wanted her to mother his children.

Coco finally reached Calhoun's table. She felt relieved that she'd been able to sneak back into the restaurant when the hostess and the security officer became distracted.

Calhoun was draining the last drop of his wine. He looked up and saw his woman and their kids staring at him. Coco glanced around but did not see anyone who resembled Samira.

"Where'd that bitch go?"

"Look, man, we not doing this tonight."

"Did she go to the ladies' room? Y'all sit

59

down and wait for me. Go on and have a seat with your daddy. I'll be right back."

"Coco, don't you make a fool of yourself."

"You think I enjoy this, Calhoun? You think I'm having fun putting you in check and trying to find out who this bitch is that you having dinner with? You make me act like this."

"I don't do —"

"Yeah, you do. A good man would not put me through the shit you been putting me through," Coco said, nearly yelling. At that moment all she could do was question her judgment, her frequent habit of making questionable choices when it came to men. She knew it was true, but she did not know how to fix it.

"Look, Ma, have a seat. Let's talk."

"No, I don't want to talk to you. I want to talk to your side bitch."

"Ain't no side bitch."

Coco left Calhoun alone to go and search the restroom. When she returned to the table with a confused expression on her face, he said to her, "Now will you sit your wild ass down so we can have a grown-up conversation?"

Feeling foolish, she took a seat. "What's really going on, Calhoun?"

"Look, Ma. You were right. There was

someone else here, but she's gone now."

"Her name?"

"Why?"

" 'Cause I have a right to know."

"All right then. Her name is Samira Idris. I had to chuck the deuces with her." Calhoun explained how when he went to Louisiana a few months ago, he'd met a woman in the casino while he was gambling at the slot machines. They kept running into each other that night. Finally, they spoke for a while and exchanged numbers. They stayed in touch; and the more they got to know each other, the more Calhoun caught feelings for her.

"We've hung out as friends here and there. But tonight, the only reason I took her out was to break up with her."

"What the fuck you mean 'break up'? You can't break up with her when you in a relationship already. Are you saying you cheated? Is that why you never came home at a decent hour?"

"No," he admitted. "It never got that far. I didn't even kiss her."

"I don't believe you."

"Believe what you want," he said with a regretful shrug. In reality, Samira never let Calhoun lure her into bed. Not that he hadn't tried. When she rejected him, it only

61

made him want her even more. Samira was different from his other women: calm, well-spoken, nurturing. And that's why he became enchanted with her.

"We never did anything, Ma. I swear to God."

"I saw you kiss her with my own eyes."

"I did it just one time. A goodbye kiss. That's it."

She reached across the table and thumped Calhoun hard across the forehead.

"Lying ass. You think I'm stupid?"

"I know one thing: Unless you willing to get popped too, you better keep your hands to yourself," he warned her.

Coco could feel a couple of diners staring at them. She didn't care. Love hurt. Being crazy in love hurt more. How could he do this to her? And what would happen now that she knew?

Calhoun apologized, which made Coco calm down long enough to keep her kids from feeling anxious. They were all staring at their mother with wide-eyed, frightened looks on their faces. Coco hated to stress out her family. She decided to lower her voice.

"Thank you for the weak apology. But it better be the last time that you do this shit. Making a fool out of me over some side

pussy. I won't put up with it."

"I know, Ma. I know. To finish my story. I told the chick that me and you getting married. And that's what we'll do. We'll do it right after this last baby is born. All right?"

"You serious?" Coco asked.

"Yeah. I'm serious, Ma. I've been thinking about things, and I think it'll be cool to get married. Time for me to grow up and do the right thing. And make you Mrs. Humphries."

It took a while before Coco could firmly grasp what he had told her. And the anger that had been boiling over melted away into calmness. She told him that she hoped that he wasn't jerking her chain. He assured her that he was on the up-and-up.

"You promise to never contact her again?" Coco asked.

"I promise."

"If you mean it, I want you to block her right now."

Calhoun instantly found Samira's info in his address book. He blocked her phone number and texts.

"Now delete all the photos you have of that whore, because I know you got that in your phone too."

Calhoun hesitated, took a deep breath, and began the process of deleting Samira

from his phone and his heart.

Coco watched him and noted the sad look in his eyes. But he continued to do everything she asked him to do, and that was what was important to her.

Mission accomplished, Calhoun apologized again. "I've been an asshole."

"Yes, you have. And a dick!"

"You right, Ma. Forgive me?"

He kissed Coco on the lips. She immediately pushed him away and wiped her lips. He apologized, then ordered a new bottle of wine. The kids were invited to get whatever they wanted off the menu. Calhoun had to make some arrangements with the waiter about adding extra people at his table. But he took care of business, then happily fed his family.

They ate, went home, and enjoyed a nice evening. And every positive action Calhoun took caused Coco to fall that much more in love with him, a love that she prayed would never end.

CHAPTER 4
GHOSTS OF TROUBLED PASTS

In early March, Quantavius Mitchell came sniffing around Coco's house.

Too exhausted to respond to the ringing doorbell, Coco asked Cadee to open the door. The little girl did it, then ran back to her room.

When Q stepped into Coco's living room, her big eyes widened even more.

"Yo, what's up?" he said.

"Are you out of your damned mind?" Seeing this man always made her start to sweat. "What the hell you doing here at my house?"

"I came over to kick that talk."

"Oh, don't tell me. You on that again?" Coco was referring to the fact that ever since she had told Q that he was the father of Chance, he'd demanded to have a bigger role in the boy's life.

"Don't tell me — you saying I don't have a right to represent what's mine?"

"Ha!" she said with a bitter laugh. "No, Q. You do not have a right."

"Oh, yeah. Well, I disagree. I want what's mine, and I think I'm gone let Calhoun know what's up."

"Q, baby, please." As much as she didn't want to do it, Coco took a deep breath and managed to pull herself up off the sofa. She walked over to Q.

"What's the matter?" she said in a sweet voice. "You want some loving? Is that why you're bugging out?"

"No, man. That ain't it. Not totally."

"Then what is it?"

He paced back and forth and looked toward the bedroom shared by all of Coco's children.

"Q, if you telling me that you want to see Chance, the answer would be no."

Right then Cadee burst from the room and ran straight into her mother's arms for a hug. But when she was done, the girl noticed the strange man in their house.

Cadee stared quizzically at Q.

"Mommy," she said, "who is this?"

"Girl, mind ya business. Go back to the room and close the door. Don't come back out till I tell you to. Now move it."

"I've seen him before. Is he our uncle?"

"If you don't leave right now, Cadee, I'll

whip your ass good. Now go."

Cadee obeyed, fearing what would happen if she didn't.

As soon as the girl left, Q got up in Coco's face. "Now I really want to see my kid. Because if you talk to Chance the way you talk to Cadee, you may as well call yourself a child abuser, because you damn sure ain't a good mama."

"Q, come on, don't say that. I didn't mean anything by it. Cadee can be hardheaded."

"That's no excuse, Coco. There is no getting a pass when it comes to how a parent treats their kid. I didn't have a daddy, and I always told myself if I ever got to be a father, I'd do the thing right. You get what I'm saying?"

Coco heard him loud and clear, but it bothered her. She felt sorry about his past, but she did not want to hear about it. She tried another approach.

"Q, baby, I get what you sayin', but look at this," Coco said and pointed to her belly. "You see this? Think about all I'm going through for a minute. I feel like I weigh a ton, my blood pressure is sky high to the point where I had to check in the emergency room last week."

"Word?"

"Yeah." It was a lie, but there'd be no way

he could prove otherwise. "They got me straight and sent me back home. But when you come around here with no notice and you talking that talk . . . Q, it stresses me out even more. And I don't need you sniffing around my house trying to start shit."

"Me wanting to be in Chance's life is starting shit?"

"Yes! Because you promised me you wouldn't be carrying on like you are, remember?"

Q grew silent. Coco continued. "Now we've talked about this a hundred times, Q, and you know we did. I laid out the ground rules and you accepted. Why are you going back on your word?"

"I said all that before I got to know him. Things are different. I have a son running around who doesn't know about me! And I love the little homie. Calhoun's ass don't give a fuck about that boy."

Exasperated, Coco swung her flabby arms around. "Why can't you be like most daddies and not give a fuck about a kid?"

Q stepped closer to Coco, his teeth clenched together. Blood boiling, he felt like popping her in the mouth for her recklessness, but he knew that would not be good if he ever wanted to file a case for full custody. "I ain't most daddies. Don't put me in the

deadbeat category. And most of the dudes I know are damned good fathers."

"Hmm, then maybe I could hook up with your friends!" Coco said, just to be sarcastic.

"I-I have a mind to — You don't deserve this kid."

"My bad, Q." Coco was almost in tears. She hated how easy it was to set her off. She was worried sick about her health, the baby that didn't seem to want to come out of her womb, and the wedding she was trying to plan. The only happiness that she recently enjoyed was the fact that Calhoun faithfully came home from work every day.

"I wish that I never told you about Chance," she solemnly admitted. "I really do. I should have just kept that info to myself. Because I told you I'll never let Calhoun know what happened between us. He just knows I had a one-night stand but not with who."

"Yeah, but if you would have told him the truth from jump, I could be in my son's life, and your boy would just have to deal with the chips that fell."

"Since that ain't how things went down, then that'll never be the case, you hear me, Q? Now please stop threatening to tell him anything. Please. If you care about me, care about Chance, or even my other kids, you're

going to have to take this secret to your grave."

"I don't know if I can do that, Ma."

"You're going to have to try. Anyway, did I tell you that I'm getting closer to my due date? I'm about to drop this one soon. And that's all I'm trying to focus on right now." She wrung her hands together, and for a moment Q felt bad for Coco.

"So, you see, I don't need you bugging me like you been doing. Seriously. I know you think I'm a bad mama, but I can't wait to have this baby. This is gonna be my last one. I swear to God it is."

She placed her face in her hands and wept. Wept about her poor decisions that made her life what it was. Why was she so reckless and wild? Why couldn't she be more sensible when it came to her relationships? Every decision she'd made so far only brought her a world filled with trouble. Coco's emotions had been all over the place lately. And Q was already familiar with the drama that went down in Coco's household. Calhoun would call Q on the phone, complaining like a little bitch. At least that's what he used to do. Lately he'd been tight-lipped, which was why Q got curious and wanted to pop by and see what was up.

"All right then, Coco. I won't bother you

70

about Chance."

"You promise?"

"I promise."

She told him thanks, then walked him to the door so he could leave her in peace.

Alita nervously stood outside Jerrod Dawson's door. Her leg was shaking and her forehead was wet with moisture.

Although the temperature was mild on that early March afternoon, her hands were inserted inside a pair of cheap cloth gloves that she'd purchased from a grocery store. She wore a long coat, dark sunglasses, and her head was covered by a slouchy cap.

Alita made sure to ignore the house that stood directly across the street from his home. She did not want to look at it. The terrible memories deeply lodged in her heart prevented her from acknowledging that house. She turned her back against it and used a gloved finger to ring Jerrod's doorbell.

A young man of medium height, thin, and with two pointed ears, he quickly welcomed her inside.

"Hey," she greeted him. Alita removed the sunglasses and glanced at the living area. "Is your mama or kinfolks here right now?"

"Nah," he muttered. "They won free

tickets to the rodeo. They won't be back for hours."

"Good!" she replied and sighed in relief. She barely wanted to see Jerrod, let alone his family members. Alita stood there checking out the impressive array of furniture and the artwork that decorated the walls.

"Go on and have a seat," Jerrod finally told her. "You act like you haven't been here before."

"Jerrod, please don't start. You know how I feel about this. I don't know why we can't meet somewhere else besides here." Feeling agitated, she went and sat on the edge of the couch. Her voice was almost a whisper as she spoke. "Coming here always feels strange — but no way I'll let you come to mine. I still feel like a shithead. Always have."

"We don't have to talk about that. We can talk about other, more important things." Jerrod decided to sit right next to Alita. He was so close to her she could smell his musty odor like his clothes hadn't been washed. She scooted over to allow a healthy distance between them.

"How are things going with you?" she asked, trying to keep her voice even and light.

" 'Bout the same."

"Hmm, I figured that. That's the only reason you stay in touch. 'Cause you say things are not good. That you can't catch a break," Alita replied, her face tight and pinched. "But somehow I don't believe you." She rose to her feet and pointed. "This furniture . . . it looks and smells brand new. It's not that low-budget cloth couch that poor folks buy. This is a couch that says I'm grown. I've made it." She allowed her gloved finger to stroke the leather sofa and eyed him. "How can you afford these kinds of things if you don't have a job?"

"I do have a job."

"Oh, really? And when were you gonna tell me?" Instead of waiting for his answer, Alita spun around and headed for the vestibule.

"Alita. Wait. Listen up." Jerrod ran behind her before she could grab the doorknob. "It's a little piece of a job, Alita, nothing to jump up and down about. That's why I didn't tell you."

"What is it, Jerrod? Tell me."

"All I do is help my cousin out from time to time at this auto shop."

"Oh, yeah? Doing what? How much he pays you?"

"It's not a 'he.' My cousin is a female. She

73

owns the shop and she teaches me how to do oil changes, battery installations, other minor maintenance. That's it."

"How much does she pay you, Jerrod?"

He shoved his hands deep in his pocket. "Apparently not enough. I'm still living with my mother and younger sisters, as you can see. In case you forgot, I'm forced to be the son *and* the daddy," he said with a smirk.

Alita's face was pinched with frustration. She was sick of sneaking over to Jerrod's house to give him money.

Perhaps this explained why she was always struggling, although she did not want to think about the true reason for her monetary setbacks. Alita was getting to the point where she wanted to end this habit of harboring the biggest skeletons of her life.

"Look," she said. "Things are getting crazy. My son . . . he wants to go to college."

"Oh yeah? But the good thing about that, Alita, is that your son has a daddy in his life that can help him achieve his dreams."

"True, but now, uh, Elyse lives with us too."

"Oh, must be nice."

"Not as nice as you think. That's one more mouth to feed. Another human being to worry about on top of all my other worries."

"I don't feel sorry for you at all, so if you want me to feel bad, stop wasting your time. Spare me with *your* troubles. We *all* got troubles."

Alita wanted to punch his face with closed fists, beat him into silence; just push him far, far away until she could no longer see him and what he represented.

Jerrod studied Alita's facial expression, her poked-out lips and an eyebrow raised so high he could read her mind.

Even though he knew she was livid, he still recognized the same fire, same beauty that he had first noticed as a kid. The Reeveses used to live across the street from the Dawsons. Their families knew each other well. Alita and Burgundy would tease Jerrod and Dru about the "puppy love" that they'd shared when they liked each other in both elementary and middle school. But once they enrolled in high school, things grew very serious between the young couple. Even though Jerrod was shy, awkward, and clumsy, somehow he and Dru connected. She was smart, a go-getter. Back then, he was too. He had ambitions, oddly enough, and entertained thoughts about becoming an architect. And Jerrod was very in love with the girl who lived across the street. But then . . . his family life grew complicated,

and things were never the same.

As Jerrod stood there fuming about his past, Alita pressed her lips together and groaned with impatience. Wanting to smooth things over, he gently grabbed her by the elbow and began to walk. When she did not resist, he boldly reached for her hand with a confidence he barely felt. He coaxed Alita back down the hallway. She followed. But instead of returning to the living room where they'd been sitting, he continued on toward his bedroom.

When Alita realized where they were headed, she stopped walking.

"Um, what do you think you're doing, Jerrod?"

"Nothing. We're just going in my room to talk. So, we can have more privacy."

"Boy, you must think I'm a fool."

"I know you're not a fool."

"You must not know, or else you wouldn't even try this. Are you out of your mind? Don't get it twisted about what the fuck I am, 'cause you messing with the wrong bitch." Alita spun around again, heading back to the living room. "I have no business being in *that* room; I barely have business being in this house."

"Oh, but you do have business here." Jerrod smiled as he followed her. "Yet you're

partially right. The person you really came to see ain't here and hasn't been here in a while."

"Jerrod, please."

Every time she looked at him she wondered how she got herself into her situation: Jerrod blackmailing her for money or else he'd expose her secret.

His mocking stare verbalized everything his words did not. Alita lowered her eyes, cursed underneath her breath, and reached inside of her purse. She retrieved an envelope thick with cash. She counted off twenty twenty-dollar bills, ten fives, and ten ones.

Jerrod glanced at the roll of bills she handed him.

He counted. "Four-sixty. Is that all?"

"What the fuck? I told you I have bills. I have old bills, new bills, all kinds of bills."

"But I gotta put some of this money on Jack's books." Jack was Jerrod's father, and he'd been in prison for going on two decades.

"I don't care if you give it all to a homeless man, that's all I got for you today."

Jerrod laughed, then nodded, not wanting to push his luck.

"Okay, cool, Alita. I'm just saying you did much better than this in the past."

"That was then. This is now. I'm sorry,

but things have changed."

"I'll bet your life hasn't changed like mine did when you and —"

"Jerrod, please. Don't remind me. I feel bad enough as it is."

"I don't care about you feeling bad. That's what's wrong with you, Alita. You only think about yourself. Not about me, my younger sisters, or even Roro. Why you never ask about her?"

Roro was short for Rolanda; she was the same age as Alita and was the eldest daughter of the Dawson family. She and Alita had been best friends growing up.

At Jerrod's question, Alita couldn't speak. Hearing the woman's name made her feel numb and lifeless on the inside. To Alita, the past was gone. Roro was dead, like a ghost that came around, hovering, poking, prodding, and needling her.

"Anyway," Jerrod continued, "even though you don't care enough about Roro to ask about her, I think you'd want to know that my sister is doing about the same. She may never be the way she used to be."

"Jerrod, y-you got the money. I did the best I could. What more do you want from me?"

He decided to back off.

"Okay, if this is the best you can do I'll

take it . . . for now. Anyway, I heard you got fired. That's probably why you're struggling like this."

"Who told you that?"

"Dru."

"Dru spoke with you?" She raised her eyebrow even further. "When was that? And how'd my name come up?"

"I don't remember."

"You're a liar, Jerrod. You don't forget shit, we all know that." Alita hated that she and he had history; regretted that she was involved with the Dawsons in ways she despised.

Alita realized she'd been at that house much longer than she wanted to be. What if his mother and sisters came home early? Even worse, what if Roro popped over?

She looked at her watch, then at him. "I don't know how you ended up talking to Dru, but I really wish you'd stay away from my family . . . just like I make myself stay away from yours. Word is bond."

Unable to stay in his presence any longer, she made up an excuse to leave, then told Jerrod goodbye.

"When will I see you again?" he asked.

"I'll be in touch" was all she could offer him. She left the house, snatched off the cheap-feeling gloves and shoved them deep in her pockets.

Alita hoped she would never see or deal with Jerrod again. But under the circumstances, a situation that could prove devastating if exposed, Alita knew that "never" was impossible.

When the Reeves sisters got together, it always seemed like an episode of *Braxton Family Values* was about to come on. Lots of talking, lots of arguing, and lots of love.

That past January, they'd gotten banned from holding their Sister Day meetings at their favorite nail salon. So for their March event, the siblings decided to meet at Dru's townhouse.

Burgundy and Coco were the first to arrive at Dru's.

Coco looked a hot mess. She was dabbing her forehead with a piece of tissue. It got soaked with her perspiration, and she looked very uncomfortable.

"Let me help you with that," Burgundy offered.

"No thanks, Sis," Coco said with an attitude. "I don't need your help."

Burgundy smiled. "And you ladies always accuse me of perpetrating. Coco, stop playing. You look miserable and sick as a dog. Dru, can you get her a cold drink of water or some orange juice, please?"

Coco growled her disapproval but let Dru wait on her hand and foot until the doorbell rang again.

Alita trudged through the doorway with Elyse walking in front of her. Elyse's long lashes were coated with black mascara. She had on light green eye shadow, and her lips were a vibrant shade of red. She was dressed in a beautiful Afrocentric dress, and her hair was pinned up and secured by a head wrap.

"Is that . . . is that *Elyse*?" Burgundy asked.

"You don't recognize your own sister?" Coco asked, even though her mouth was wide open in shock just like Burgundy's.

"Isn't she beautiful?" Dru asked with a smile. "She looks like a Nubian queen."

"Why you all done up like that, Sis?" Coco wanted to know. She tried to sit up and take a closer look. She could tell that Elyse had gained a little bit of weight. The young lady had actually sprouted some hips since the last time Coco had seen her. And those two little mosquito bites that used to function as her breasts? Well, now the mosquito bites were swollen like plump, juicy oranges. Coco waved around her flabby arms.

"Lita, why you been hiding Elyse these days? What y'all two up to? You keep her from her family like you own the girl or something."

Alita hesitated. "As usual, I don't know what the hell you're talkin' 'bout, Coco. I sure wish you'd go on and have this baby 'cause your attitude sucks. You've been pregnant forever."

"And? So?"

"So . . . the only thing known for being pregnant this damned long is an elephant."

"I swear to God, if I wasn't stuck to this chair, I'd —"

Alita laughed good-naturedly. "I'm just playing with you, girl. No need to get violent."

Alita set her purse down and looked around. "Can I please get something to drink? What does it take to get some service around here? Dru, I know your fridge is stocked with the good shit. Hook a sister up."

Dru smiled at Alita, knowing she enjoyed getting waited on from time to time. She obediently went to gather more cold drinks for her siblings. The ladies all settled around the living room. Elyse sat close to Alita and pointedly ignored Burgundy, who'd tried to facilitate eye contact with her.

"I hope y'all hurry up and get through this meeting," Alita said as she swallowed some hibiscus tea.

"I agree with you," Burgundy said, ready to get down to business. "The minute we wrap up, I have to head over to Morning Glory. A group of minority female entrepreneurs is holding a brunch there in one of our private meeting rooms. I'll have to oversee everything and make sure it goes perfectly. If things go well, this could become a quarterly event."

"Oh, yeah?" Alita said. "How many people are coming?"

"Um, around fifty to seventy-five. Maybe even more. And at thirty-five bucks a head plus that administrative fee . . . hey, it adds up."

"Show-off," Alita said. "Another way for you to take people's money."

"Excuse me. We're not *taking* anything," Burgundy objected. "We do a great job catering these events. It's top-notch. Plus, we provide a valuable service to the community."

"Excuse me back," Alita said. "A service is *free.* You and Nate charge up the ass. Y'all are like banks trying to rip folks off. Last time I was at Morning Glory, I saw the new menu and the prices went way up. It used to be affordable to eat at your restaurant. Now you gotta be rich to eat some waffles, scrambled eggs, hash browns, and a damned slice of bacon."

"Alita, shame on you. It's not like you ever have to pay, or even leave a tip for the waiters when you come there."

"I'm just saying," Alita told her. "I'm thinking about your customers. Why black business owners always gotta rob the black customers by getting all bling blingy and marking up those prices? You do know we can go to McDonald's and eat for less than five bucks."

"Are you serious, Lita?"

"I damn sure am."

"Look, you cannot even compare McDonald's to us," Burgundy replied in an exasperated tone. "Plus, I know what this is really about. And I don't have time for Lita to be hinting around about her money issues right now —"

"Not only that," Coco butted in, "y'all better hope my water don't break. Dru will have a fit if I mess up her carpet and so will Tyrique."

"Don't even sweat it, Sis," Dru told Coco. "I'm not worried about any carpet. In fact, why don't you drink this tea that I made? It's healthy, and it'll be good for you and the baby."

"Thank you, Dru Boo," Coco told her.

"At least one sister is really concerned about me."

"I am, Sis," Dru said, relieved that the topic had changed. "And why is it taking you so long to give birth? Is everything all right?"

"Yeah, I'm good. The baby is good. She or he is just taking their sweet time."

"Speaking of time, let's get this meeting rolling," Alita complained. "I sure wish I could take over the meeting because so far we've talked about everything except the assignment."

Burgundy frowned. "And aren't you part of why we couldn't get to the topic?"

"No! You were the one going on and on about that fancy schmancy bacon and eggs party."

"You know what? Since you think you know everything and want to be in charge, I'm agreeing with you for a change, Lita. You are now in charge. Go ahead. Take over the meeting, Sis."

Dru, Coco, and Elyse smiled. This change of events was unprecedented, and no one could predict how things would end up with their big sister holding the reins.

"Good. 'Bout time you made a decent decision," Alita said as she stood and walked to the center of the room.

"First of all, are y'all good with the January assignment?"

"What was that assignment again, Lita?" Burgundy asked.

"Huh?"

"In January? Do you remember what we were supposed to focus on?"

"Fuck you, B."

"Lita, now don't curse me. I told you about that a hundred times. Don't you ever curse me again."

"All right, okay. I apologize." Alita sighed. "No. I don't remember it. But you do. So be nice and remind us, B."

"The January assignment was for us to learn to say 'yes' to something you've always said 'no' to."

"Who came up with that bullshit?" Alita asked. "No wonder I couldn't remember it. I definitely didn't try to do it."

"Lita, you're wrong for that. Even if you don't agree, you should at least have given it an honest try."

"I'll honestly try to do it the next time." Alita turned to another sister. "All righty then, Dru Boo. What you gotta tell us?"

"I was glad for that assignment because it gave me another opportunity to try and look up my ex. You know, Jerrod Dawson."

Alita froze as she stood in the center of

the room. "And what happened? Did you find him?"

"Yeah, in fact I did. It was through Facebook, of course. I got in touch with him via Messenger. And we actually got a chance to talk."

Coco hooted and hollered. "I hope that Tyrique didn't find out about y'all hooking up."

"It was not a hookup, Coco. We just met for coffee. Had a face-to-face. I needed closure. You all remember how close Jerrod and I had been. Ever since we were seven years old. We'd run back and forth across the street all the time to play with each other. Our families hung out sometimes." She swallowed deeply. "By the time we got in high school, things got really serious. I felt so comfortable with him. We'd talk about everything. Jerrod had plans to design houses. Become a CAD designer. And me, I was going to conquer the medical field. Occupational therapist. And we were planning to apply to the same college. In the tenth grade we were inseparable. But something happened. He broke up with me with no warning. We used to walk to the bus stop together, ride together, eat lunch every day in the café. All of that shut down. I racked my brain trying to figure out what I did. I asked him what was wrong. He avoided me. Acted like he hated me. You all were there. You have to remember."

"I remember hearing you cry yourself to sleep every night," Coco said. "We shared a room, and I felt sorry for you, but I got so sick of hearing you boo-hoo throughout the night."

"Thanks for the support," Dru said sarcastically. "Anyway, fast forward to now, I was shocked Jerrod responded when I messaged him."

"What happened then?" Burgundy asked.

"We met up. And let me tell you, I was in for a surprise. It's been, what, about ten years, and Jerrod looked like hell. But I played it off and tried to catch up. I asked what he'd been doing all this time. And he kind of avoided my question."

"That's weird," Coco replied. "All I can remember is that his daddy went to jail. And his mama almost lost her mind behind it. Remember that, Alita? You had to have remembered 'cause you and their older sister — what was her name? Rolanda? — you two were thick as thieves."

Alita's eyes misted up. She hoped to God that Jerrod did not have any photos or postings of his family on his Facebook. She wanted to ask but fear held her tongue.

Maybe she could sneak and look up his profile herself. If he did have family pictures, would it be wrong of her to ask him to take them all down? Make his page private?

"Alita, are you listening? Why you got that faraway look in your eyes?" Coco wanted to know.

"I wish Dru would get to the damn point," Alita finally responded. "I'm bored as hell. Time is flying by. We need to talk about the *next* assignment. Fuck January. It's almost April. And you still ain't had that baby."

Everyone laughed, and Alita swiftly changed the subject. She read over a document that Burgundy had prepared concerning their meeting.

"Okay, sisters. Check this out. The March assignment is to create a bucket list. Oh, I like this one, B. Good job."

Burgundy told her thanks. "Before you all go to making a list, I have an idea. How about we go on a girls' trip?"

"Oh, yeah, I would love to do that," Dru told her. "I have vacation coming up, so count me in."

"Wait a second. When would this be? You know I gotta have the baby, then get married and go on a honeymoon. I don't know if I can handle all that, y'all."

"Coco, it would be this summer. Like in

June. How does that sound?"

"One question!" Alita said. "Who's paying?"

"I got you."

"Are you serious, B?"

"Very serious. That's why I need to leave and take care of this catering event and make that money," she teased.

"Oh, yeah. If that's how you're paying for my trip then yes, you need to be headed out the door." Alita calmed down, feeling humble and in a daze. "And thanks in advance. That's very generous of you, B." Alita was impressed. "Where we headed?"

"I was thinking New York," Burgundy said.

"Count me in," Dru said.

"Me too," Coco answered.

"Me three," Alita shouted.

"Glad to see that we're all in agreement. I can buy everyone's plane tickets and pay the hotel expenses. You'll be on your own for food and souvenirs, of course."

"Okay," Alita said. "That's fair."

Burgundy continued. "I'm thinking we can stay in the middle of all the action, near Times Square. Go shopping and maybe see a Broadway play or a Mets game."

"Damn, I'm getting excited. Is your hubby going?" Alita asked.

"Hell no," Burgundy said. "He is not allowed to go. It's a girls' trip."

Alita told her that a getaway was something to look forward to and she couldn't wait to leave. She desperately needed to get away from it all. She needed relief from the bumpy and dangerous road that life had driven her on.

CHAPTER 5
MARCH MADNESS

March twelfth — Coco's due date — came and went.

"What's up with you, girl?" Alita asked on the day that Coco was scheduled to give birth.

"I don't know," was Coco's honest answer.

"What you mean, you don't know? Does the doctor still hear a heartbeat?"

"Yeah. Everything's good. This baby's just taking its sweet time. It probably has heard me fussing at its daddy so much —"

"And you've got little Cypress Humphries scared already," Alita concluded.

Coco's ultrasound had determined she'd have a girl. And she felt bad about it because she and Calhoun already had two other girls. She knew that Chance wasn't his, and it would have been great to give her man a baby boy.

"I know one thing. I can't wait for Cypress to show her sweet little face. 'Cause as soon as I can lose a good twenty pounds, I'm getting married. And nothing in the world will stop me from staying married," Coco said. "I don't ever wanna be like you, Lita. No divorces for me."

"Marriage is tough," Alita told her. "And you don't know what you'll do in a bad situation until you find yourself in it."

A week and one day later, Alita drove over to Coco's.

"Look," she sputtered with impatience. "You need to drink some castor oil. That'll get Cypress and *you* all shook up." She laughed. "I'll bet my life on it. Keep a pair of clean underwear nearby, though."

Sick of being pregnant, Coco took Alita's advice. She asked Calhoun to go to the twenty-four-hour pharmacy to buy her a bottle. Alita was still at her house when Calhoun got back. She opened the cap then poured one spoonful and shoved the laxative into Coco's mouth.

"Damn, this tastes like Wesson oil mixed with soap."

"You want that baby to come out, don't you? Then get ready for round two, 'cause one swallow won't be enough."

"Lita! I don't want to. I can't do it. Hell, I can stay pregnant two more weeks."

"Do as I tell you, Coco."

"You ain't my mama." She frowned. "Besides, how you know 'bout all this?"

"Don't worry about how I know. One more time. Open that sassy mouth of yours. And once you're done, drink lots of water to stay hydrated."

Coco did as she was told. And soon thereafter, in the wee hours of the morning, her womb was ready. Cypress made her appearance, red-faced and screaming after she took her first breath.

While at the hospital, Calhoun stood by Coco's bedside when their daughter was handed to him.

He held her in his arms, curiously staring at Cypress with an odd look on his face.

Exhausted yet happy, Coco told him, "She's yours; don't even try it."

Alita and Burgundy, who were also witnesses to the birth, looked at each another and burst into laughter. They asked to hold the baby and began cooing at their niece and filmed several videos that were posted to Snapchat and Facebook.

The joy of another Reeves child could be felt throughout. Pink balloons, flower bouquets, and baby booties dotted Coco's room.

"I hate to be the one to tell you this, but fuck it, I'm 'bout to say it anyway." That was Alita.

"What, Lita, what?" Coco said.

"You know what today is?" she asked with a smile.

"It's the day my last baby was born. She completes our family," Coco snapped at Alita, feeling exhausted from everything she'd recently gone through.

"Well, I saw this on the Internet earlier this morning while we were waiting for Cypress to make her appearance. But Coco, girl. Today is March twenty-first! *Single Mother's Day.* Ain't that a mess? I thought it was funny as hell. Too funny." Alita handed the girl back to her mom.

Coco reclined on the bed, her baby settled in her arms, a frozen smile etched on her face. "Don't embarrass me like that, Lita," she said and took a long look at her engagement ring and an even longer look at Calhoun.

When she was released from the hospital, Coco felt as if she was floating on a wonderful cloud. She got numerous well wishes. Even her father called and told her "Congrats." But a couple of days later, everything changed.

She was able to stand around in her kitchen and make sure that the kids had a decent breakfast to eat.

Calhoun, who'd taken a week off from work to help her out, scolded Coco.

"Now Ma. I know you think you can do it all, but you need to lay it down and try not to do so much. I can cook some eggs."

Coco laughed. "Man, please. I've seen your watery eggs. You go on back in the bedroom and play with the kids till I get done fixing a real breakfast. Thanks, baby. Now leave. Get out."

Calhoun did as Coco told him. Soon Chance wandered into the kitchen. At first, he was trotting in a playful run. But then he abruptly hit the floor. His skin turned yellow.

"There you go again," Coco scolded him. "Get up, boy, and stop all that playing."

When Chance still lay out like he was paralyzed, she stopped what she was doing and came to see about him. His skin felt cold and hard. Coco screamed for Calhoun. They called 911 and arranged for Dru to drop Cypress and her other kids off at Henrietta Humphries's place. Calhoun's mother was happy to watch her grandkids.

After a short drive, Coco and Calhoun arrived at the emergency room.

Coco got Alita on the phone, her heart pounded wildly in her chest. "He's breathing, Lita, but I'm scared, really scared." She described how Chance had acted. "This is what I get, huh? I haven't been the best mama, and now God is punishing me by —"

"Don't say it, Coco, don't. Chance will be fine. I'm on the way. Stay prayed up."

Once the physician examined him and gave him all kinds of tests, Coco and Calhoun got the news.

"He doesn't have enough red blood cells and he's been diagnosed with anemia. Plus, he has a rare blood type, so we'll need to get some donated blood. Chance must have a transfusion."

Coco screamed. "What? No!"

The doctor looked at Calhoun. "Are you the father?"

Coco wanted to die. "Um, no, he's not," she answered for him.

"Nah, I ain't the biological daddy." Calhoun was grim. "I've raised the kid since he was little. But I've always wanted to know who the real father is. I guess now I get to find out, huh, Coco?"

"But I told you, Calhoun," she said. "I don't know what the baby's father is."

The doctor shook his head disapprovingly. "Well, whatever the situation is, it would be advisable to locate the father. And do it as soon as you can, ma'am. It could be a matter of life or death."

A groan escaped Coco's mouth, and she asked to be excused. Calhoun stared at her, knowing for sure that she was about to make a phone call. He ran behind her.

"Anything I can do?" he asked. "Oops, no. I can't. I am *not* the father."

"Calhoun, please don't be like this. You know how the situation went down. We were on a break and I hooked up with someone else. For just one night. That's it. I'm sure that you had sex with other girls when we broke up."

"I may have done that, but at least I didn't fuck her so good that she got pregnant. And kept the baby!" He gave Coco a sad look then turned around and walked away. Regardless of his hurt feelings, whatever she had to do, she'd be forced to handle this crisis on her own.

Coco proceeded to leave the building. When she located her car in the parking lot, she got in and quickly dialed Q. She told him everything that was going on and asked if he could help.

"Damn. Yeah, hell. I'll give blood, you know I will."

"Thanks, Q. But how we gonna do this? Calhoun is here at the hospital, and I know he will not leave until he figures out what man in that waiting room is my child's father. And if he sees you walking up in there, all hell is gonna break lose. He'll put two and two together. Oh, God, why is this happening? Why my baby boy gotta get sick? I'm so scared, more scared than I've ever been in my life."

"Calm down, Ma. What's the worst that can happen?"

"Think about it. Calhoun has been suspicious of me ever since we got back together three years ago. And if he finds out that you were my one-night stand, he'd kill me, kill you, then you'd never get to be a father, you know what I'm saying. Everyone's dreams would end just like that." She paused for effect. "So please be real careful, Q. Get here when you can, but let me know the second you arrive."

"Okay, I'll do that. But look at the situation like this," Q said. "Your boy may surprise you. If I give blood and the baby turns out fine and makes it through, that may be the most important thing. Calhoun may not even care that I'm the father."

"Are you stupid or just dumb? That Negro won't give a damn that Chance made it through. He will tell you thanks for the donation then pack up and leave me quicker than you can say 'Hasta la vista, baby.'"

"Who cares if he leaves? What does he really do for you anyway? You act like he's the only man in town."

Coco quieted down. In a way, Q was right. She was sure there were better men out there. But in all the years she'd been with Calhoun, she never imagined herself with anyone else besides him. Why? She did not know. Love was funny like that.

Coco returned to the emergency room. She drew Alita to the side and asked for a huge favor. Alita listened with wide eyes but then nodded. "I got you."

For the next ten minutes Alita expertly distracted Calhoun, engaging him in all kinds of conversations, steering him to another section of the large facility, until Q was able to enter the area undetected.

Q rolled up his sleeves, pumped his fists to get the blood circulating, and let the nurses draw a pint of blood. He did all that he needed to do and left just as quietly as he came.

Coco called him and thanked him. Then she hung up and prayed.

But later on, when the doctor privately informed Coco that the blood from Q wasn't an exact match, she broke down. She sobbed into her hands. Alita heard Coco's wails from around the corner. She hurried to the room and asked the doctor to give them privacy.

She patted Coco on the back and tried to whisper words of comfort. But then Alita shut the door and folded her arms across her chest.

"Dark Skin, I remember we talked about this situation months ago. And I asked you if you would ever be real with me and tell me who's the daddy of Chance. You told me that you know who the father is. Now, I was shocked as hell that you slept with Calhoun's boy. But that's another story. We all make mistakes. But seriously, Sis. If not Q, then who?"

Coco sniffled and avoided eye contact.

Alita got in her face. "I asked you a question. Who is Chance's father?"

"I-I don't know."

"You're a damn fucking liar. You don't remember who you slept with? Was it a whole football team?"

Coco said nothing. Although she had never gone as far as being sexually active with five to ten men in one week, she still clearly recalled the day that Chance was conceived. And the nightmarish quality of it made her want to die. Forget a new marriage. Forget her kids.

"Coco, let's be real with each other. You

likes to get down in the bedroom. Nothing wrong with that. But it sounds like you ending up sleeping with more than one man in the same day. Is that what happened?"

Coco slowly nodded as large tears streamed from her eyes. Her sister was blurry, but the memories of her betrayal were not.

"I see. Damn, Coco." Alita could only process the information she'd asked for. But Alita was in no position to judge. She tried to sound understanding yet realistic.

"Coco, listen to me and listen good. I'm sorry you're in this situation. I wouldn't wish it on my worst enemy. And you're going to have to forgive yourself for what happened, because nothing you can do will change the past. It's all about the future. And we're talking about a child's life here. Somehow, someway, baby girl, you're going to go back in time and remember who you slept with. You're going to have to contact Chance's father and tell him what's going on. You better hope he's man enough to give that blood so our nephew, your son, his son, can live a long life."

"But, Lita, you don't understand. I-I-I just can't contact the father."

"Why not? He's still living? Is he in Houston? Do y'all stay in contact?"

Coco could only nod. The words escaped her. If her family knew her dirty little secrets, they'd never have anything to do with her again. She'd be hated. Scorned. She could not afford to lose her family.

With a critical decision to make, Coco wondered how to choose. Would it be her fiancé whom she loved very much, her family that meant the world to her, or would she sacrifice her only beloved son?

At that moment, she had no idea what to do or who to turn to.

After Alita left the room where Coco had been hiding out, Coco received a call that she'd been expecting.

"So Ma, is everything cool?" That was Q. He told her he felt a little dizzy after giving blood but he had to know how everything turned out.

How could Coco admit to this this man that he wasn't Chance's father? He was so into the boy that the truth would destroy him. She lied again. "Everything is great, Q. The baby is okay. He's gonna make it."

"Word? That's cool, Ma."

"Yep, sure is. You saved the day, Q."

"I'm glad. So glad. Thank God my son is gonna pull through. I wish I could be there in the hospital with him, but that's not the most important thing. He's gonna be all right, Coco!"

She heard pure joy surge through Q's voice. She silently thanked the Lord regarding Chance. But Coco couldn't totally rejoice. In fact, if she could go back in time, she would probably pick the very day that this nightmare began.

As she listened to Q continue jabbering on and on about how thankful he was that the little boy would live, her heart sank. She mumbled a few words to Q then told him that the doctor had entered the room and she needed to go.

"Ms. Reeves, time is of the essence."

"How's he doing?" she asked.

"It's not looking good."

"What are my options? Since I don't know who the daddy is, that shouldn't stop my son from getting well. What if the daddy is dead, then what would happen? Can't we find a stranger that matches my son's blood type?"

"That is a possibility. It could help, but you'd have to contact a rare donor program. In fact we have one in the Houston area. See my nurse and get the information. Good luck, Coco."

Feeling hopeful for the first time in a long time, Coco paid the nurse a visit and decided to leave the emergency room.

Calhoun agreed to stay behind with Chance. She bit her bottom lip as she watched him sitting next to Chance holding his limp hand. The child was unconscious but still breathing.

"I've got important business to take care of, baby. I'll be back as soon as possible. Call me if anything and I mean *anything* happens."

Coco got on the road but she needed to make a pit stop. First, she called Baller Cutz, the second business establishment that Nate and Burgundy owned.

A barber answered the phone.

"Hey, is Burgundy around?" she asked.

"Yep, she is here. You want to talk to her?"

"No! Nah, I was just checking. Um, did she just get there? This is her sister."

Coco purposely left out which sister she was. The barber confirmed that Burgundy had just arrived.

"Cool. I may check back with her in a bit. No need to tell her I called. Thanks." Coco hung up. She drove over to Morning Glory.

As usual, Nate's car was parked in his reserved spot.

Heart beating wildly, Coco rushed inside the restaurant and went straight to the business office, which was where he could usually be found.

She saw him seated at the desk, and she quietly shut the door behind her. He looked up from his computer.

"Hey there. What's going on?"

"Um, Nate. I need to ask you a huge favor." Coco remained standing.

"What is it, Coco? Are you following up about getting put on payroll? If so, that's already in the works —"

"It is? That's good. But no, Nate, I want to talk to you about something really urgent. I-I need you to go to a blood donor center and anonymously donate your blood. See," she continued, "I know that you are someone that has this rare blood type. As it so happens, my baby *boy,*" — she barely kept herself from bursting into tears — "he is in the emergency room, Nate. He's anemic. I had no idea until now. Anyway, my baby boy needs a blood transfusion or else . . ."

His eyes wet, he nodded as if he understood.

"I'll do it. Where do I go?"

"Thank God. Um, and as you already know this has to stay on the low. I don't want anyone to get the wrong idea. See, this guy I know named Q, he donated and I told him that his blood actually has done some good. But it wasn't true, Nate. You know how it is. And, well, that is what he needs to

106

believe even if it ain't legit. It's complicated."

Nate nodded again, his face growing ashen. "No need to explain. I'll do my best. Give me the info and we'll make it happen."

Coco thanked her brother-in-law and went to get back in her vehicle. She sat there for a full ten minutes, hopeful that the blood was a perfect match, then something good could finally happen for her.

But how long the goodness would last was something she did not know.

Dru stood next to Elyse in front of her bathroom mirror.

"All right, Elyse, repeat after me. 'Ay, eee, I, oh, oooh.' "

"Dru!" Elyse protested.

"Go on. I know you probably feel like you're still in elementary school but do it anyway. These exercises are going to help you."

Right then Gamba stepped into the bathroom. Elyse smelled him before she saw him. That fragrant cologne of his made her want to touch him.

"Listen to your sister," he said. "Do every single thing she tells you."

Elyse instantly obeyed Gamba. And when Dru insisted that she repeat sounds like

"Bee, cee, dee, ee, ef, and gee," the girl did that too.

Twenty minutes later, Dru felt satisfied. They left the bathroom and went and took a seat on some barstools in the kitchen. Dru presented a tiny plastic storage container and opened the lid.

She handed Elyse a tube of mascara.

"Go ahead, Sis. Fix your face. You have ten minutes to do everything I've taught you."

Feeling energized, and not even minding that Gamba was a captive observer, Elyse went to work. She sat before a lighted mirror and applied mascara, curled her eyelashes, swiped her lips with glitter gloss, and dusted her cheeks with blush.

It was early Saturday morning in late March. Based on the coaching that Elyse received from Dru and Gamba, she felt ready. More confident.

It was almost time for Elyse to head for work. She excitedly grabbed her purse and cell phone.

"You look beautiful. And you did this all yourself." Dru beamed at her.

"Thank you," Elyse answered, careful to remember the proper enunciation.

"She's doing excellent," Gamba agreed as he walked with them to Dru's car. He opened the door for her and watched her get in. "And don't forget to walk around with your back up straight and your head held up high."

"I won't forget," she promised. On an impulse she hopped out of the car and rushed into Gamba's arms. He laughed and swayed with her back and forth, patting her on the back and giving her much needed encouragement.

She lifted her lips up to him and closed her eyes. But instead of feeling his mouth on hers, she felt two fingers. She opened her eyes and looked up at him. He shook his head no. She was disappointed but understood. She needed to remain focused. Her emotional recovery depended on that.

As Elyse thought back on the past few months, things had been going well. So very well that she could not remember a time when she felt more alive. Her lessons with Gamba were growing more intense, and she felt like a caged animal ready for battle. And Dru had been so generous lately, buying her things like hoop earrings and bangle bracelets. She'd also purchased new items for Elyse's wardrobe, which badly needed updating: items that she would take with her during the trip to New York and casual pieces she could wear on the weekend; she even splurged and bought Elyse a lovely sleeveless black dress that she could put on for a more formal affair. Gamba had been with them when Elyse tried on the outfit, and she came out of the dressing room to see how he liked it.

He nodded and smiled with much approval.

"Every woman needs a nice black dress. They are always in style. Plus you need to show off your legs, girl," Dru told her.

"I can't believe I'm wearing more dresses," Elyse muttered.

"I must warn you, you're going to attract a lot of attention from men. But don't let it freak you out. Stay calm and in control."

Elyse shot a worried look at Gamba. Could he witness the changes in her? The fact that she was becoming sexier than she'd ever dreamed. Did he even notice? And furthermore, did Gamba mind? Was he afraid that some other guy would finally snatch her up right from under him? No, she concluded. He gave her little compliments, but overall it seemed like he was just as unbothered as he'd always been.

And Elyse, not ever having had a real boyfriend, did not know if his nonchalance was evidence of his good character or if it was something to worry about.

110

Once the two women were settled in the car with the engine running, Dru started driving Elyse to Morning Glory. She turned on the radio, found the NPR station, and said, "Elyse, I want you to listen to these newscasters. Repeat everything they say."

"Why?"

"Because you're going to learn how to pronounce your words properly and how to enunciate like I know you can."

"That's dumb."

"No, Elyse, talking like you're stupid is what makes people sound dumb. Go ahead and don't resist me. I'm trying to help you. You're about to go among all kinds of people at that job: business people, politicians, preachers, attorneys. They may not even say one word to you, but if they do, you must be able to talk to anyone and look them in the eye no matter what level they're on."

Elyse agreed to give it a try. She listened. She repeated the news. She laughed when she messed up but started the process all over again.

"Great job," Dru said and beamed at her with pride.

Elyse got dropped off in front of the restaurant. She walked in with her head held high, feeling ready for whatever. And she continued doing the menial tasks that she'd been paid to do since she was first hired: replacing bottles of ketchup and hot sauce on the tables and making sure the salt and pepper shakers were filled and washing dirty dishes by hand.

She handily did her job, plus other minor tasks that the shift manager assigned to her. And an hour later, when Nate emerged from the business office and saw her, at first his face registered shock. Elyse felt just as surprised as he looked. She did not know he was there. She felt an urge to turn around and run, but something made her stay put.

"Who is this woman? Is she a new hire?" he asked.

Elyse hadn't come across Nate in months. Alita insisted that she work when Nate wasn't around, and Burgundy had agreed to that plan.

And right then, instead of letting the manager answer Nate, Elyse felt a surge of boldness. She stepped up to her brother-in-law.

"Hi, Nate. It's me, Elyse." She raised an eyebrow at him and did not welcome him with a smile.

"Oh, uh, um, hmm. I didn't recognize you." Embarrassed to see her, he started to scurry away. He knew that his wife had forbid him to even be near the girl. But Elyse noticed his nervous reaction and she stopped him.

"Dat's fine. I mean, that's all right, Nate. I'm good. No need for you to run scared."

The manager eyed them warily.

"Uh, no," Nate finally said. "I do have to go. I have, um, errands to run. That's what I meant. I'll be back in a few . . . a few hours."

When she could no longer persuade him to remain in the restaurant, it gave Elyse great pleasure to watch him leave out that door. Running like he was trying to evade an arrest.

"It's working," she said to herself. "And it's just the beginning."

CHAPTER 6
WHY DID I WANT
TO GET MARRIED

Alita paid a visit to her man's house one morning in mid-April and brought Elyse with her. They were in the living room, Alita comfortably sitting on Shade's sofa.

Elyse was perched on the floor between her legs as Alita braided the young woman's hair.

"Hey, Alita, that's looking pretty good." Shade stood nearby watching.

"It's all right. I couldn't get hired to work in a salon, but this'll do. It's way better than how she used to wear it . . . all nappy and covered up."

"You have a lot of skills. In fact, I'm proud of you and how you've stepped up to the plate to help care for your sister."

"Yeah, well. I'm just doing what family does. See, remember, I'm the oldest, and ever since I could count to one hundred, I remember having to help out with all the girls. Dru, Coco, this one here." She laughed. "I was so much older than the younger sisters I felt like their mother a lot of times."

"Did you feel robbed of your childhood?"

"Something like that. But it was all good." Her funny-sounding voice fell to a faint whisper. "Too late to change things anyway. What's done is done."

"Alita," Shade said. "Everything all right?"

"Everything is the way it's gone be."

"That sounds negative."

She said nothing.

"C'mon, love. Talk to me. You've been acting a bit distant, not like yourself. What's going on? Is it Leno?"

Alita's face brightened. "There you go. My knucklehead son has been screwing up. I guess since basketball season is over he's acting like he's lost his damned mind."

"Doing what?"

"Hanging out with his fellow knuckleheads. Whoever you hang around is who you'll end up becoming."

"Maybe," Shade said with a smile, thinking about how crazy his woman acted a lot of times.

"The scouts are always watching," Alita replied. "And that means that Leno has to practice in and out of season just like LeBron does. Stay ready. That's the only way he's getting drafted to the pros."

"Alita, sweetie. I told you that there are no guarantees."

She stopped braiding Elyse's hair and stood to her feet. "I guess I'm wasting my time then, huh? I guess driving Leno to basketball camps and paying for extra coaching lessons and making him feel like he is something special is a total waste? Is that what you're telling me, Shade? That my son is only guaranteed to be a failure?"

Shade tried to hug her, but she pushed him away.

"I'm sick and tired of dreams that turn into nightmares. I just am!"

"Go on, sweetie, get it all out."

"They tell you to prepare for the future. Have a plan. Write it down. And work on it to make it all happen. You can have whatever you like. That's total BS. Life isn't easy like that. Real life throws curveballs. And sometimes the balls hit you in the head and knock you out."

"True, sweetie. Bad things can pop up. But even if they do, that's no reason to give up on life or your dreams. No reason to be afraid that things can't turn around for the good."

"Save it, Shade. Those types of fairy tales happen to everyone else. People whose

116

stories get told in *People* magazine. Not to average people like me."

"You're not average, and don't you ever say anything like that again."

At that moment Alita was afraid that her man did not know her as well as he thought.

"Come here," he said. This time when Shade tried to hug Alita, he forced her to accept the warmth of his arms. She calmed down. His arms felt soothing and strong as he whispered words of encouragement.

"No matter what, you have to trust that things will be good. Everything's going to work out fine."

Alita drew strength from him right away. It was amazing that no matter how despondent she felt, Shade could ease her fears.

Alita stared at Shade Wilkins in fascination. If she looked at him too long, would he disappear? Why did good things last so long before they turned into something else?

"I want to believe, but I'm afraid."

"Alita, baby. Stay strong no matter what happens to Leno. You have to set the example." He released her and looked pointedly at Elyse.

"Technically, you are now her guardian. And you are coparenting Leno. You must stay strong and positive for the both of them. Forget about yourself. Think about the kids."

She agreed. "Again, you're right. I gotta be strong even when I don't feel it."

"That's the thing, Alita, the strength is there. It'll come out at the right time to prove to you that you're stronger than you think you are. You're an overcomer. Most of us find these things out eventually."

Just then the doorbell rang. Shade went to the door and welcomed Gamba. Elyse's face lit up when she saw him. By then her long, thick hair was half braided; the other half was wild looking, but she didn't care. She leaped to her feet and flung herself in Gamba's arms. He hugged her back, then asked her to sit back down.

"How'd you know she was here?" Alita asked. She returned to the couch and started working on another section of Elyse's hair.

"Elyse FaceTimed me a little while ago. I think you had gone inside of a gas station to pay for gas. That's when she called and told me where she'd be."

"Aha. You two must be in love. I just hope you ain't doing the —"

"We're good, Ms. Alita. That's all I can tell you."

In spite of herself, Alita felt genuinely happy that Gamba had taken Elyse under

118

his wing.

Alita checked her watch. "Well, I better hurry it up, because I know Elyse will be going to work in a bit. She does the hostess thing at the restaurant now. I'm happy for her."

"How is that going? Has she had any more troubles with Nate?" Shade asked.

"None. He knows better, all I can say." Alita assured him that at least for Elyse life was going very well.

But when it came to Coco, life had gotten quite interesting.

It was the first week of May. And she was deeply entrenched in the last preparations for her wedding. They had planned on holding a brief ceremony that Friday. And they'd throw a nice reception later that night.

"Dru Boo, you good?" Coco was asking. She was at her house with all of her sisters.

"I can't believe you're finally doing it," Dru said. "I'm honored you want me to stand next to you. You deserve all the happiness in the world."

"I do, don't I?" Coco laughed. "We've got to go through all kinds of hell before we end up with the man we want. Lita, don't you be depressed. Your day is coming."

"Oh, don't even worry about me and

Shade. We're good."

"Where is Calhoun?" Burgundy wanted to know. She had recently deposited two grand in Coco and Calhoun's joint bank account, a happy marriage gift of some sort.

"He's probably going to see about his suit he picked out. It's nice too. Real nice."

"Well, I know one thing. Y'all sure enough waited long enough. You got the marriage license and the paperwork all in order? You ready for this, Coco? Ain't no backing out. No changing your mind, nothing." Alita was adamant that her sister fully realize what she was getting herself into. "Once you say 'I do,' That's it. Do better than I did, all right, Sis? Work out your issues."

Coco's eyes misted. "That means a lot coming from you. Sounds like you are finally cosigning on me and Calhoun being together."

Alita said nothing. What more could she say? Grown-ups were determined to have things their own way. But she did wish her sister the best.

By ten forty-five on Friday morning, the ladies had arrived at the courthouse for the wedding. Coco went ahead and paid the seventy-two-dollar fee and presented her marriage license to the window clerk. They waited another fifteen minutes. Calhoun

120

was nowhere to be found.

"Did you go by Henrietta's house?" Dru suggested.

"Yes!" Coco snapped. "I went earlier today before I came here. His mother ain't there. No one is at that house. I called five times already."

"Maybe they are on their way here." Burgundy tried to stay upbeat. "It's Friday mid-morning. Rush hour traffic has kicked in."

"Rush hour traffic has nothing do to with this. It would never keep my man from answering his phone," Coco said. "Something else is up."

A couple of hours later, Coco decided to no longer waste anyone's time. No refund would be issued. She left the courthouse in humiliation. She decided to go home, decked out in the dress that she'd been so happy to see herself in because it fit her slightly tinier frame.

And later, when she got a text from Calhoun, it included a video message.

"Hey, Ma. I would tell you I'm sorry for not showing up. But you're the one that should be saying you're sorry to me. I finally know the truth. That you fucked around with my boy. That you lied and made a fool out of me, all this time. And because of that there's no way I'm marrying you. Why don't you hook up with your baby daddy? 'Cause I ain't trying to be in no fake relationship."

The video abruptly ended.

And Coco felt totally numb.

"What's wrong?" Alita asked when she walked into the room. "Did you hear from Calhoun?"

Because Alita was the only other adult still at the house with her, Coco did something she never thought she'd do. She handed her phone to Alita. Opened the text. And she replayed the video for her.

When she was done watching, Alita asked Coco to have a seat.

"Start explaining, Dark Skin. It sounds like he found out info that you been hiding from me, from everybody."

"All I can say is everything I've been banking on the past few years is now all gone. I-I am officially a single mom. With four kids. And no man."

"Don't you dare start crying, Coco Chanel Reeves. I mean that." Alita saw how far Coco had poked out her lips. And she hated to see her distressed.

"I want so bad to say 'I told you so,' but I won't go there. What good will it do? You need to forget that man and start thinking about the future."

"Are you serious? Who'd want to think about a future that is so fucked up it ain't even worth thinking about? I know it sounds crazy, but that's how I feel."

"Fine. I'll give you a minute or two to feel sorry for yourself, but after that, Sis, you're going to have to do better. I mean it. We're Reeves women. We're tougher than steel. I know people look at us and laugh at us like we ain't shit, but we gotta prove 'em wrong, Coco. We'll show 'em. And I'll help you."

"You will?"

"Yeah, dummy."

"But why would you help me? I thought you feel like if I make bad decisions then I'm on my own."

"Yeah," Alita said. "But I know you're hurting. And I hate when any of my family is in pain. It was real tacky of him to dump you through a videotape. Like who the hell does he think he is acting like he's Tyrese filming messages on tape? If I could I'd kick Calhoun's ass up and down the street. But he ain't worth the jail time."

"You damn sure right about that." Coco wiped her nose with some tissue.

Alita went and made a pot of black coffee and poured her sister a cup. They sat at the table and shared stories of how they'd messed up when it came to men.

"When you put all your dreams into the hands of one person, that's giving 'em way too much power. Trust me. I know." Alita sounded very mysterious, but Coco decided not to probe.

"You gotta learn from this, baby girl. Can you do that? Promise me you'll think about it."

"It'll be tough, but I'll give it a try. Thanks, Lita. Love you, girl."

A month later, Q asked if he could come by. Coco told him it was fine. When he arrived at her house, he held a plastic bag filled with toys and clothes. Ever since Coco indicated that Chance had a successful blood transfusion, Q had been calling and checking on Chance every day, but this was the first time she let him stop over.

"Q. You didn't have to buy these things."

"Yeah, I do. Now that your boy is out of the picture, I feel I should be able to come around my son like I been wanting to."

"Dammit, Q." Coco got up and began pacing. Should she open up to him and tell Q that the kid was not his son? No way. There'd be no telling how he'd react.

"What's the problem, Ma?"

"I just don't want Chance to get spoiled."

"What you talkin' 'bout? He's a kid. Kids

like and need toys. It's normal."

"Yeah, but . . . She thought quickly. "I love that you bring him new things, but my girls will get upset. They act jealous. And they play with Chance's toys and sometimes they break them." That was the truth, but it wasn't because of envy.

"No problem. Next time I come by, I'll bring something for them too. I don't mind."

"Quantavius!" Her heart was touched and torn. She decided to keep her mouth closed and let him be a blessing to her children.

But when he visited her again two weeks later, not only did he have a bag filled with goodies for the kids, Q also presented Coco with a large jar of bath bombs and a tall bottle of bubble bath wrapped in a pink ribbon. He even got her a dozen roses.

"Gifts for me? That's so sweet. But why'd you do this, Q?"

"Well, I just was thinking about you . . . you do so much as a mama . . . and I thought you'd want to know . . . Hold on a sec." Q fished through his cell phone and let her see a photo. Calhoun Humphries and Samira stood cheek to cheek. She wore a veil that was flipped open and uncovered her smiling face. Calhoun broadly smiled as well, and he wore the very same suit that he'd purchased for his and Coco's wedding ceremony.

"Did he?" she asked.

He grimly nodded.

"Please, Q," she wailed and pushed the phone away.

"One of our friends sent this to me. I wasn't invited. And I see you weren't either. But you should know the truth."

"But why show this to me?" she sobbed. "If the truth messes up everything, why tell it?"

"Because lies do the same thing. And both of 'em hurt."

Coco stood motionless. It seemed like all the memories, decent vivid memories of Calhoun, were something she couldn't forget. The boisterous joking; the evenings of all of them sitting at the table and eating dinner together as a family. The nights they hung out with their kids and just laughed at every silly thing they did. That's when she'd had the most fun. Where did those times go, and why did everything have to change? And more important, why did another woman come from nowhere and live out her dream?

"Life is so unfair," she said.

"Ain't it, though. It's something I think about every damned day." He hated seeing the hurt on her face, but Coco needed a good dose of reality.

"Maybe now you can go on with your life, Ma. That man you was crazy about? He's gone."

"As much as I hate to admit it, yeah. My man is gone."

The May Sister Day had convened. This time they were gathered at Coco's. And she wasted no time letting the sisters know how she felt weeks after finding out that Calhoun up and married someone who she didn't know was still in his life.

"Honestly, I feel like whipping that bitch's ass."

"Why, Coco?" Dru asked.

" 'Cause she stepped out with a man that she knew already had someone."

"But you two didn't officially live together. And you have no idea what Calhoun told the woman. Some men do lie about their real status."

"True that," Alita said. "Maybe in this case, your anger needs to be at him, not at her. You don't even know her, but you fully knew Calhoun's ways."

"All I know is that he needed to be loyal to me just like he demanded that I be loyal to him." Coco thought again about how she hid the truth from him about messing around with Q. Perhaps this was her punishment for keeping shameful secrets.

"It doesn't matter what you say, Lita," Coco continued. "That lady, Samira, is dead wrong. Why mess around with a man that's in a relationship?"

"Coco, I know you're heated and pissed off, and I don't blame you," Alita told her. "But it took me a long time to learn that a side chick could never exist if the man wasn't disloyal. She didn't aim a gun at his dick and tell him 'if you don't fuck me I'm going to blow it off.' Nooo, it did not happen that way. And you already knew he was immature and inexperienced. Did you think he would never be curious about sleeping with another woman?"

"If that man loved me the way he claimed —"

"Love has nothing to do with a man wanting to have sex with a new chick. Even I know that," Dru claimed. "Tyrique and I discuss this type of thing a lot. And he said that for men, sex is not emotional. That's why a married man can go sleep with a woman, and when he's all done, he can leave the girl in her bed and return home to his wife and kiss on her and act like nothing ever happened. He got sexually satisfied and now his mind is focused on that 'honey do' list. And he's ready to resume being a 'good' husband until the next opportunity comes along."

"That's coldblooded," Coco said.

"It's real," Alita said. "And it happens every single day out here. Next time, if you find yourself a good one, you better hold onto him real tight, because the good old days of men being old-fashioned, decent, and faithful, and holding the door open and pulling out her chair, unless you're lucky, that shit is long gone."

"Talk that talk, Lita," Dru chimed in.

Alita was tired of Coco wallowing in self-pity.

"For this Sister Day meeting, let's talk about truth again. Something that keeps coming back to bite us in the ass over and over." Alita wanted Coco to hear her, really understand once and for all. "Calhoun is off the market. You got that?"

Coco nodded.

"Forget him. But don't try to kill him or his new wife either. If anything, be nice to the lady. That'll throw her off. Become really good buddies with her, and that'll scare her more than threats ever could. You getting what I'm saying?"

"Nope, not really, Lita."

"Put it like this. No matter how hard it is, the truth of your situation is what you need to face. Truth is not something that you believe. It's something that you accept."

"I get it," Dru said in agreement. "That's how you're able to move on, because, Coco, at this point there's nothing left for you to do. And you now can give your beautiful kids lots of love. A lot of women wish they had what you have, even as a single mother."

Coco knew Dru was referring to the fact that she could not get pregnant and did not know how it felt to give birth.

"I guess I never looked at it that way," Coco admitted.

"Right. Be thankful for the good things you have," Dru told her. "You have your life, your kids, a decent house, clothes on your back, you're a great cook, and you're loving and funny. You're pretty. You've got your own transportation. You can see, you can walk, talk, hear, and you're not in prison."

"Not yet," Alita said.

"Okay, okay," Coco said, finally laughing.

"And the most important thing, girl," Dru said. "You've got us. And we'll be around to help you do whatever you need for the kids. Right, sisters?"

Alita, Burgundy, Dru, and Elyse gathered

together in a tight circle, pulling Coco into a much-needed group hug. Alita even gave her a kiss on the cheek.

"Girl, stop it, now, I ain't playing with you," Coco said as she tried to duck.

For her sometimes it seemed as though the tears would never stop falling. But this time, she shed happy tears.

"You will be all right," Alita assured her as she wiped her lipstick off Coco's cheek. "And instead of looking at things like not marrying Calhoun as the worst day of your life, flip that shit around and see it as the best day of your life."

"Okay, now you're stretching it, Lita," Coco told her. "I loved him and wanted to be his wife till death. But now another woman is living my dream!"

Burgundy added, "Take it from me. Samira may be happy for now, but the grass might not be greener on the other side."

Then Dru added, "That's why Tyrique and I are still happily cohabitating. If you're not a hundred percent ready, then you should never feel pressured, or even try to force your man into getting married. I think you would have eventually left him anyway because you would have gotten tired of handing him all your power. Now, you've got your power back. Do something good with it."

Coco surprisingly drew strength from her sisters' honest opinions. Not wanting to reject the truth as she'd so often done in the past, she listened and agreed.

She could no longer run from truth.

It was time to face it.

CHAPTER 7
SEX AIN'T BETTER THAN LOVE

Nate could not believe what he was seeing. It was late on a Friday evening. He was downstairs in the family room. And a pair of his pajamas, plus several large pillows, had been spread across the sofa. A makeshift bed for husbands in the doghouse.

He went and stood outside their bedroom, pressed his ear against the door.

He heard light voices.

Nate rattled the knob. It was locked.

He banged his fist against the hardwood. "Burg, what the hell is going on? Why is this door locked?"

"You know exactly why." Nate heard his wife answer him from the other side of the door. She was chatting with Alita on speakerphone while this was going on.

Nate banged the door three more times. "Unlock the door, Burg."

"Tell him to go fuck himself and swallow his own semen, B."

"Girl, be quiet. This doesn't concern you, Lita."

"Like hell it doesn't," Alita snapped back. "As long as you're still married to that poor excuse of a man, everything y'all do affects me."

"Burg, if you don't open up this door right now, you'll wish you had." Nate sounded more frustrated than enraged. Nevertheless, she pictured her husband, his height, and how he towered over her. His big hands that, even when he was just playing around, could hurt and bruise.

"No, Nate. It's better this way. You can stay out there. Sleep on that couch or you can use the guest room on the first floor."

Her meaning did not go unnoticed. Nate couldn't believe that his wife thought he'd actually go upstairs and touch his daughters. No way. He adored the girls.

"I don't like this," he complained. "I don't like being locked out of my own room."

"Oh, yeah," she said. "It could be worse. You could be locked up."

He fell silent. This was her first time talking to him about the "incident." Ever since Alita had come to their home and practically kidnapped Elyse last December, Burgundy had barely mentioned what happened. It was too painful to think about him having sex with her sister. She wondered how long it had been going on and told herself that it had happened only one time. And no way she'd ask Nate. All he'd do is lie and make up excuses.

It was so very hard to love a man whom you thought you knew but didn't.

And these days, repulsion was the best she could give him when it came to intimacy.

"I don't want to sleep next to you, Nate."

"Why not?"

"Are you kidding me? You know exactly why; don't act stupid."

"Sis," Alita interrupted. "I'm sorry but you're the one that's acting stupid." Her voice loudly rang out. "You don't fuck the man anymore; you're making him sleep on the couch, which is totally understandable, yet you still want to be married to him? That makes no damn sense."

"It's complicated," Burgundy answered in a wistful tone. She lowered her voice. "I-I don't want to get divorced. I just want us to take some time out to work on our relationship. When that will happen? I honestly don't know. Right now I need to stay focused on the girls and on our businesses. And being like I used to be: the good wife, the perfect yet stupid wife, is dead last on my agenda."

"You sound bitter," Alita responded with a knowing laugh. "You sound vengeful too. Just like your big sister. Maybe it runs in the family."

For once Burgundy could not argue with Alita. For the trials and tribulations that she'd gone through, the struggles, and the disbelief that her husband could have it in him to exhibit inappropriate behavior toward Elyse — it was beyond her comprehension. Why did people think they knew other people like the back of their hand just to find out they were living with a stranger? Nate's behavior disgusted her. She wanted to kill him, not forgive him. Yet she felt that letting go of the anger and offering him some semblance of forgiveness could happen, just not overnight.

So she'd given Nate the silent treatment at times. And that would send a shock to his system and caused him to plead with her to stick by his side. But every time her husband begged her to look past his "crazy ways," as he called them, she shrank back in disgust. Each time he tried to play off his behavior as just temporary poor judgment, she wanted to weep. And when he stooped so low as to even blame his indiscretions on her, saying that if she had not withheld her wifely duties from him, he wouldn't be so desperate.

In those moments Burgundy was one step away from changing the locks on the front and back doors and blocking him out of her life for good. She hated the lies, the disillusionment, and the misplaced blame for his unwise, felonious actions.

"Look, B. Take it from me," Alita continued. "I've been where you at right now. Trying to make that decision. Should I stay or should I go? Should I stick with him for the sake of the kids? Or should I kick his ass out and put my life back together again?"

"Look, Alita," Burgundy told her. "I appreciate your advice, but truly, you're the last woman that I'd take relationship advice from."

"Oh, yeah?" Alita said feeling insulted. "Then why don't you tweet Iyanla Vanzant and see if you can go on *Fix My Life*. 'Cause your life sucks, B. It's fraudulent as hell. And I never ever thought I'd see the day that those words came out of my mouth. Bye, bitch."

Feeling frustrated, Alita hung up. She hated that so many of the Reeves sisters were going through terrible situations. It was as if the family was cursed. It made her angry and sad. But soon, Alita dismissed those thoughts from her mind. When a woman purposely chose to be in her situation, she'd always get what she had coming to her.

After thinking and praying for ten minutes, Burgundy decided to unlock the door. When she opened it, she saw Nate seated on the floor outside their bedroom, his back pressed against the wall, head slumped over. She heard him snoring, the noise resembling a tiger.

And in spite of herself, she giggled. He looked exhausted, yet endearing.

"Nate," she whispered. "Get up."

"Huh?" He struggled to open his eyes. She nudged him with her toe. "What's wrong?" he said groggily.

"You fell asleep. I'm sure your butt must be hurting by now." He wiped his eyes with rounded fists and stood to his feet.

"That's not the only thing that's hurting." He actually grabbed the front of his robe.

"Don't start. Don't play the sympathy card with me, Nate." She walked to the kitchen, and he followed behind.

"You may not want to make love to me," — he yawned — "but the fact that you're still talking to me gives me some hope. I guess showing love is more important than having sex."

"You got that right," Burgundy said and

opened the cabinet to reach for a box of tea bags.

"Wait, let me do the honors." She gave him a dubious look then shrugged. He proceeded to pull out the tea, sugar, a bottle of honey, and fresh lemons that he set aside on the counter.

"Go right ahead. Knock yourself out. But my letting you make me some tea doesn't impress me. I'm not as easy as that, Nate. You have a long way to go before you impress me again."

"Ouch," he said. He looked around at their large beautiful home, which he'd paid for with his hard-earned money. The expensive furnishings with custom made drapes. Her tasteful clothes and jewelry that she still enjoyed wearing. Compared to other wives, she didn't have it so bad.

"I don't know that I deserve that judgment."

"Are you serious? You deserve jail, Nate. Don't you get it?"

Soon Burgundy was talking to the back of his head. Because every time she tried to tell him what was on her mind, he turned away from her. He covered one ear with one hand and tried to open the refrigerator for a cold bottle of water with his free hand.

"You may not want to hear it, Nate, but

for us to move forward in our marriage, in this family, you have to listen to me and listen real good." She paused, carefully selecting the tender yet firm words she needed to express.

"In some odd way, I still care about you for whatever reason. I can't turn love on and off like it's a water faucet —"

"Thank you, Burg. I needed to hear that."

"Hold on. On the other hand, you must realize that you hurt me deeply. Not just me, you hurt my family, Nate. My sister. You embarrassed me with your actions. Do you understand?"

He nodded and poured cold water into two large mugs. "Go on," he mumbled.

"You have daughters. Girls that you adore. How would you feel if a grown-ass man did to Natalia and Sidnee what you did to Elyse?"

He walked to the microwave, popped open the door, inserted the mugs, then slammed it. He set the timer to three minutes and listened to the hum of the oven as it boiled the water.

"You wouldn't like it, Nate. I know you wouldn't. Not as much as you dote on our girls."

"But she's not a kid. She's grown. She only did what grown-ups do."

"What? I can't believe you said that." Burgundy eyed both of the cups of water that were bubbling inside the microwave. "Surely you can't think that age is what makes it okay to sexually force yourself on a woman? You wielded power over Elyse even if she is almost twenty. If a woman was sixty-five and a man strong-armed her into sex, do you truly believe the fact that she's old doesn't make her feel violated? Or powerless? Every woman has the right to choose when she wants to make love. When she's not given a choice, it's rape!"

This time Burgundy did not ask Nate if he got it. If his predatory actions were unwanted, then that's what mattered the most.

Burgundy continued. "Furthermore, let's get something straight. Even if she had said yes —"

"She wanted it, Burg. She did not mind at all. That's the part that no one knows."

"Oh, save it, Nate!" Hearing him speak those words hurt her deeply. The idea that Elyse, shy little Elyse, could lust after him and beg her husband to make love to her was totally unfathomable.

Or was it? Why, anyone could see that the girl dressed like a seductress these days. But still, Burgundy did not want to imagine that scenario.

"The end result is that that girl is traumatized. She is trying her best to get through this situation. Thank God for the psychotherapy sessions. And believe it or not, Alita has stepped up to the plate. She takes damned good care of her. And I think that Alita is right. She told me —"

"The only thing Alita can be is wrong. She fills your mind up with all kinds of crap. And you fall for it every time."

"That's my sister you're talking about."

"And I'm your husband. You don't owe her a thing. You haven't made any vows to her —"

"And I don't have to."

"Then you're stupid, Burg. Because last time I checked, that sister needs a psychiatrist too."

"You know what. Be quiet. I don't want to hear anything you have to say, Nate. As intelligent as you are, you still don't get it. And until you stop putting the blame on everything and everyone else but yourself, this conversation is over."

Burgundy thought long and hard as she stared into the cup of tea that he'd made for her. Finally she poured the liquid down the sink and walked out of the kitchen.

Chapter 8
Basic Training

The key of imagination allows you through doors that you've never gone through before.

"Come on, Elyse," Dru said. "Repeat after me. 'I'd think twice about doing that if I were you.' Go ahead, say it."

Elyse tried hard to speak as intelligently and precisely as Dru. But she felt frustrated. Some days she could get into talking like she was powerful, other days she felt defeated.

"I don't want to talk like that, Dru. It's too hard."

"It's not hard, sweetie. The words you hear and the way I pronounce every syllable, you need to do the same thing. You're going to get yourself good and ready. And stay ready."

Besides Alita, Dru was the other person that Elyse trusted with her secrets.

"You can confront Nate and never allow

him to put his creepy hands on you again. Do well in your job and one day, Sis, you may end up getting a better paying job in the Texas Medical Center."

"What?" Elyse said, looking aghast. The TMC was where Dru was employed as an occupational therapist. It was much larger than Morning Glory. There was no way she could imagine herself working around so many people.

"Come on over here," Dru demanded. Elyse followed her to the bathroom and was instructed to face the mirror. Brilliant lights shone upon each delicate feature: Her large doe eyes that looked afraid. The downward turn of her mouth. The deadness of her eyes.

"We're going to change all of that," Dru said. "We have to."

Dru was starting to sound a lot like Gamba. He was at work. And oh, how she missed him.

Elyse allowed Dru to fix her hair and they practiced enunciating words. But Elyse had a lazy tongue. Anytime she got nervous, she would lapse into her former self. But she tried very hard to do exactly as she was told.

"You don't have a right to speak to me like I'm nothing. I'm not scared of you. I won't let you abuse me anymore," Elyse said, pretending she was talking to Nate.

"Hey, a long time ago I used to be like you. When I was in high school I lacked self-esteem. Afraid of my own shadow."

"You? I don't believe dat."

"It's 'that' Elyse, 'that.' Don't be so lazy."

"I can't help it."

"Yes, you can. If you want a better life you'll do whatever it takes to have it," Dru told her. "And if you want to keep Gamba interested, you need to step up your game. He's a good guy. He's been around the world. If you have nothing to offer him, he's going to go about his way. Because you're not giving the man any reason to stay."

At that Elyse's little ears pricked up. She could not imagine Gamba losing interest in her. And she could have kicked herself for not letting him know that she was starting to truly care about him. But she was scared. What if he laughed at her? What if he didn't feel the same way she did?

Life and love could be so confusing, and Elyse desperately wanted to do things right.

"I will give him a reason to stay," she defiantly told Dru. "Watch me."

Dru smiled and high-fived her sister.

The time had come. Elyse wanted to be nervous but couldn't do it if she tried. She felt very prepared and ready to do battle.

Dru dropped her off at Morning Glory. Elyse felt at ease when she noticed Burgundy's car sitting in the parking lot.

"He's not here now," Dru read her mind and quietly assured her as they walked inside. "But there's no telling when he'll be back. You just want to remain professional and do your job. You are now a hostess and that's good. That means you'll be up front and center, and never really have to be anywhere alone in the restaurant."

Elyse nodded. She was in full makeup. And as she walked inside the restaurant, she could feel all eyes upon her. She walked with confidence, not slinking around the way she used to.

"You are black girl magic, Sis." Dru gave her a hug and told her goodbye.

"I know it. I know."

Dru departed, then made sure she had Elyse on speed dial and that video chat was ready at all times.

Elyse placed her things behind the counter and greeted the other girls.

"Hi, Elyse," said her shift manager. The other coworkers stood back carefully observing the girl who used to switch out salt and pepper shakers.

In no time at all, Elyse grew comfortable greeting the guests, handing out menus, and deciding which tables they'd sit at.

Standing all day on her feet took a lot out of her. By the time she was finally able to take a break, she kicked off her shoes and found an empty booth in the back.

Elyse was fiddling with her phone, answering Dru's texts, when she felt a presence hovering over her.

Nate stared at Elyse as if she was a dazzling beauty. And she was. Elyse felt more feminine and womanly than she ever had in her life. Even though her body was covered by the hostess uniform, her makeup was impeccable and her hairstyle made her stand out.

"You look good, Elyse," Nate told her. "Way different than you used to look."

"Did I tell you it was okay to speak to me?"

"W-what did you say?"

"You're not even supposed to be here. And why are you talking to me? Will you please leave me alone?"

He felt indignant. The girl had never spoken to him in such a manner in her life. "Need I remind you that I am your superior? Don't take that tone with me."

"Don't talk to me and you won't hear this tone."

"How dare you —"

"And how dare you do what you did to me! I never liked it and I never asked for it, so stop going around spreading rumors about me." She felt righteously angry at him. Thankfully, there were no customers around to witness their confrontation. Elyse's transformation seemed amazing, but it was also draining. She felt like she was playing a role. She felt like she was drowning and throwing out her own life preserver to save her life.

Shame him! That's what Dru told her. The abuser needs to hear the truth, the facts about what he did and how those things made you feel. Shame him!

Elyse walked over to Nate and said in his ear, "If you ever try to touch me again without my permission, it'll be the last thing you ever see yourself do."

She stormed away and told him she needed to go to the ladies' room.

Her heart beating wildly, she had to get Gamba on the telephone.

"Gamba," she said. "I'm sorry to bother you."

"What's wrong? What happened, Elyse?"

"He showed up again and I told him how I felt."

"Okay, and how did he respond?"

"He didn't say anything. I dunno. He

might be mad. I don't care." Her voice was filled with stubbornness. "I do my job and I don't mess with anybody. He should leave me alone."

"Where was Burgundy when this happened?"

"I don't know. I don't want to be around her either. I-I hate working at this place, but in a way it's good because I felt I had to confront him. At the same time, it's hard to be around him and her. I wish I had another family."

"Sweetie, you're just upset right now. You get off in, what, forty minutes? I'd like to come pick you up. I'll call Dru to let her know."

Her face lit up. Just knowing she'd see Gamba made her heart swell with happiness. He was the brightest of sunlight after the darkest of days. Oh, how she loved him. She only wished that he loved her too. Sure, she could rely on Gamba to look out for her. He was always there when it counted, but why didn't he ever tell her that he loved her? Why didn't he voluntarily kiss her? Wasn't she pretty enough? What more could she do to get him to care for her?

Once she finished using the restroom, Elyse returned to the front station. By then she felt better and more confident. She allowed herself to be extra outgoing, laughing with the customers and giving them a friendly smile. A little while later, Burgundy entered the restaurant. She had left that morning to attend to some business and had not yet crossed Elyse's path. But now she noticed how the young lady seemed to be the center of attention at the hostess station. Several electronic pagers were clutched in Elyse's hand. She proudly walked the male guests to their booth. Her ponytail was set high on her head. Burgundy watched the girl's hair freely swing back and forth while she traipsed through the restaurant. All the men enjoyed being served by Elyse equally, and Burgundy steamed with envy as she watched them laugh and joke.

"Who the hell does she think she is?" Burgundy asked under her breath.

She waited for Elyse to return.

When she got back, several other men, including some older gentlemen, were waiting.

"Um, our other hostess can help you out," Burgundy offered.

"No, thanks. We want Elyse. She's our favorite."

"Your favorite? Oh, all right," Burgundy told them. She fumed inside as she watched Elyse attend to those guests as well.

And when Elyse returned to the hostess station, this time Burgundy was ready for her. "Elyse, can you come to the business office with me?"

Burgundy's tone and facial expression caused Elyse to feel weak in the knees. She felt her heart jump inside her chest. Her breathing intensified.

"How long will this take? I'm 'bout to punch out."

"You are *about* to punch out. Not 'bout."

"I know dat," she snapped back.

"You know that. T-H-A-T. It's pronounced *that.*"

"I said I know that. Leave me 'lone, B."

Burgundy impatiently asked her again, "Are you coming or not?" Elyse passively followed behind her sister, her mind racing as she wondered what was wrong this time. Burgundy shut the door behind her then turned around. She gazed at Elyse, noticing everything about her that stood out. Elyse was wearing the company uniform that consisted of a gray-and-pink polo with the Morning Glory logo embroidered on it. She also had on dark slacks along with comfortable shoes, but Burgundy noticed something different about her. Covering Elyse's shoulders was a smart looking black jacket with the sleeves slightly rolled up. They exposed

151

some gold bracelets that Burgundy had never seen before. Gold earrings dangled from her ears and were so long they almost touched her shoulders.

"Where'd you get that blazer?"

"Dru got it for me. Why?"

"I'm asking the questions. And I think, no, make that I *know* that you are in violation of our company dress code. You are not allowed to wear earrings that big and pretentious. Take 'em off. Now!"

"No!"

"Elyse? Did you say no to me? Your boss?"

"What difference does it make? I'm *about* to leave."

"You leave in ten minutes. You're still on the clock. Remove the earrings and the blazer or I will dock your pay."

"I don't care. Go 'head. Tired of you." Elyse was young but she knew when a woman viewed her as competition, and it hurt her to think that Burgundy would treat her in such a manner.

"You can dock me all you want," she continued. "You do everything else you want to do."

"What did you say?"

"You heard me. Why you messing with me? Threatening me? You getting on me about petty stuff and stayin' on my last nerve." Her frustrations bubbled over, and she was unable to stop. Just because Elyse was mostly quiet did not mean she had no feelings, that she appreciated being bullied and ostracized.

"Why you hounding me over dumb things? I do my job. I do it real good. That's what you should focus on."

"Well, um, I . . ." Burgundy was startled. In her entire life she never recalled her sister defending herself with such conviction. In a way it was admirable, but on the other hand how could she speak to Burgundy like that, like she forgot the definition of respect?

"Elyse, I agree that you've caught on fast and you do this job pretty well, but you need to straighten out that uniform next time, so we won't have this issue again."

"What issue, B?"

Elyse removed the jacket. And it was then that Burgundy noticed that the young woman's breasts had filled out even more. Same was true for her hips. Elyse had become a woman and somehow had graduated from her girlish nature. Had Nate noticed? Did he like it?

God knew that Burgundy had recently shunned all his attempts to get sex. Maybe he would turn to her sister again. Burgundy stared at the big executive desk that stood before her and imagined Elyse propped up with her legs spread and Nate standing in the middle of them.

No! No way!

"Put the jacket back on, Elyse. It doesn't look so bad after all. In fact, I want you to wear it every time you check in to work. And since you only have five minutes left on the clock, you may leave now."

"Good." Elyse walked away with an angry look on her face.

"Who's picking you up?" Burgundy called after her.

"None of your business," Elyse responded. She opened the door and slammed it, leaving Burgundy feeling resentful and confused.

Days later Elyse was too sick to go to work. It was early morning on a Friday. She was at Alita's place. And she was sulking. Even though she'd gotten Burgundy all together by then and kept the woman at bay, Elyse still wasn't completely happy.

Especially that morning.

Gamba had visited her as usual. But as soon as he got there he had to step outside of the apartment to take a telephone call.

When he returned inside, Elyse was sneezing, coughing, and wiping her eyes with crumpled pieces of tissue. Every part of her body ached, from her muscles to her head. She felt like she'd been run over by an eighteen-wheeler.

"You look tired. Beautiful, but terrible all at the same time," Gamba said to Elyse in his easygoing manner.

"I already know I look and feel like crap." She coughed loud then blew her nose. It felt embarrassing for him to see her in such a sickly condition.

"Hey, I need to step out for a minute," Gamba replied. "I'll be right back."

She was so relieved that she did not even respond to him as he left her alone.

Why doesn't he love me? What will it take for the man that I love to love me back?

After a while Gamba returned holding a couple of grocery bags. He set everything on the counter and retrieved a package of cough drops, a carton of orange juice, a box of cold medicine, a can of tea bags, soup cans, and several boxes of tissues.

"Here," he said. "I got something for you." He unwrapped a cough drop and made her open up her mouth so he could insert it.

"Suck on that for a minute."

She silently obeyed and stared at him in anger and misery.

Gamba proceeded to open up a can of

chicken noodle soup, found a tiny pot, and heated up the food. He doctored it up with his own special seasonings and stirred it until it was smoking hot. The savory smell of chicken broth filled the apartment.

When the soup was ready, he scooped a large amount in a bowl and carefully placed it on a serving tray. He poured some orange juice and dropped some ice cubes in the tall glass.

All this time Elyse had been reclining on the sofa, her legs curled underneath her, as she silently fumed about her circumstances and wondered what she could do to fix them.

She took one look at the soup. "Can you add crackers?"

"Sure."

Elyse instructed him to place eight to ten crackers in the bowl and crush them up for her. Gamba did exactly as Elyse instructed. When the soup was just as she liked it he asked her to open her mouth, and he spooned a good bit of it, all the juices and noodles and chicken pieces together, and served it to her.

She slowly began to relax and eat as he sat beside her. She ate until she was nice and full. Then he grabbed the Fire stick that he had previously taken the time to program for her and Alita.

"What do you want to watch?" he asked.

"*Black-ish* or a good movie."

"Which do you prefer?"

She gave him a thoughtful glance. "My favorite movie is *Beyond the Lights*." Elyse loved that romantic film about a female R & B singing star and the handsome young cop who is assigned to help her.

Gamba set up the movie to begin streaming. He then sat next to her and watched TV in silence, unaware of the glances she kept giving him.

He's a dummy, that's what's wrong with him. He doesn't know I love him and it seems like he's not into me. What's wrong with this guy?

After the film was over, he turned off the television.

"Open your mouth," he commanded. Elyse decided not to argue. He whipped out a thermometer, placed it underneath her tongue, and took her temperature. The instrument beeped.

"Looks like you're going to live, young lady. Your temperature is normal. You'll recover in time. I need you to keep getting your rest, drink lots of liquids, and just take it easy."

"I need you," she blurted, in an almost pleading way. To Elyse, Gamba looked so

157

handsome she could eat him up and enjoy him way more than some soup and crackers. He was wearing army fatigues that day, and she loved a man in uniform. It was his day off from work, and she did not understand why he was spending it hanging around a sick woman.

"I need," she said. "Um, I need."

"What did you say?"

"I-I need you to hand me that box of tissues." She coughed and gave him a sad look.

"Right, of course, I'll get that for you, sweetie." He opened the box, yanked out a few sheets, and thrust them at her.

"Here. Elyse. Blow hard. You'll feel better once you get everything out that's inside of you."

"No shit."

Although she did not want to do as he told her and dreaded that he could see her in such an ugly, unattractive state, Elyse was too mad to argue. She was ready to give up. This love thing was too complicated. It did not matter if she nicely combed her hair, or carefully applied her makeup, or dressed sexily. She concluded that the man she loved would never love her.

Gamba brought her a warm blanket and spread it across her lap. He stuffed two pillows behind her back until she said she felt comfortable.

"I'm ready to watch *Black-ish,*" she said.

"Yes, ma'am."

He sat next to her tending to her every need while she distractedly watched the television. She nursed thoughts of hurt and rejection. Why hadn't he tried to kiss her? What good was her hand if he didn't try to hold it?

When the medicine took effect, Elyse began to nod off. She gradually fell asleep. Gamba picked her up in his arms and carried her to Alita's bedroom. Since Alita wasn't home, he thought she'd be more comfortable resting in a big bed.

Gamba gingerly set her down and watched her cough and yawn and struggle to get comfortable. After a while he unlaced his shoes and slid in bed next to her, still fully clothed. He held her close to his side and listened to the way that she breathed in and out, snorting and coughing. At times she moaned like a baby, and the sound was music to his ears.

Eventually, they fell asleep next to each other, breathing in perfect harmony, like two that became one.

But when you're asleep you're not conscious enough to know what's going on, and Elyse had no idea that Gamba had grabbed her hand and held it as they rested.

Hours later Gamba woke up. Elyse was still fast asleep. He stared at her in silence then left. He came back and sprayed the room with Lysol.

He walked over to Elyse, leaned over, and started to give her a quick peck on the lips. But he thought about her brother-in-law and changed his mind. He in no way wanted to take advantage of her like Nate had.

"I'll be back," he whispered to her, then closed the door behind him.

CHAPTER 9
UNFINISHED BUSINESS

Alita and Leno were standing in his bedroom when her heart sank. She couldn't believe it as she stared at Leno. She tilted her neck to peer closely at him. "Did you grow a couple more inches, son?"

He nodded and shrugged, acting like his growth spurt was no big deal. But when you were a single mother who had to keep forking over dollars to buy new shoes that no longer fit, and pants that kept getting too short, it was a huge deal.

She asked him to do her a favor.

"Um, Leno. I want you to lie down on your bed. Get in it and act like you're about to go to sleep."

"Yes, ma'am."

Leno crawled into his bed, the one he'd been accustomed to sleeping on during the past few years. He spread out on his side, shoved a couple of pillows under his head, and curled into a ball.

"Damn!" Alita said.

His feet hung out, legs too long to fit comfortably; she watched as he clumsily lay on his side.

"I feel so bad, Leno. Can you forgive your mom?"

"What are you talking about?"

"No wonder you've been complaining about back and neck problems. You need a new bed and a mattress. And they need to be top of the line."

She did the quick math. For a decent mattress, Alita would shell out more than a thousand bucks. The box spring plus a new headboard could easily double the cost. She did not want to go cheap.

"I may as well get you a king-size bed because what if you grow some more? You're definitely not about to shrink."

"I dunno."

"Sounds like you don't care, but I'm not you. And from the bottom of my heart please forgive me. Let's go, son. We'll head over to Gallery Furniture."

It was a Saturday morning in June. The weather was so beautiful that the freeways were crowded with cars; passengers speeding along the road to visit shopping malls, water parks, the lake, or a nearby beach. It was a beautiful summer day and felt like it should be celebrated.

But when Alita coasted into the furniture storeroom and asked to be shown the king-size beds, she hardly wanted to break out into a cheer. Why did everything cost so much? Once she picked out a suitable Tempur-Pedic mattress and box spring, she agreed to max out the only credit card she was lucky enough to own. That single expenditure would set her back by five grand.

"Thanks, Mom." Her generosity was totally unexpected.

Alita whispered back, "You're welcome, Big Foot. That's my new nickname for you."

He laughed.

They arranged for the bed to be delivered that night and walked out of the store to look for her car.

"You're the best mom in the world."

"I'm a fool, that's what I am."

"Why you say that?"

Worried, she explained to Leno. "This means no more goofing off. You gotta stay on top of your b-ball. And hope and pray that your Big Feet gets picked by a decent team."

"What? Is that all I am to you? A prospective NBA player?"

"I'm sorry, Leno. That came out all wrong.

I love you to death, but Lord knows I had no idea that I would have a child who eats like a horse and grows like a weed. I mean, hell, this five-thousand-dollar expense is like buying a used car."

"Right. And you told me that you were going to buy me that too. Remember? You told me that when I was thirteen."

"That's because back then you and your silly little friends thought it would be fun to try and steal a car. Thank God I caught you just in time. After I whipped your behind good, I had to tell you something to make you act right."

He looked appalled. "Guess what? I believed you, Mom. Plus, I straightened up after that. I think you should go on and get me a car."

"Leno, that's out of the question. Right now a comfortable bed is way more important than a car."

"What? Why? You promised."

"Promises get broken."

"Then why promise me?"

"Sometimes things change."

"Then change 'em back!"

"What?"

"Make things different, make 'em better," he pleaded. "You're my mom. That's your job."

"Leno, you seem to forget that I'm not the only parent you have. Shit! Your daddy sells cars."

"I know that, but he never promised me one."

"Oh, Leno." He was starting to stress out Alita. "It doesn't really matter. Ask him to help you anyway. Get him on the phone and see what he says."

"I don't want to bother my dad because you already told me —"

"My God, will you please stop worrying me about getting you a damned car? Do I look like I can afford it?"

Leno's eyes were blank with indifference. Seeing her son leer at her as if she was inadequate filled Alita's heart with sadness. There was nothing worse than being a parent who lacked the resources to care for her children.

"I want to do it for you, son, believe me I do. I just can't afford it."

"That's what you always say. You've been saying it forever."

"Leno, you act like I do nothing for you."

"That's the thing, Mom. The stuff you end up doing, you complain about it, and you act like it's just so hard for you to be my mother. Why do things for me if you're just going to complain?"

"You're wrong! That ain't the truth and you know it. It's not complaining. It's realizing the hell I go through to make it happen. I-I bust my ass to take care of you and Elyse."

"This is not about her. It's about *me*. Why help me out if you're just going to bitch about it? How do you think that makes me feel?"

"Leno? Are you out of your mind? As long as you live under my roof, don't you ever talk to me like that. Like we're on the same level."

"Tell you what. Since I'm such a burden that you can't afford, maybe I should leave home? How about that?"

By then they both were breathing hard and shouting at each other in the middle of a crowded parking lot. They were bound to attract attention. And Alita did not care. But the one person Alita did not expect to be watching them quietly came and stood in front of her.

"Hey, Alita. I thought I recognized you. What are you doing here?" It was Jerrod. She'd been avoiding him for the past few weeks.

"Taking care of some business," she told him. "Come on, son. Let's go."

"Wait," Jerrod said and held her arm to

keep her from leaving. She hated that.

"Do you mind? I don't like people touching me like that."

"Okay, sorry. I just wanted to meet the little fella. Or should I say big fella. This must be Leno, your son? Hey, nice to meet you. I'm Jerrod Dawson."

Leno eyed the guy warily. But he eventually said, "Hey."

"Your mom has told me a lot about you."

"Oh, yeah. Well, who are you? Who is this, Mom?"

"An old friend. Nice seeing you, Jerrod. C'mon, Leno."

"Hold on a second, Alita. We have some unfinished business that we need to discuss. Um, can you do something for me right now?"

"No, Jerrod. I can't. Can you see I'm trying to leave Gallery Furniture? It's not like you can find anything in there for less than a hundred." She laughed and tried to make another joke. But Jerrod did not join in. His jaw was rigid and tight with anger.

"I don't really care about all of that. Because you see, Leno has two parents that are in a position to help him. My own father is in prison," he explained to Leno. "Aggravated sexual assault was the charge. He got the maximum sentence too. I was about six years old when my daddy got arrested. That was twenty years ago."

"Damn! That's too bad."

"My daddy was convicted and locked up in the state prison a little while after your, um, aunt Elyse was born. Yeah, my dad's been in prison almost as long as Elyse has been alive. Let's see, he should be turning fifty-seven at the end of this year. Imagine having twenty birthdays pass by while you're locked up from the free world. Twenty long years with no candles to blow out."

"Uh, sorry to hear that," Leno told him.

"I'm sorry too. Breaks my fucking heart that my daddy got taken away from me. Taken away from my mother. Our family."

Leno looked confused.

"Oh, my bad," Jerrod continued. "Your mom and I lived across the street from each other when we were kids. I used to date your aunt Drucilla from elementary school to high school. That was my girl. Did she ever mention me?"

"No, the hell she has not, Jerrod. Now if you don't mind, we gotta be somewhere else." Alita grabbed Leno's arm to drag him along. She knew that Jerrod would finish explaining to Leno what happened. That he did not find out until he was fifteen who his dad was accused of sexually assaulting: his girlfriend's sister, Alita. And that would explain why, later on, Jerrod's mother never wanted him and Dru to be boyfriend and girlfriend. His mom suffered in silence and had spared him of the truth for years. And after he discovered the truth, he did not want anything to do with Dru or her family. That is, until he got the idea that Alita should personally pay him for everything she'd done to destroy his family. And initially, Alita agreed to fork over tiny amounts of cash to him because he'd convinced her that what happened between her and his father was partly her fault. And when he threatened to tell her then-husband Leonard about the baby, she offered to pay him more money. Plus that's what her mother, Greta, had encouraged her to do when she'd been alive. Greta kept Alita's name out of the news during Jack's trial. The lies began. The cycle continued.

These days Jerrod felt Alita should pay. "I don't care where you gotta be, Alita. You think you can ignore my calls and not answer me when I've texted you twenty times." Jerrod was angry and unrepentant.

"That's 'cause I'm kind of busy right now, Jerrod."

"You think I care that you got better

things to do than to give me money like you've done for the past ten years?"

"What?" Leno said. "Mom, what is he talking about? Why would you give him money? Is that why you can't afford to buy me a car?"

"H-he's lying," Alita said. She despised Jerrod for his lack of concern. "It's a big misunderstanding."

"One thing I can't stand," Jerrod replied, "is being called a liar. Not when I know what I'm saying is the truth, and you know it too, Alita."

"Jerrod, please. Leno, baby, go get in the car, I need to handle something real quick."

Leno reluctantly returned to the car, but he looked back at his mother a couple of times before he got inside the vehicle.

And it took everything inside of Alita not to fling Jerrod to the ground and stomp him across his face. "Jerrod, please, please don't do this anymore. Leno doesn't need to find out like this."

"I knew it. You're a fucking scammer. You're stringing along your son and Elyse just like my mother did to me until I found out the truth. She made up stories about what really happened to my dad. And now they don't even know what a liar you are."

"I can handle this situation any way that I

choose, Jerrod. It has nothing to do with you. The truth is mine to tell, not yours."

"The truth is anyone's to tell." He came so close to her face that she could smell his breath. "And if you don't tell it, I will."

His voice sounded so threatening that Alita felt herself shrinking before him. That was something she never wanted. And the fact that Jerrod could make her feel panicky caused her to grow angrier. "Jerrod, I'm warning you one more time. Leave us alone. Stop asking me for money. I don't owe you shit."

"You serious?"

"Hell, yeah. Because what you're doing could land you in jail just like your no-good daddy. You're extorting me. And you're taking money, food, and clothes out my child's mouth."

"You think I give a fuck about the money I'm taking from Leno so you can pay me for taking my only father from me? You should have thought about all of that before your ho ass starting sleeping with Daddy."

"I didn't start sleeping with him."

"My parents were happily married. And you weren't raised right, Alita, or you never would have fucked an old man, a man with kids, and got pregnant by him."

"Jerrod, please lower your voice."

"My voice is the *only* thing you've left me with." He actually choked back tears. "It's all I've got."

Alita hated seeing how hurt he was, and she wondered how the truth about this situation might affect Leno. And Elyse. Maybe it was time the young woman learned that Alita was her mother. But what if she wasn't emotionally strong enough to handle that type of news? And how would Leno feel when he found out Elyse was his sister? And Dru? Poor Dru. She could not fathom how everyone would act upon knowing her secrets.

"You may not agree with or like the decisions I've made, and that's fine," Alita continued. "But I was young back then. I was still a stupid, clueless teenager. And your daddy took advantage of me, Jerrod. I'm the true victim! So don't get mad at me. Your daddy should have known better than to fuck around on his wife with me or any other female. Because quiet as it's kept, mine wasn't the only neighborhood pussy he toyed with."

Jerrod swung his arm and smashed his balled fist against Alita's mouth. The impact cracked her lips. Her mouth began to swell, and she felt numbing pain. She ran her tongue across her teeth and tasted the saltiness of blood.

"You sonofabitch —"

"What? Who you gone tell?" Jerrod asked.
"Nobody! Because you can't handle telling
the truth. I want my money, I don't care
how you get it. If your son starves to death,
let him starve. If you end up homeless,
tough shit. Get me my fucking money."

Oh shit, what should I do?

Alita was scared that Jerrod would carry
out his threats. But she had no more money
to give.

When she got back in the car, Leno took
one look at Alita and yelled, "What the hell
is going on, Mom?"

"I don't want to talk about it."

"Did he hit you?"

"Don't worry about it."

"You're strange." Leno looked back as
they sped away from the furniture store. "If
I ever see that guy again I'ma bust him
upside his head."

"Don't say that. Stay out of this. I'm
handling it."

Leno gave her a knowing look. "Yeah, it
looks like you're handling it all right."

Alita shushed her son and drove along the
freeway, thankful when Leno finally stopped
questioning her. Soon he grew tired. His

head leaned back against the seat. And his mouth fell open as he snored. When he completely fell asleep, Alita retrieved her cell phone and texted as she drove.

Dru Boo, we need to talk

Alita felt nervous after she pressed send. She knew that when she finally told Dru what had happened between her and Mr. Jack Dawson, the truth would have to extend beyond the sexual sin she committed with a married man.

Dru called her right away.

"Hello, Sis. What's going on? What are you doing on this beautiful Saturday morning?"

"Um, well, me and Leno, he's with me in the car right now, we had to go to get him a new bed and mattress. He's still growing like a wild plant that's out of control. But as his mama, I did what I had to do."

"Oh wow, you should have told me. I could have helped chip in some money. Or you could have asked B. You two may butt heads, but Big Sis always has the wherewithal to help you out anytime you're in need."

That was Dru. So intelligent, reasonable. Warm and compassionate. "You are amazing, Dru. Have I ever told you that?"

"Nope, not that I can recall."

Alita laughed at Dru's honesty. And she

realized that on many days, condemnation kept her tongue from expressing to Dru how much she loved and admired her. She was the levelheaded, kind-hearted Reeves woman. Very bright, goal-oriented, and someone to be proud of because of her common sense and decency.

Oh, how Alita did not want any of Dru's wholesome qualities to worsen if the whole truth was ever disclosed.

Oh well, she thought. *Let's get this over with.*

"Anyway, Dru. I need to talk to you . . . in person . . . about something important."

"Sure. Is everything good?"

"Uh, it's complicated . . . that's all. And messy as hell . . . point-blank, it's all fucked up."

"Now you're scaring me. Can't you tell me right now?"

"No! Leno is with me. I don't want him to hear this conversation. I'll explain later."

She dropped Leno off at their home and attended to her busted lip. A half hour later, she arrived at Dru's.

"Tyrique here?" Alita asked.

"Um, yeah, but he's upstairs being a sleepyhead right now. I can't wait to join him. Hey, what happened to your lip?"

"Cold sore," Alita fibbed.

"Looks terrible."

"It'll heal."

"Oops, excuse my rudeness, Lita. You want some hibiscus tea?"

"Yeah, that'll work," Alita told her. But then she thought about how scorching hot a cup of tea could be, and she had a quick change of mind. "You know what, scrap that. Just get me a can of soda. I'll pour it in a glass and add some ice."

Dru got her sister the ginger ale and started the microwave to prepare a bowl of popcorn.

"Now, what is it that you want to tell me?"

Alita stared at the counter then looked up at Dru.

"You know how with Sister Day we are supposed to tell the truth? And how it's something that our mother wanted us to do, to stay in touch and help each other out through thick and thin?"

Dru nodded. "Go on."

"I remember one time you told us at our meeting that you have trouble with truth. And, to be honest," — Alita nervously laughed — "I have a problem with it, too."

"Now that's something I find hard to believe."

"Well, believe it, Sis, because depending on what it is, sometimes I struggle with it.

Truth can cause misunderstandings. And it can make people's lives change . . . in a bad way. Like when you find out a husband is unfaithful. It may be their truth . . . but it can mess up other people when it's revealed."

Dru told Alita, "Hold that thought." She rummaged through the cabinets and found two small bowls then carefully poured the popcorn in and sprinkled some seasoning on top.

This minor diversion gave Alita more time to think and consider what she did want to tell Dru and everything she wanted to leave out.

"Okay, done. Now go ahead with your story. But will you please just tell me what you're trying to say?"

"All right. Um, I just wanted to say that, a long time ago, back when you were six or seven, and I was around seventeen, maybe younger . . . um, it was a Sunday afternoon and I was at home. And I went outside and walked across the street to visit Roro."

"Jerrod's sister. I remember her."

"Good. So you should remember back then we were tight, like sisters. I was always welcome over at their spot. I could come up to their front door and if it was unlocked, it was nothing for me to just go right in, no problem." Alita could visualize in her mind's eye how everything played out on that fateful day.

"And, um, so on that day, I ran up the stairs to Roro's bedroom, and I saw that she was passed out asleep in her bed. I thought I'd leave her alone and catch up with her later. And back then it was nothing for me to just hang around the Dawsons' house like I lived there. So, um, I ran back down those stairs and I decided to see what they had in the fridge. Their mom was a great cook, she was from Memphis and she could grill a mean barbecue. And she would leave big pieces of ribs and homemade potato salad in the fridge and she always encouraged us. She would say, 'My house is your house. Feel free to get whatever you want.' And so we did."

Dru stopped tossing popcorn in her mouth. All she could do was stare at her sister and listen and wonder about the wayward method she was using to tell her something that she had described as "very important."

Alita sadly laughed to herself. "Like I said, we were like family. So as I'm reaching in the refrigerator trying to move bowls of food out the way so I could get that BBQ, and I-I, um, I felt this big hand. And it touched my back, right? I turned around. It was Mr. Jack. Mr. Dawson. And he was —" Alita closed her eyes and took a sip of her beverage.

"Go on, Sis, tell me what happened. No judgment."

"Jack started rubbing my back all slow and heavy-handed."

"What did you do?"

Her eyes popped back open. "I looked at that bastard like he was crazy."

"Good."

"He stopped rubbing me and he was like, 'Hey, Lita. Those pots are too heavy. Let me help you with that.' I moved out the way and let him. And he got the food out for me and got me a plate and set it on the table. Except I didn't feel hungry anymore, Dru. But I wasn't sure exactly how to tell him. And while I stood there thinking all kinds of thoughts and trying to figure out how to leave, I noticed that Jack was staring at me something fierce. And he, um, he finally told me that his family was planning a surprise party for Roro real soon and he asked me if I wanted to be in on it. I guess I said okay because next thing I know he tells me to follow him. And he gets me to go down the hallway, and we wind up in his bedroom."

Dru's eyes were enlarged. "His bedroom?

Lita, no!"

"Yes." Alita's normally loud and boisterous voice grew smaller and feeble. "He takes me inside of that cold-ass, dark room, and at first I'm sitting on a chair that's next to a small desk. He turns on this lamp and I noticed a calendar sitting there with Roro's birthdate circled and some notes written down about what they wanted to have on the party menu. But, Dru, he took me by the hand and, um, he asked me to stand up. So I did. And Mr. Dawson's creepy ass then told me to excuse him for saying so, but he thought I was pretty. Told me I was sexy. And that's when I kicked him in his balls and smacked his hand so hard that it made my fingers sting. He asked me what I did that for. I told him don't say shit about how I look. That it was none of his business. And I guess I shocked him. Because his face grew all ugly and crazy looking. And he yells at me, then grabs me by the hair and yanks it. And he asked me why I assaulted him like that. He tells me that he can call the police and report me because women were getting arrested for hitting, punching, twisting arms, pushing, slapping men, you name it. He was holding his balls all this time he was telling me this stuff. I could tell the man was in pain and, hey, I got real scared.

180

I felt confused. Even though I did not trust him, I knew he was the adult, so I believed what he told me. Then Mr. Dawson told me he hadn't even done anything to me to make me do that to him, and because I was so aggressive and went Billy Bad Ass on him for no good reason, he had a right to defend himself. And he wanted to teach me a lesson so I would never pull that with any other man again. And he pretty much forced himself on me, Dru. Pushing my head down to give him oral sex, all kinds of stupid shit that I hated but did anyway. I thought if I didn't do it he'd kill me."

"That sounds messed up."

Dru jumped up and hugged Alita. "Oh, my poor sister. I'm so sorry you went through that. Had no idea. I've never heard this story before."

"Sometimes things happen that people never tell. Or they wait a long time before they tell it."

"That's horrible, Lita. Did you file charges?"

"I'm not done with my story. Have a seat."

Alita continued. "Long story short, nine months later, Dru, I-I gave birth to a baby around the same time that Mama had a baby."

Dru stared at her sister, her face registering confusion.

"What are you saying?"

"No one knew I was pregnant. I didn't gain a lot of weight. The pregnancy was hidden."

"By who?"

"By Mama and Daddy. Mama faked her pregnancy."

"She what?"

"Yup. Mama stuffed padding into her shirt, walked around with her hand on her hip, and knew how to make herself throw up."

"I don't believe it."

"It doesn't matter, because I was there. She and Daddy covered it all up to protect me and our family. You were only seven or eight and no way you could've guessed what was going on. But remember when I left to go stay with Grandmamma for a few months? That only happened after I reached my seventh month. And I got homeschooled for a quick minute, and she took care of me till I gave birth. Then we moved from that house to the one where Coco stays now."

"My God," Dru exclaimed, her eyes widening with every shocking revelation that Alita exposed. It felt odd to hear such things and know that it had happened right under her nose. "And the child that you had?

Where is it these days?"

"Um. I-I don't know."

"What do you mean you don't know?"

"Mama, our sweet, image-conscious mother, took that baby from me, Dru."

"Wait a minute. She did? But how? What are you talking about?"

"It's true. You may not have known, but I lived this shit. This unfair, demoralizing shit became my life. And to have my child taken away from me, snatched out of my arms as if I did not matter, it messes my head up to this day."

"I don't understand," Dru said.

"I was a minor. I guess I had no rights. Mama said if I fuck around like an adult then she'll teach me I'm not as grown as I thought I was."

"But weren't you raped?"

"Mama knew I'd had sex at fourteen. Even though she didn't say it out loud, she acted like I must've had something to do with that man messing around with me. But I didn't, I swear to God."

"This is all too much." Dru was pensive as she tried to collect thoughts that made no sense to her logical mind. "I-I hear what you're saying. I believe what you're telling me. But I still don't understand, Alita."

"Hell, you ain't the only one."

"How can you not know what happened to the child? Because I know you can't be referring to Leno since he obviously lives with you and was raised by you."

"That's the thing, Sis. See, it's like this . . ."

As Alita continued with her messy confession, Dru could no longer listen. The story sounded partially true and partially filled with lies. As a result, she did not know what to believe. With a grim look on her face she backed away from Alita. She raced up the stairs and shut the bedroom door solidly behind her. Dru sat on the edge of her bed, her head in her hands, as she thought back on many strange occurrences that had happened within her family. The day that a newborn baby came to live with them. She remembered how their mother's tummy looked bigger for a while. And all she would tell the girls was that there was going to be a new member of the family. And then this little girl whom their mother named "Elyse Reeves" was now their youngest sibling. Soon thereafter their mother's stomach seemed flatter. It seemed she dropped the baby weight really fast. But Dru was too young to understand those types of things.

All she knew was that everyone called Elyse "Baby Sis." But maybe that's all

"Baby Sis" was — just a title.

Dru choked back painful tears as her mind took her places she did not wish to go. And when she heard persistent knocking on her door, she did not respond. She blotted out the noise of Alita's knuckles loudly tapping. Dru shut her eyes and stiffly remained seated in complete silence. She sat there until Alita decided to go away.

Even though Calhoun had wed Samira more than a month earlier, that Saturday morning would be the first time Coco officially got introduced to his wife. Coco stood in the doorway of the home that she'd shared with Calhoun for the past seven years. He and Samira had just driven up. She watched him open Samira's car door and extend his hand. So polite and gentle. Coco stared at the father of her kids, who seemingly overnight had changed into a stranger.

They took their time walking up to her.

"Hey, Coco, this is Samira."

"Hey," she said. "How you doing? Come on inside. That's where the kids are." Under normal circumstances, Coco would have been traipsing around the house wearing a nightie covered by a long bathrobe. Her feet would have been stomping about in some old tattered house slippers. But today, she wore a purple wrap dress that hugged her slimmer figure. She'd dropped a good forty pounds since giving birth to Cypress, and she felt she looked fabulous.

"Wait right here," she said to Samira. "Um, Calhoun, can I talk to you in the kids' room?"

"No, whatever you need to say, you can say it in front of my wife."

Coco offered a smile that her heart did not feel. "All righty then. No problem. Just wanted you to make sure and drop the kids off here tomorrow no later than six. And I'm putting Cadee's homework in her backpack. Can you help her with it, please? Don't forget. And try not to give Chloe any cheese. She's allergic to cheese," she explained.

"Oh, poor baby," Samira said.

"Yeah, it ain't nothing nice," Coco said. "But she can drink a little milk. But it can't be cow milk. Understood?"

"Yes, of course." Samira nodded and typed some notes into her cell phone. Even though the ladies were cordial, the atmosphere felt awkward. Like a pink elephant was in the room staring right at them.

Coco had always been one to speak her mind. But she felt like she was on a job interview. Like she was in someone else's house instead of her own. She shuddered and then walked over to Calhoun.

"Um, can you excuse us, Calhoun? I want to talk to Samira woman to woman."

He was silent.

"Go ahead, honey. It'll be fine," Samira gently urged him. Calhoun hesitated and ducked inside the kids' room. When Coco heard them squealing in delight, she felt herself relax. She gave her competition a sincere smile.

"Have a seat, Samira. I-I've wanted to chat with you going on a minute. Now what's done is done and ain't nothing I can do about it. But I have some things to get off my chest."

"Go ahead."

"How much has Calhoun told you about me or our relationship?"

"Um, I don't see what that has to do with anything . . ."

"It doesn't, yet it does. Because even though he went on with his life, he pretty much shocked the hell outa me. He just did. And I was pissed. I wanted to kill that sonofabitch."

"Seriously? You wanted to do all that? All because a man determined that he wanted to do something else with his life?"

"Oh, save that shit." Coco laughed.

Samira gasped.

"Look, if you gonna be around me you'll have to ignore some things. Just because I use certain words doesn't mean I'm mad. Speaking my mind is just how I am. I keeps it real." Coco observed Samira and noticed how stiff looking she appeared while she sat on the edge of the couch. The stark contrast between Coco and Samira did not go unnoticed. And it truly hurt her that her ex had picked someone so different from herself.

"Coco, I don't know what to say. We did not plan this wedding or marriage behind your back. It was all of a sudden."

"You pregnant?"

"What?"

"It's a simple question, Samira."

Samira rose to her feet. "No, not that I know of. But that would be of no concern to you. The only thing that matters now is the coparenting of Calhoun's children. I want to be friends if possible. I know it sounds strange and maybe even insulting. But where I come from women try to rally around each other."

"Right, you from Africa or some shit like that?"

"Yes, I am. I'm a proud African woman."

"Mm hmm. I'm not surprised. Well, did you put some type of voodoo shit on Calhoun and make him marry you? Because all of this happened a little bit too fast for my tastes, unless he was creeping around on me for the longest when I had no idea."

"Creeping?"

"Don't act dumb. You know exactly what I'm talking about, tramp."

Calhoun stepped into the room. Cadee and Chloe clung to his long legs as he tried to walk.

"That's enough, Coco. We came here to get the kids and that's what we about to do. Don't you ever disrespect my wife again. If you got a beef with me you need to speak to me. Leave my wife out of it."

Every time he said "wife" Coco felt as if she'd been slammed into by a tractor trailer. The pain was unbearable.

"My wife is a good woman, and she doesn't deserve your bad attitude."

"I don't have an attitude."

"You're trying to hide it like you want to be the bigger woman, but it's a complete fail. You're salty, Ma. Take the L and go on with your life."

Calhoun's biting words dredged a hole in her heart. She could not believe she'd ever been in love with him. When you believe in people and they let you down, that's when the hurt pours in. And Coco did not know what to do. How could she get rid of the pain?

"I try hard to work with you," Calhoun said as if to pacify himself. "But you need to do better."

She'd had enough. "Calhoun, you're wrong and you know it. You can't sit up here and act like I'm supposed to go and accept the fact that you dumped me on my wedding day and then up and married this African bitch —"

"Let's go." Calhoun grabbed Samira by the arm and led her out of Coco's house. The girls scrambled behind their father.

Calhoun left Coco alone with Cypress. There was no way she'd let them take care of her youngest. And she had already known that he wouldn't bring Chance with them. In fact, little Chance could only stand on his toes in front of the window. His nose was mashed against the cold glass. He yelled after them with his eyes looking as sad as she'd ever seen them.

"Come back," Chance yelled, but they couldn't hear him. They drove off. Chance backed away from the window. He closed his eyes and burst into tears.

"Come back," he screamed again and

stomped his little feet. Coco went and picked up her son and tried to comfort him. "Baby, it's okay. That means you and me get to spend time together. You my little partner."

"I don't want you. I want my daddy."

Calhoun had been the only father Chance had ever known. He did not understand why he was no longer invited to hang out with the man and his other siblings. Coco learned she'd have to be his mother and his father.

Chance screamed and yelled and tried to bite Coco when she attempted to hug him.

After a long while she managed to calm him down then went to place Chance in his bed. She lovingly read to him until he fell asleep.

Coco then got Alita on the phone and told her everything that had just happened.

"He's a fuck boy, that's all, Coco. And guess what, you picked him. You gotta be more careful next time."

"Won't be a next time."

"Girl, please. There will be a next time and you know it. As soon as you get horny again —"

"Oh, hush up. I ain't thinking about sex."

"Anyway, once you're over your ex, you gotta learn not to just run up and be with any old body. Life is too short, as you found out. And you wasted all those years on a man that did not feel about you the way you felt about him. On Valentine's Day he told you y'all was gone get married. He went with you to get the license. Then he dumped you like you were burnt-up furniture after a house fire."

"Lita, please hush."

"Truth hurts, Sis. But the good thing is now you can see that he ain't shit, and you can get ready for someone better. Once you get Calhoun completely out of your system, you'll be open to love again. With a good man. You'll see."

"I really hope so, Lita. If not, I can't see myself forgiving him. It hurts too badly. And because of the kids, me and him will always have unfinished business."

"Right. I know all about unfinished business."

"Enough of my sob story. What's been going on with you?" Coco asked.

The fact that Coco called and did not mention Dru meant that Coco did not know the latest.

Alita sighed. "Girl, I don't know where to begin. So much is happening my little head is swirling."

"Can't be as bad as what's happening in

my life."

"It's probably coming in as a close second."

"Tell me about it." When Alita thought about her own drama, she was not ready to tell Coco a thing. Not yet. Some things you held onto for as long as possible — held onto until you couldn't hold on any longer.

CHAPTER 10
DAUGHTER

Alita was worried. Dru refused to respond to her calls, her texts. And it was killing Alita. Who could she turn to at a time like this? Family meant everything. She had always believed that there was strength in unity.

Alita knew she was taking a risk, but she hoped that this one would turn out in her favor. She decided to pay a visit to someone that she felt loved her.

The moment he opened his door, Alita rushed into Shade's arms.

"Baby," she told him. "We need to talk. I always knew this day was gonna come and now it's here. First, I want to say, you know I love you with all my heart. For you to put up with me, put up with my mouth, my family, well, that means everything in the world to me. But after I tell you what I'm 'bout to tell you . . ." Alita expelled a loud breath. She could not imagine Shade not wanting to be in her life. He'd become her rock. But when people think they know people, and find out additional stories about their true character, a risk is always involved.

"Come out with it, sweetie. Just start from the beginning."

"Oh, no. I can't do that Shade. It would take too long. It's too complicated. But, Jesus, I guess I should just go ahead and tell you . . . My family is a great family. But we have a lot of secrets. Little things that some of us know about, and big things that barely anyone knows."

Shade looked confused.

"Oh, don't give me that. Every family has dark secrets that they don't like to bring up. Stuff that we know about but we won't talk about. We go on with life, year after year, pretending like things don't exist, and we try to sweep it all under the rug and hope it never leaks out. Am I right?"

"Yes, Alita. I agree with you."

"Good. Then I know you won't judge me for what I'm about to say. Well, it's like this." She stared into space for a long time. To admit something that you've never spoken out loud took a great amount of courage.

"Elyse is not my sister. She's my daughter. I'm telling you this, but I don't want you to tell a soul. I was forced to tell people that

Elyse was my sister ever since she was born."

"Are you serious?"

"Yes, I am, Shade. And now I have to learn how to deal with this and how to do it without losing my mind."

"Why are you just now telling me?"

"Because of Elyse's other side of the family. They've always known the truth, and one of the people is trying to start some trouble." She did not want to go into detail and hoped Shade wouldn't pry further.

"Are you in any danger?"

"No. Just dealing with some threats. Someone threatening to tell, that's all."

Shade sat and absorbed what Alita wanted to share with him.

"Now you know," she said. "Now you understand why it seems I'm like her mama."

"Okay. I must admit I'm shocked," Shade said. "But who's the father?"

"Um, the father of Elyse is a guy that . . . see, he pretty much . . . the bastard raped me when I was in high school."

"Elyse is a product of rape? You're kidding."

"I wish I was. And after I got pregnant, my mama told me to have it. Told me that she'd raise the baby as her own. Mama said, 'No need to blame the child for how it was conceived. We will love her just the same.' I knew that I wasn't supposed to tell anyone I was expecting. So that's exactly what happened. I could never say Elyse was my daughter. I had to pretend. It was all a huge mess and Mama didn't want things to get any messier. Then after I switched schools, everything changed."

"How did that make you feel, Alita?"

"I was pissed at the man; and very mad at my mama. She stole my child. She didn't give me a choice. She just told me how everything was going to play out and that I needed to do what she said so we could protect the child and keep her safe."

"I'm sorry to hear that . . . What about your own father?"

"My dad did everything my mother wanted him to do. Basically she ran him and the whole house. Daddy was a good man and he should have stepped in and taken charge but he didn't. But that's another story."

"How have you been able to pretend all this time?"

Alita shrugged. "It wasn't easy, but basically I just grew into that role. I called Elyse 'Baby Sis' and that's what she became. After a while it really seemed like she was my mother's daughter. My mom made me concentrate on continuing my education. Getting my diploma and trying to work off my depression. She also felt that work would keep my mind off of things, and so I started getting jobs to stay busy. I helped with my sisters and acted like everything was normal even though it wasn't."

"But then your mom passed away."

"Right. And I was somewhat glad."

"Seriously?"

"Yeah. Mama was sick, and I hated to see the woman suffer. I loved her even though I didn't agree with some of the things she did. But then after she was gone, it's like I knew I didn't have to live by her stupid rules anymore."

"She was a major influence, huh?"

"Very strong-willed. Always wanted to have her way. Always had something to say."

Shade smiled. "Did you inherit some of her personality?"

"You know what? Because I love you I will let you get away with that *shade,* Shade!" Alita laughed along with him and quieted down as she thought how relieved it felt to pour out her heart. But she knew there was much more to tell, and she didn't want to run the guy away.

"Basically, that's the burden I've carried inside of me for a while."

"Stupid question, but did Leonard know about your past?"

Alita wrung her hands. "Um, at first he didn't. But eventually he did."

"He did?"

"Yeah, he did. He was my husband. If I couldn't tell him, then who could I tell? But I regret opening my big mouth, because it caused some issues in our relationship, to be honest. My confession probably made him change from a decent man to a bad man. So now can you understand why I've hid the truth?"

Oh, God, it was so hard to unveil dirty, dark, terrible secrets about one's past. Most people wanted their secrets to remain buried, never to be unearthed. Truth could cause strange reactions, and many did not possess the character to handle it.

"But we got through it, Shade. That's the only thing I want to share about that."

"But your son, Leno . . . does he know?"

"Oh, Shade. I feel so bad. Neither of them know. Elyse thinks she's my sister. Leno has no idea. I honestly don't know what to do. Babe, I don't want to fuck up my family even more than what it is. But it's all eating me up inside." She could not tell him about the extortion money that had been paid to Jerrod Dawson . . . It made her feel dirty and like a common criminal. And that was something Alita didn't want.

"I don't know, Shade. Sometimes we say 'yes' to things, not really thinking it through and being able to see the damage it can cause. And so you agree to shit and it gets all fucked up and then you try to make a better decision but you never know how anything will turn out. That's what I've learned. Whether I lie or tell the truth, I can't control what happens."

She sighed. Even though he smiled outwardly and seemed to appear calm and supportive, she wondered what was going through Shade's mind. Some men were difficult to figure out. Men could go ghost on you over the pettiest of things. A woman could do one little thing that irked the guy and, boom, she'd never hear from him again. He wouldn't call, text, or come by anymore. And she'd want to call him, but pride wouldn't allow her. Screw him, she'd tell herself. There's more fish in the sea, and if he ditched me over bullshit then he ain't the one. She would pretend like she didn't care that he blew her off, blew off what they'd built up. But deep inside, she'd be hurt and disillusioned. Stunned that the man did not care about her the way she believed he did.

Alita began to tremble. "Please, Shade, baby. What are you thinking? Tell me!"

"You've been to hell and back. You've survived something that could have destroyed you. And your revelation gives me a little insight into your personality. You always seem defensive."

"When I no longer had a daddy in my life, or a daddy that wouldn't stand up to his wife, who else is going to defend me?"

"Me, that's who. Because you have me."

Alita could not suppress the joy she felt. A big smile spread across her face. She flung herself in Shade's arms again, plastering his cheek then his lips with tender kisses.

"It's going to be all right, Alita. There are people out here going through worse than you, and they're making it. We'll just take things a day at a time."

"You mean it?"

"I do. Just stay real with me and we'll be cool."

"Okay," she promised him. "I'm sorry for just now telling you, but I wasn't sure how you'd take it."

"I know how hard it must have been for you to admit that to me. But never apologize for telling the truth. Truth shines light on injustices, and telling the truth is the impetus for change."

"What?"

"Sometimes truth causes change."

"Okay, I get that. But why didn't you just say that in the first place?"

"I'll remember that next time," he said with a laugh.

"Do that."

Shade grew serious. "Truth scares us, Alita. And a lot of times people feel they can't do it, can't tell it. They are scared of what might change."

"I know that's right." Alita nodded. "Because I was hoping you wouldn't hate me for telling you my truth. I was scared as hell that you wouldn't trust me anymore."

He wrapped his arm around her and hugged her tight. Then Shade lifted her chin and stared into her eyes.

"I'm glad you trusted me enough to share that with me. But don't forget. I'm not the one whose favor you need the most. You'll have to find the guts to share that same info with your kids and other family members too. And if they love you the way I love you, then things will work out in the end."

"You love *me?"*

"What do you think?"

She sighed and savored the good feeling of having him in her arms as well as in her life. But at the same time she wondered what might happen if she dropped other truths that she was hesitant to release.

At the May Sister Day, Alita calmly stood before all her family members. They were meeting to review the travel itinerary for their planned girls' trip that would take place the following week.

"I wanted to make an announcement," she told them. "I don't want to spoil everybody's good mood and excitement about the trip, but thank God the tickets are nonrefundable." She laughed.

"What are you trying to say?" Burgundy asked.

Alita stared at Elyse; the girl had made such an improvement in the past few months. She hoped she wouldn't relapse with everything that was about to go down.

"I want to tell y'all something, but first I need to run it by Elyse."

Burgundy frowned. "Elyse? Why her? What's she got to do with anything?"

"Burgundy, don't worry. This has nothing to do with that husband of yours."

"I didn't say it did," Burgundy replied, but she still was racking her brain to try and figure out what Alita was up to this time.

They were over at Coco's. Alita asked

Elyse to come to Coco's bedroom so they could speak in private.

She grabbed the young woman by the hands. "I'm so proud of you, Elyse. You've grown up. You're beautiful. Strong. You're handling therapy like a pro. And it seems like being around people doesn't bother you the way it used to."

Elyse shrugged. "I'm glad too. But I still have a long way to go."

"Right. Well, Elyse, um, on the other hand, I hate that those bad things happened to you with Nate. The way he violated you. And he was wrong for sure."

"Yes, he was. I hate him."

"I don't blame you for hating him. But you should also forgive him one day."

"What?"

"I'm just saying. You're too pretty of a girl to go around holding all kinds of hatred on the inside. You've seen the face of hate. It's never pretty."

Elyse nodded. "I don't *hate* him, hate him. But I can't stand him. I think he should be punished for his sins." She paused. "Why do some people get punished and others go free?"

"I wish I had an answer." Alita shrugged. "But a lot of times things just aren't right, they ain't fair, they are totally fucked up, and it makes us so angry that we just want to go and hurt someone when we feel we've been wronged. An employee who wants to harm the horrible boss. A man that wants to get back at his cheating ex."

"No one wants to be treated bad for something they did not deserve."

"Exactly, Elyse. And see . . . I-I know how that feels too. To be wronged. By an adult. Someone that should know better."

"Why did he do that to me?"

"Elyse, baby, I simply can't answer. Maybe some of us are messed up in the head, Elyse. Some folks do wrong over and over again and get away with it. Others are just plain evil and they don't know how else to be. In Nate's case, I don't know what his excuse was. But the good thing, the best thing is that you don't have to deal with that anymore." She paused. "He hasn't tried to do that to you again, right?"

"No," Elyse said in anger. "I'd kill him if he did."

"Elyse, I hope you're joking. Because two wrongs don't make a right. I mean, I understand your feelings, but seriously, there has to be a better way to handle this."

"What is it then, Lita? What? 'Cause he seemed to go on with life like nothing ever happened. And Burgundy. She ought to be ashamed of herself."

Alita loved that Elyse was speaking her mind. Speaking her truth.

"I agree with you, baby girl. Nate is worse than B, and he'll get his one day." Alita coughed and cleared her throat. Dammit, how could she find the words to tell the girl that she was her mother? It wasn't as easy as she'd pictured it to be.

"I love you, Elyse, I do. That's all that matters. You hear me?"

She nodded. "Yeah, I hear you."

"But do you believe me?"

"Yeah, I do."

"Why?"

"Because you tell me. That's how you know that someone loves you, 'cause they say it."

"But that's not the only way, Elyse. People also tell you by the way they treat you. The good things they do for you to show you how they feel."

"Really?" she asked in wonderment.

"Yes. So if you get it both ways, count yourself lucky. That's a whole lot of love right there."

"Hmm, I see," Elyse told her then sighed. "Is that all you wanted to tell me?"

Suddenly there was a sharp knock on the door. Exasperated, Alita told Elyse, "I guess we'll have to finish this conversation some other time."

The two women exited Coco's bedroom and were met by Burgundy, who had a warning: "Um, Lita, I just thought you'd want to know that I invited someone else to this month's Sister Day."

"Oh, yeah? Who'd you invite?" Alita asked. She got her answer when she walked back into the living room and saw Julianne, Nate's sister.

"Hey there, cutie pie," the woman said and waved at Alita. The two women spoke and hugged. It had been a few months since they'd last seen each other.

Julianne took a seat next to Burgundy and smiled at everyone. "I feel honored to even be at one of these meetings," she said. "Now I really feel like I'm part of the family."

At first Alita was annoyed by her presence. But after a while she felt glad that the woman was there.

"What you been up to, Julianne? . . . When's the last time to you talked to Nate? . . . Um, may I ask you a quick question? Did your mom and dad teach Nate how to respect women?"

Julianne raised her eyebrows. "What are you asking me that for? Has my brother done something that's made you feel disrespected, Alita?"

"Not exactly. I was just curious, you know. Because a lot of times we don't understand people, or can't understand them, unless we know the way that they were raised. We need that background info to help us out."

"Well, I guess the proper values were instilled in Nate and my other brother, who is now dead. Nate was the baby boy. I was older than him, and I'll admit I used to beat him up."

"Really?" Alita smirked. "I sure would have loved to see that."

"Oh, trust me, things got ugly. Because Nate would always fight back. He tried his best to get his licks in."

"That sounds pretty normal, though, Julianne. I want to know the dirt. Did he do freaky things like —"

"How would I know?"

"Because you're his family. You grew up in the same house."

"That's true but it's not like I was with him twenty-four-seven."

"I'm sure that things get back to you, Julianne. You had to have heard something."

"Look, no one knows what anyone is like when they are alone or behind closed doors. Who are you when no one is looking?" Julianne asked. "It sounds like you want me to spill all my brother's secrets, and for what? Do you want any of your sisters to spill yours? Because as quiet as it's kept, you —"

"Oh, we don't need to be talking about that type of stuff, now do we?" Burgundy said. "What's on your meeting agenda? I definitely don't believe that Nate Taylor is at the top of the discussion."

Alita refused to back down.

"We'll get to that in a second. I just want Julieanne to answer me this one question."

"What?"

"Does your brother have a history of messing around with little girls? Playing doctor with the neighbors? With you? Playing house and pretending to be the daddy?"

"Even if he did, just about every kid in America has played those little childish games, even you, Alita."

"Yeah, but there's a big difference between playing house and molesting —"

"Um, okay. This conversation is going to stop right now," Burgundy loudly said as she stepped in. "I'm taking over this meeting. This is the reason why Mama wanted me to run Sister Day. We need to stay focused. Okay, we already know that our bucket list is to travel to New York in a couple weeks. But our new assignment is this: Make a decision that you've been putting off."

"Wow, another assignment that just sucks. Who comes up with this shit?" Alita said.

"Do you really need to ask? I gotta agree with Lita. We need to shake up the box and come up with some better assignments. Every thang is so damned depressing," Coco said.

Burgundy broke out into a smile. "Fine. I give up. We'll do the July assignment as I've just stated it. But after that, you ladies can all come up with them. Since what I'm doing isn't appreciated or valued."

"There you go." Alita couldn't help but laugh. "We won't tease you this time, B. But thank you for letting us have some input for future meetings. We need to liven this shit up, make it more fun and exciting."

She went into high theatrics mode, trying to lighten the mood. But she was secretly directing her antics at Dru. Her sister had remained calm, composed, and seemingly unemotional since the meeting started.

"Hey, Dru Boo, can you get me something good to drink?"

"Sure," Dru replied in a clipped tone.

After ten minutes she couldn't take it anymore. Alita pulled Dru to the side. "I think we need to talk. We need to keep talking till we get everything off our chest."

Dru cocked her head. "Everything? Really, Alita?"

"What's that supposed to mean?"

"I had another conversation with Jerrod," Dru replied.

"Oh! What did y'all two talk about?"

"His *father.*"

"Okay."

"And how he may be getting out of jail next year."

"Really?"

"Yes, really." Dru was no-nonsense.

"What else did Jerrod say?" Alita asked.

"He told me that you seduced his daddy."

"Oh, that's a damn lie. Everybody knows that a minor can't give consent. Plus, wait a second, is this why you acting all funky toward me all of a sudden?"

"No. I'm acting funky because what happened between you and his dad is something you should have told me. I mean, I'm twenty-six now. How many times have you heard me mention in the past decade how I never got closure from Jerrod? But you, Alita, you knew the whole story all along. And now I feel stupid!"

"One thing you aren't is stupid. But you are sensitive, Dru. You are the one person in the family that I know doesn't like to deal with different types of drama. Who's the first person to not get involved with mess? You, that's who. But that's no excuse. I still could have told you instead of having you wonder all this time." Alita paused. She honestly did not mean any harm, and she never wanted this issue to come between them. "It might be too late, but for what it's worth, Dru, I'm sorry. Will you forgive me? Even a little bit?"

"Forgiveness isn't something I can simply hand over to you — like someone would hand over a twenty-dollar bill to help you with gas money."

"What? Did you really have to go there?"

"Yes, I did. That's nothing compared to what you've done."

"Okay, I get it. It's 'crucify Alita' again."

"No, it's not. Don't think you're the only one in the family that's gotten crucified. Save the dramatics, Alita. Everything isn't about you, and your pain, and what awful things you're going through. Get over yourself."

Alita looked shocked but tried to play things off. "Oh, c'mon, Dru. Other than this bombshell I just dropped, your life is rosy. It's freaking perfect compared to mine. You may have a few troubles but nothing like what I've been through."

"Even if that's true, it doesn't mean that I don't feel hurt and pain too. I-I can use some help and sympathy. Just because I seem strong and independent and nonchalant about some family issues doesn't mean I can't use a helping hand at times. That's what the family doesn't know. Everyone assumes because I'm calm and reasonable that I'm doing great. Well, don't believe everything you see."

"You have big problems? Ha!" Alita snickered. "I'll believe it when I see it."

"By the time you see it, it might be too late!" Furious and disappointed, Dru sadly shook her head and simply walked away.

CHAPTER 11
GIRLS' TRIP

Alita brimmed with joy. It was early June. Their plane had just landed at the Newark International Airport. And now she and her sisters were traveling in a huge van that was carrying them over the bridge to Manhattan.

Shade, who'd been convinced by Alita to join her on the trip, sat next to her in the back row where they were surrounded by an abundance of luggage. Yet the crowded space felt cozy and romantic.

He placed his arm around her shoulders, and they shared a juicy kiss. Alita stuck her tongue way down his throat and laughed hysterically at the same time.

"How you feeling, woman?" he asked after he came up for air.

"Like I'm in a damned dream. Like I'm a Cinderella who just escaped from her evil stepmother."

"Is that a good thing?"

"It's all good, as long as this taxi won't turn into a pumpkin," she replied.

"I'll do my best to keep that from happening."

"Will you?" she asked as she searched his eyes. He nodded and seemed quite serious. Alita trembled with happiness deep on the inside.

"Then I guess it's okay to say that some dreams do come true. Because if someone would have told me that I'd ever find my ass in the Big Apple, I would have accused them of lying through their crooked-ass teeth."

The sounds of the city included honking car horns, big trucks with their yellow flashers popping on and off as the drivers set about to deliver packages and goods to area businesses. Every time they turned a corner, Alita saw and noticed things she'd never seen before. From stretch limos fighting traffic to dozens of school children surrounded by teachers who were obviously enjoying a pedestrian field trip. Street vendors hawking food, artwork, key chains, and t-shirts.

"Shade, on the real? This is something I've only seen on TV or in that movie *New Jack City,* shit like that."

Shade threw back his head and laughed.

"There are many good things in life that's just waiting for us to enjoy. You see, Alita, you've been like a lot of other people. Too scared to step outside the house, too caught up in work and family drama. Making a lot of excuses when really there is no excuse. You just got to get out here and live life, no matter what happens."

"I know that's right."

Alita quieted down and watched in awe as they viewed the magnificent Manhattan skyline. Traffic was brutal as hundreds of cars were trying to make their way into the city.

It took almost an hour for them to reach their hotel, which was located in Times Square.

Once the couple checked into their room, Alita grabbed Shade by the hand and led him straight out of the door, down the hall where they waited a while to board the elevator.

"Let's roll," she told him. "Forget my sisters. I called Coco to see what's up. Can you believe they all hanging out in her bathroom trying to get their lace fronts and makeup straight? I ain't got time for all that. That's why we had to get out of that room, which is very nice, by the way, and go see some NYC shit."

"Let's roll," Shade told her, feeling just as excited as their elevator door opened up.

Once they made it to the first floor, they hurried through the lobby and walked out onto the streets. Holding hands, they casually strolled up and down Broadway and checked out large store windows that displayed souvenirs, clothing, and other paraphernalia.

"Yep, I'm dreaming. Do you know that?" she asked. She stopped to take a photo every few seconds.

"Alita, this is your life. It's not just a dream. You're really here."

"I know it, but it doesn't feel real." She paused. "I just wish that I could have taken Leno with us. But he's hanging out with his dad this week."

"And there's nothing wrong with that. Two people created that boy. And you need a break sometimes. You deserve that."

She nodded and leaned into the warmth of Shade's body.

When you're used to the doldrums of a routine life, visiting a vibrant city such as New York can be an amazing stimulus. Alita's perspective was transitioning. Her mind and spirit were getting awakened.

Possibilities.

That's what she felt stirring around inside

of her. She no longer wished to dwell on family troubles and how she was perceived by people. She wanted to forget it all and make time to do fun things, like going to Macy's on 34th Street, taking a carriage ride in Central Park, and maybe even being brave enough to hop on a ferry that would take them to Ellis Island.

But for now, she was enjoying the feeling of her own two feet gracing a New York pavement.

"I swear to God, this ain't nothing like Houston. Don't get me wrong, H-town is cool, but this is on a whole 'nother level."

"I'm so glad you're saying that, my love," Shade told her. "If you had a mirror you could see how your eyes are lighting up." His voice sounded emotional. "I was worried about you for a second. And to see you this happy, it's worth every penny we're spending."

Alita nodded emphatically then beamed till her cheeks hurt. "And I know I'm looking like a damned tourist, but hell, I don't care."

She swirled around in a circle, stopping to gaze at the skyscrapers, the throng of people rushing back and forth, and listened to all the various languages that she heard as people from all over the world were chatting up a storm.

They slowed down long enough to enjoy the alluring smell of mozzarella cheese, zesty tomato sauce, and pepperoni. The delicious aroma filled her nostrils and made her head spin.

She took a moment to study the nicely done menu that was displayed outside the window of a pizza place.

"You hear my stomach growling, Shade?"

"Nah," he said.

"Well, you need to clean out your ears, because I'm hungry as hell. There's so much to choose from I don't know where to go."

"Don't even sweat it," he said. "Before it's over with, I want us to try a lot of different places."

"You sure?"

"I'm positive. Just enjoy yourself, sweetie."

If Shade only knew how badly she wanted to do just that. But Alita was like a lot of other people in the world: folks that felt they could not enjoy themselves because one thing or another made them feel undeserving. They only knew self-loathing. Talking themselves out of getting the thick slice of cake, or the biggest piece of chicken. That's what other people got to do and certainly not anyone like Alita Washington, who knew more about problems and how to solve them than about taking it easy and living in the moment.

Even though they ended up walking almost five miles, Alita did not complain. Their journey caused them to end up outside of a delicatessen with a menu displayed in the window.

"Can we go in here, please?" Alita asked.

"Your wish is my command."

She and Shade walked into the crowded restaurant and observed all the food displays that were in hot and cold bins. There was fresh fruit and all kinds of meats and vegetables.

They ended up grabbing several Styrofoam containers and piled them high with cold chicken pasta salads, a couple of hero sandwiches, grilled vegetables. And they could not leave without adding two slices of New York–style cheesecake.

Shade paid for it all and looked at Alita like she was crazy when she tried to reach for her wallet.

"Really? You nuts?" he asked.

"You know I am, but I'm sure you picked up on that when you first met me." They emerged from the delicatessen loaded with heavy bags and decided to take their time returning to their hotel room.

"I wonder what the sisters are doing?" she

said, almost talking to herself.

"Are you still down and out about Dru?" Shade said, asking the question that he'd been wanting to know.

"Not really," she lightly told him.

"Alita. It's me. I've been around you long enough to know when —"

"Hey, it's cool, all right." She shrugged, and her voice grew thicker. "I know Dru and she ain't like Coco or Burgundy. She won't hold a grudge forever."

"But have you two really talked things out? Like," Shade said in earnest, "I would hope that you ended up apologizing to Dru. Not making any more excuses about what happened. Maybe putting yourself in her shoes for a change?"

"Shade, I'm getting around to it, all right? I just have to pick a time and a place." She looked about. "Where in the world can I find a good place to talk to my sister about the fucked-up things I've done? It ain't easy, I tell you. I came here to get away from it all. And it was Burgundy's big idea to do the sister trip." Alita could only let out a bitter laugh.

"But, B, I know her. She wanted to get away just as much as me. Her drama is way bigger than mine."

"You think?"

"Okay, we all got big-time drama going on. And I never knew it would get to this level." Her eyes misted, but she quickly wiped away a tear. She let out a big sigh and shuddered.

"Okay, enough of that, Shade. We had the conversation, and now let's get back to the good feelings." She drew one bag that she was holding up to her nose and inhaled. "You smell these strawberries? That's what I'm talkin' 'bout. We are here to party and have a good time. Isn't that what you told me, sir?"

"Yeah, I did, but —"

"So let's get back to doing that, all right?"

He nodded and agreed to try and stay out of family business. God knows he did not want to do anything to get on his lady's bad side. More healing was needed, of that he was sure, and he decided to allow time for things to work out between the sisters.

Alita continued taking in the sights and sounds of the city. It was getting to be twilight. And everywhere she looked she saw lights flashing, all colors of the rainbow, and the connection of life going on.

"I want things to stay like this forever," Alita finally said, opening up. "Life feels real good for a change. I-I just want them to stay good."

He took a moment to lean over and give Alita a kiss on the lips. She started laughing, unable to help herself.

"What's wrong now?" Shade complained.

"Nothing's wrong. Everything is just perfect."

She exhaled. Feeling peace, joy, and happiness was something that Alita had craved for a number of years. When things were rocky years ago, she felt cursed, like she was doomed to a life filled with misery, drama, and reaping every bad thing that she'd sown.

"I think God is sort of kind of liking me these days," she said, almost in a whisper.

Shade laughed. "He's always liked you. You have fallen into that trap, the perfection trap that made you think that God hates imperfect people. It's not like that at all. It's a fallacy."

"A what?"

"A misconception. It's a flat-out lie." Shade paused, wanting to make sure his analogy would be received. "Leno has messed up bad, right? It made you mad."

"He pissed me off."

"Right, but deep inside the love is there."

"Yes."

"You haven't disowned Leno."

"No way. I love my son . . . no matter how badly he screws up."

Shade could only look at Alita and nod. He watched her until a light began to sparkle in her eyes. Until she beamed at him. She gratefully squeezed his hand.

"You da, you da, best," she sang. "Best I ever had."

And they went on to enjoy the leisurely walk back to their high-rise hotel, feeding each other their delicious food, and making passionate love until they fell asleep, happy and exhausted, in each other's arms.

The next day was filled with planned activities. Alita rose out of bed before the sun came up. She and Shade took a shower together, got dressed, and hit the streets. No matter what time of day it was, the energy of New York was apparent. People rushed to ride the subway, hailed cabs, or did what they're known for: walking. Alita and Shade happily joined the throng of people. They visited a museum, walked into some boutiques, and caught a cab so they could hang out in Harlem. They came back to the hotel, and Alita decided to get one of her sisters to tag along so they could build sweet new memories together.

In the afternoon, Coco pulled Alita to the side as they were walking through the iconic Macy's store located on 34th Street. "Tell me something, Sis."

"What's that?" Alita said.

"Why did you get to bring your man on this trip? This is supposed to be a girls' trip."

"That was Burgundy's rule, but B needs to know that she does not run me. So, I wanted some male company on my getaway, and he had some vacation time, and that's why he's here."

"But if I would have known that, I would have brought my baby along."

"Who? Cypress?"

"No, fool. Q."

"What? Are you serious? Y'all two are actually seeing each other?"

"For the time being, yes."

"But that can't last for long, because once that man realizes you've lied to his ass about Chance, Lord have mercy, Coco. Why you keep getting into the same type of drama, over and over again? No man on earth is going to put up with your constant bullshit."

They were headed to the women's shoe department, and Alita immediately tuned out any response Coco gave her. Footwear was placed in well-lit cases or set on white circular displays with boots strategically placed on top. Alita had never seen so many wonderful, sharp-looking shoes in her entire life.

"No wonder they call this place the world's largest women's shoe department." She happily collected boots, leather sandals, wedges, and pumps. Soon Alita's hands were completely filled with all the types of shoes she wanted to try on.

"Really?" Coco said. "You really about to buy all these damned shoes? Who do you think you are? A Kardashian?"

"Ha, Kim wouldn't be caught dead buying shoes at Macy's."

"Right." Coco frowned. "You can find her shit at Sears."

Alita ignored Coco, found an empty seat, and waited for her shoes to arrive so she could try them on and strut up and down the walkway, pretending like she was a model.

"You're having way too much fun, Lita."

"Hello! That's why we're here. Do you know how long it's been since I've had a real vacation? I can't remember when. And it's sad. I'm almost forty and I really need to start living, you know what I mean? Going to work, struggling to pay bills, dealing with family issues day after day, that ain't living. It's surviving. I want to do more than barely make it."

Coco was impressed. "I'm glad you thinking like that, Sis. Because I thought you would have jumped out of a window by now since you got fired from your customer order clerk job."

"Nope, not doing that. I may get sick and tired of some stuff, but I still have hope."

"Well, I sure hope your man is prepared to pay for all this stuff you wanna buy."

Alita's eyes sparkled with brightness. "That's the thing. He already told me he'd do it, Dark Skin. He will help me out and buy me what I want. See, *that's* what I'm talkin' 'bout. I hate when a man makes a hundred thousand a year and will barely help the woman that he says he loves. Cheap as hell, but always trying to tap that ass for some pussy. Shade ain't like that at all."

"Alita, when have you ever dated a man that made a hundred grand?"

"Coco, I have a man right now that brings in that type of money. So chew on that!"

"Alita, you're in love. And it looks good on you. I'm mad as hell yet happy for you."

By the time the women were done inspecting all kinds of footwear, Alita called Shade from her cell phone. He'd been in the men's department, but when he got her call, he came right away to help her out.

Shade liked everything she selected and agreed to buy Alita six pairs of shoes.

"This feels like Christmas in July," Alita

said with a laugh. "Thank you, baby. It's been a long time since anyone has made me feel this good." She kissed him on the lips, and all he could do was smile. It made him happy to make her happy.

After he paid for the merchandise he made a suggestion. "What if we take the escalator down to the basement and go to Herald Square Café? We can get some coffee or espressos. Then we can get some sandwiches and salads. Let's take a break from all this shopping, sit down, and people watch."

"I'm game," Alita said and grabbed him by the arm. He carried one bag for her and she carried the rest. What pleased Alita even more was the fact that Shade even offered to buy Coco a pair of shoes. His gesture stunned the hell out of her. Of course, Coco said yes. And as the trio walked to board the escalator to go to the lower level, Coco had a dazed look on her face.

Shade and Alita stepped onto the escalator first. Coco followed behind them. But she was so deep in thought, she lost her footing. She tried to grab hold of the handrail but it moved much faster than the steps. Coco fell against the wall and soon began to slide about till she was lying sideways. Her body began to rotate and soon her legs were sprawled up in the air.

She looked like she was riding a Ferris wheel.

"Oh Jesus," she yelled. "Can someone please stop this damned thing?"

Alita looked behind her and watched her robust sister lying upside down on her back as the escalator descended. She screeched with laughter, gasped for breath, and wiped the tears that rolled down her cheeks.

"Lita, I hear you. I'm going to kill you, I swear to God." Coco struggled to pull herself up from off the stairs that were still in motion, but after a few seconds she gave up and just went along for the ride. But she managed to look over her shoulder. "Lita, you need to stop recording that video and come help me."

"I'ma help you. But this is too good not to tape. It's historic. Love you, Sis."

After Alita and Shade helped Coco recover from her embarrassing fiasco, they managed to make it down to the ground floor to enjoy a soothing hot coffee and eat a nice, healthy lunch.

"Damn, Sis, you really made this trip very memorable for me," Alita told Coco as they ate.

"Don't start."

"Too late."

The two sisters giggled at each other and

enjoyed the bonding they rarely got to indulge in. It had been a good while since they'd spent time together without fighting.

And right before they got up to leave, Coco finally gathered enough courage to look Shade in the eye. "It's official. I may not have made it to the altar, but it looks like y'all two just might do it. Welcome to the dysfunctional family. Don't say I didn't warn you."

CHAPTER 12
BACK AT GROUND ZERO

After the trip had ended, the memories of their joyous experience began to impact their lives once the ladies returned to Houston.

One morning in early June, Burgundy woke up to the sounds of their lawnmower. She assumed that it was their landscaper, Marty, who was paid to tend to their expansive property. But when she put on her robe and walked into the kitchen, she looked through the window and saw Nate. He was dressed in a t-shirt and some workout pants. And he was seated on the mower as it steadily moved across the yard.

She went outside and called to her husband.

"Hey Nate," she said. "Why are you out here?"

"Can't a good man cut his own lawn, take care of his own maintenance?"

"Yes," she said, perplexed, "but you usually pay other people to do that. What happened to Marty?"

"I had to let him go."

"Oh. And when were you going to tell me? Or why haven't you simply replaced him?"

"What's with all the questions, Burg? I'm just doing the things that a husband does. That's all."

Burgundy raised her hands. "Suit yourself. It looks odd, but whatever."

Later on that day, she could hear Natalia and Sid screaming with laughter. She ran from her bedroom to see what the fuss was all about. Nate was on the carpet, perched on his hands and knees. Sid straddled his back with her little hands braced around his neck. She held on for dear life as he gave her a boisterous ride around the family room. It was a big room, filled with all sorts of large sofas, chairs, and tables located everywhere.

"Oh, so that's the racket I keep hearing. Y'all out here playing and having a good old time."

"Yeah, Burg. That's what I do with my girls. Just spending quality time with them."

"Daddy is so cool," Natalia said. "Hurry up so I can get my turn." She turned around and told her mother, "And after this we're going to play hide and go seek."

"Really?"

"Yes, and I always come up with some good hiding places so Daddy can't find me. Sid tries to follow me around, but I tell her she needs to come up with her own hide out."

Burgundy walked from the room with a smile on her face. She was happy that there was some sense of normalcy in their lives, that the girls saw their father as their dad and not as a sexual abuser.

That night Burgundy was exhausted from all of her activities. But one ritual that she insisted on lately was the girls crawling into bed with her.

Burgundy sat squarely in the middle, with Natalia settled on her right and Sid on her left.

They chatted for a couple of minutes, when Sid asked, "Where's Daddy? Why isn't he with us?"

"Um," Burgundy said. "He is busy in the other room right now."

"But is he busy all the time? Because I never see him in this bed anymore."

Burgundy's heart sank. She'd forgotten how kids notice every detail. Even if they did not understand what was going on in the house, they still saw and felt its impact.

"Well, tell you what? How about you go

and find Daddy and ask him to join us, okay, sweetie?"

Both Natalia and Sid yelped, jumped out the bed, and ran from the room. When they returned, both leading Nate by the hand, he looked puzzled and nervous.

"Am I in trouble?" he asked Burgundy.

"No." She smiled. "You're just missed. So why don't you take a break from what you were doing and hop in bed with us for a little while."

Nate got in bed next to his wife. His eyes thanked her.

Natalia wasted no time with her requests. "Daddy, I heard some people talking about the father-daughter dance. I want to go."

He laughed. "You're only seven, way too young for that, Natalia. That's for when you get older or get married."

Sid spoke up. "I want to do a daddy-daughter dance too."

Burgundy shook her head. "They are too cute, but they're trying to grow up much too fast."

"Right, I can remember the day both of them were born. Even then I was thinking about how they'd one day mature, graduate from high school and college, and maybe get married and give me some grandbabies."

"Really, Nate?" Burgundy asked. "I don't

think you need to be thinking about things like that. Let's just enjoy our kids at the ages they are. I don't want to rush them to grow older and be independent or teach them how to cook and drive a car until the day that all of that is supposed to happen. And we have a long way to go before that takes place, don't you agree?"

"I do agree with you, Burg. All I want to do," he said in a rare emotional voice, "is to enjoy my family. Enjoy all the wonderful stages they're in right now."

At hearing the word "stages," Natalia took that moment to share the exciting news about how she'd be participating in the drama club for the new school year. She loved to act and sing and was taking dance lessons. She proceeded to talk her parents' ears off. They laughed and smiled and took great joy and pleasure in interacting with their kids.

As Burgundy silently beheld her husband's gentle loving ways with their daughters, it was difficult to mentally reconcile what he allegedly did with Elyse. How could the man that she married be a rapist? Why would a grown man want to exert power over a young, helpless woman? Nate was so large that he easily towered over Elyse. Did he make her have sex with him? Or was it consensual? Burgundy shuddered. Then she thrust the horrible images from her mind and concentrated on the here-and-now.

Five-year old Sidnee sang and joyfully swung her father's huge hand as she held it tight. He laughed then tickled her underneath her arms, causing her to squirm and yelp, which made Nate play with her even more. Then Natalia protested, "When will it be my turn? I want you to tickle me too, Daddy."

They horsed around for ten more minutes and engaged in lovely conversation. Nate's eyes glistened with thankfulness. Burgundy loved what she was seeing at that moment. It easily made her forget anything bad had ever happened.

"We've got great kids," Burgundy said.

"Yes, we do. And I love them with all my heart, Burg, I'd never do anything to —"

"Shhh. I know you wouldn't. I know you love the girls. And you love me."

"I do, Burg. I do."

"Shhh," she said again, feeling overcome with emotion. She wished she could turn back the hands of time in so many ways, that what was currently happening in their lives would just quietly disappear.

As Sid and Natalia chattered on and on, everything felt so perfect. Burgundy decided to teach the girls some lyrics from *The Sound of Music.*

" 'So long, farewell, auf Wiedersehen, good night.' "

"What's that mean, Mommy?" Natalia asked.

"It's a nice way of saying good night or goodbye."

"Cool." They continued singing together until they learned the song.

Again Nate mouthed the word "Thanks" to Burgundy. She whispered back, "You're welcome," and they enjoyed putting the girls to bed as the evening came to an end.

Alita was seated at her desk at her job as a bill collector. She was in the midst of harassing a woman who was late paying her bills when she felt someone approach her. She looked up and was handed a pink slip.

She hung up on the woman and asked, "What's this?"

"Read it," her supervisor told her. "And if you want to talk to me you only have seven minutes. We pretty much need you to pack up and get your personal things right now. Then you'll be escorted out the door."

"What? Why? What did I do?"

Right then another manager entered her cubicle. Everyone in the company was very used to the loud outbursts of Alita Washington. But they were in no mood for her antics today.

Alita stood up, her face turning red with shame.

"You know what, fuck this shit. I don't even want anything from my cubicle. Why? What good will photos and coffee mugs do when I need a check? Y'all can take this bullshit job and shove it right up your fat asses."

Alita stormed from the building and tried hard not to cry. She couldn't believe it. How could she get fired from two jobs in less than a year? Why was the Lord shitting on her like this? Or was it the devil? She did not care who it was, she didn't like it one bit.

First thing she did was go straight home and open a kitchen drawer. Alita pulled out a bill organizer whose file pockets were bulging with papers. She took a seat at the dining room table and glanced at each bill: water, electricity, car insurance, cell phone, gas, cable, credit card, and some medical expenses regarding Elyse. She also remembered that Leno had an upcoming dental appointment for a deep cleaning that would cost a hundred seventy-five.

Alita mentally added up the numbers of

what she owed versus what she had. She pushed back from the table and ran to her bedroom closet. She started rummaging through shoeboxes. She made a mess searching through purses, old dresses, costume jewelry, and music CDs.

"Let's see what I can sell." After searching for ten minutes, Alita gave up. She laughed and slammed the door. "This shit ain't worth ten cents."

Alita debated if she should pawn the lovely shoes she'd gotten in New York and loudly muttered, "Hell no."

Hating to do so, but without any other solution, she placed a call to Burgundy.

"What up, B. Look, you're not going to believe this," she started out saying. "But I just lost my job."

"You lost what? Lita, stop playing."

"You think I'd play about something as serious as that? Sis, I just can't go through this again. All this stress is getting to be too much." Between her still hiding secrets from Elyse, and from the agony of Leno recently getting kicked off the basketball team due to some juvenile antics, she felt like her world was ending.

Her voice trembled. "B, tell me the truth. Am I a bad person? Am I? Do I deserve all this shit that's happening to me? When will it stop? Why do I feel like God is trying to hide my happiness from me?"

For the first time in a long time, the words that came from Alita's mouth made a solid connection to Burgundy. The two sisters were so unalike it was as if they came from two different sets of parents. But knowing the pain from extreme hurt? Burgundy could relate.

"I don't know why things seem that way, Lita. Everybody feels like they're getting messed over at some point. Or like they can't catch a break."

"Ha, even you?"

"Even me."

"But you got money."

"Money can't buy everything."

"Okay, B, then what's the answer? 'Cause I'm up a creek with no paddle."

"Well, first of all, maybe you should calm yourself down. Slow down enough to think things through."

What her sister proposed sounded about right. But functioning in a logical, calm manner wasn't a natural part of Alita's character.

So instead of waiting for Alita to do that, Burgundy began to map out a plan for her frazzled sister.

"I'm sure there's something I can do to

make the situation better —," Burgundy told her.

"There's plenty you can do. For one, I need to pay off this one credit card that got maxed out," Alita replied. "And if I can get some help with the car note that would be good too." She informed Burgundy how she had to buy Leno some furniture and she chose not to go cheap this time around.

"What you did for your son was true love. And the least I can do is help you with that balance and plus some car notes. Don't even sweat it, Lita."

"Seriously?"

"I'm serious."

"Oh, Jesus, thank you, 'cause that interest rate for Visa is off the charts."

"Doesn't matter."

"But you don't even know how much I owe," Alita said in a hushed tone.

"It can't be more than five or ten thousand. Surely no more than fifteen. No credit card company would be crazy enough to spot you more than that. Whatever the amount, I got you."

All of the saliva left Alita's mouth. She yelped. Then she laughed. Because to her ears it sounded like her sister was playing God and was powerful enough to rescue her. Again.

"B, you don't know how much this means to me."

"Forget about it. That's what family is for."

The very next day, Alita drove over to Morning Glory to meet Burgundy. She mentioned to Dru that she was going there to pick up Elyse from her job. Dru said it was fine. And when Alita arrived at the restaurant, Burgundy was true to her word. Alita handed over the most recent bill to her sister so she could reference the account number. And Burgundy wrote out a check to Visa for ninety-five hundred dollars.

"B, you're the best sister ever. I mean that." Alita snatched the check from her hand, then jumped up and down and gave Burgundy a lovable squeeze. And when Burgundy also wrote a check to her to cover two car payments, Alita kissed her all over her cheeks. "You're my favorite, B, I swear."

Burgundy smiled and kissed her back. "I will remember that the next time you call me out of my name, Lita."

"Girl, I just be playing with you." Alita calmed herself down, then glanced around the restaurant. It was busy as usual. She inhaled the aroma of coffee, waffles, scrambled eggs, and fried bacon. "I guess I can eat some of this expensive food before I leave."

"Go right ahead," Burgundy told her. "Get whatever you want."

"It sure is nice to know black folks with money, I swear to God."

Burgundy laughed and told her she needed to go take care of some business.

Alita took a seat at her favorite booth and placed an order. She continued glancing at the pricey menu and sipped on a cup of hot tea, when something caught her attention. She looked up. Jerrod had slid into the booth.

"Hi, Ms. Alita," he said.

"What are you doing here? How'd you know I was here?"

"Facebook is like breaking news when it needs to be."

"What's that supposed to mean?"

"Dru and I are Facebook friends. I can see all her posts and all her photos. I was in the neighborhood when I happened to check her page. She had posted about how happy she was that you were at Morning Glory about to eat breakfast. And then I started looking through her photos. I saw you in them. And I remembered how you cried broke a little while ago, yet based on all that grinning you were doing, you were living it up in New York. A trip to NYC costs a grip."

"So what? My sister paid for that trip. For all of us —" Alita thought twice about her words. But it was too late.

"Oh, yeah. One of your sisters got it like that!" Jerrod looked around. "I read in the papers about her. Burgundy, right? She's Taylor now? I see that she and her husband opened up two more barbershops earlier this year. The barbershops that cater to the members of the Rockets, and the Texans, and a few of the Astros. Must be nice to have a sister that's securing her bag."

"Jerrod, my sister ain't your business. Leave me the hell alone."

Right then she saw Elyse breezing by clutching menus in one hand. She was leading patrons to their booth. Alita broke out in a sweat. Did Jerrod know what Elyse looked like? What if he tried to talk to her? What if he told her that Alita was her mother?

She thought quickly. Once her credit card payment cleared, that would free up her balance. She could take out a cash advance and help him that way.

"Look," she whispered. "I can get you a thousand dollars in about three days. How does that sound?"

"Sounds hella good. But how I know I can trust you?"

"If I had a stack of Bibles I'd swear on them."

"That's not good enough." He thought for a second. "Why don't you friend me on Facebook and then post on my wall that you're about to hook me up financially? Kind of like an early birthday present."

"What? Are you insane?"

"Pretty much. You see, I gets real crazy when it comes to my money. If I had a daddy, I could ask him for some, but you know how that goes."

Alita wanted to jump across the table and smack Jerrod. But she knew she couldn't make things worse.

"Jerrod, I swear to God I will get you the money. I will stop by your place on Friday. I promise."

His eyes flickered with doubt, but he agreed to her suggestion. "You make sure and get me my coins. If you don't do it, I'm coming for you and your daughter," he said. Jerrod pointed at Elyse. Then he got up and left.

CHAPTER 13
EVERYTHING MUST CHANGE

No one wants their past to catch up with them or, worse, for the past to repeat itself. But that's what life felt like. Burgundy stepping in to help out felt good. But Alita knew she couldn't keep begging her sister for money.

It was now the week after Alita had visited Jerrod and paid him one grand. Elyse had just gotten home from work and was hanging out in the living room.

"Elyse, baby, can I talk to you for a minute?"

"About?"

"I need to have a tough conversation with you, sweetie."

"Are you going to finish telling me what you tried to tell me before . . . when we were at the last Sister Day?"

Damn. Why did Elyse have to remember that?

"Um, no, sweetie. This time I wanted you

to know, I just lost my bill collector position. They let me go. I'm down to one job."

"You lost your job? Again?"

"Yes! It happens. Anyway, my current little gig as a stock clerk, hell, it doesn't pay me enough to afford the rent on this place. And I-I think I may have to move. Leno might even need to go live with his father. Things are about to change."

"What's going to happen to me?"

"I'm not sure, sweetie."

"I'll go stay with Coco."

"Dark Skin? Ha! She's too unstable. She has all those damned kids and a heart that's broken. She's still trying to heal from getting dumped."

"How about Dru?"

Alita laughed. "That child tries to act like she cares a lot, but if your troubles get too overbearing, she won't take you in. Dru is cool, but her help is only going to go so far."

Elyse twisted her lips, thinking. "I'll go stay with Gamba, then."

"Gamba?"

"Yeah."

"Is that your way of saying that he's your man? Does Gamba love you like that?"

Elyse honestly could not answer the question right then. What they shared felt like love, but she still wasn't sure how to categorize it.

And later on that night, when Gamba stopped by Alita's apartment to visit Elyse, she greeted him with a tight hug. She pulled him against her breasts and squeezed him with all her might.

"Is everything all right?" Gamba asked after they stopped hugging. They were alone in the living room. Alita was taking a nap in her bedroom.

"I-I'm not sure what's right anymore. I feel mad about somethin'." But Gamba wasn't listening. He had his own news to tell her first.

"Elyse, I came over to tell you that I've gotten my orders to help handle a hurricane situation that's hit the state of Florida." It was late June and the hurricane season promised to be busy. The troops were called in to assist in the recovery effort in thirty-one counties. Gamba would be leaving early the next morning with no idea of when he'd return to Houston. The prospect of Gamba leaving her, even for a day, frightened Elyse. It was only when she was with Gamba, or when her thoughts were filled with him, that she felt strong and capable and willing to face everything in her uncertain world.

"No," she yelled. She leaped into his arms,

pressing her chest against his, and tried to become one with him. "Don't go, Gamba. Please! Don't go. I won't let you."

Gamba could only smile. He kissed her forehead. "You're too cute."

"I don't want to be cute." Oh, how she ached inside for this man. She was dying for him to notice that she was a woman, and she felt more than ready to receive his love. Her ears ached for him to tell her how he felt for her. Her body ached for him to be inside of her. All she knew was that the US military sounded dangerous and risky. Things happened. What if she never saw him again?

"Gamba, I don't want you to leave me."

Gamba lovingly patted her hair and pulled it back from her face. He looked into her eyes. "I could never leave you, Elyse."

She stared up at him, her eyes big and round with wonder. "Why not?"

Go ahead, say it.

Her insides screamed at him. Her heart moaned in agony. *Tell me that you love me.* But he gave her a blank look, as if the words escaped him.

Unable to help herself, Elyse grabbed Gamba's head and pulled him toward her. She pressed her lips against his mouth. She took the initiative and gave him the kiss that she'd always wanted to give. At first his lips felt tight with resistance, but as she poked her tongue gently into his mouth, his lips parted, then softened. His tongue was soft and wet. A grunt escaped her mouth and landed in her throat. Her chest felt hotter and hotter as if she were melting.

Gamba felt something too, as evidenced by the hardening of his penis. She felt good in his arms. Warm and nurturing. He closed his eyes and allowed Elyse to take control. He kissed her back. Elyse got so excited that she reached inside his shirt. She fumbled around until her fingers touched his nipples. They felt hard and thick. That made her more excited, and she rubbed his erect nipples over and over. She began to feel an erotic wetness between her legs that made her cry out loud.

At first what Elyse was doing to Gamba did not bother him. But when she unzipped his slacks and reach inside to caress his penis, Gamba surprised himself when he moaned. Her hands felt gentle, yet there was urgency as she rubbed. She flicked her fingers across the tip and tried to stimulate him even more.

It had been so long. He wanted Elyse. But he thought about it and gently removed her fingers that now clutched his dick, clutched so tight it felt like she was part of him.

Gamba gave her another gentle kiss that let her know that he cared, but he felt they should stop.

"Okay," he said. "That's enough." He opened his eyes and wiped his lip. Elyse trembled and was breathing hard.

"But I want. I want more. I want you."

"Elyse, you don't know —"

"I do know. I know what I want."

His heart was torn. He knew she considered herself mature enough to handle a man like him, like she was on his level. But he cared about this woman; it was amazing to watch her recent transformation. Making love at this point would feel premature. Everything had to be just right. And Gamba had promised himself to never do anything to hamper her growth or ruin her survival.

"Look, I hear what you're saying, sweetie, and we'll talk about this when I get back. Promise!"

"When will you be back?"

"I don't know, but I don't think I'll be gone that long." Gamba wanted to refocus. He tried his best to let go of the memory of what he had just shared with this very desirable, passionate woman whose pure love he felt each time he was in her presence.

"There wasn't extensive damage to the

infrastructure and that's good. But the governor asked the military to deploy a few troops and that's what we must do. But I'll be back, Elyse." He narrowed his eyes, taking in her beauty, from her large eyes, to her hair, upswept and sexy. And he took care to notice her pouty lips that felt soft to the touch, the fiery warrior look in her eyes; eyes that rarely concealed her feelings.

"You swear?"

"I swear to you, Elyse."

She thought a second. "You going to Florida? I heard they have alligators. You a good swimmer?"

He threw back his head and laughed. "Damn straight I am. I got all kinds of skills."

"I don't know how to swim that well, but I guess I need to learn. I'm about to go back and live with Burgundy."

"You are? Be safe. You have what it takes to learn and grow and be that woman that I know you can be."

"I can be that woman as long as you teach me everything you know, Gamba. If you do that, I'll wait for you."

"It's a deal."

Before he left, Gamba impulsively backed Elyse against the wall. She looked up at him with expectancy. He spread his legs wide and watched her throw her arms around his neck. He gave Elyse another soulful kiss. As they embraced each other, he ran his fingers through her hair and felt her body press against him. She moaned and sucked on him, and he knew that her tongue was talking to him. It was saying that Elyse adored and respected him. In his mind and through his lips, he told her he loved her too. He moaned again as his body ached for her. His eyes filled with tenderness. Then Gamba ended their kiss. He wanted to stay, but he had to leave. He placed two fingers against his lips then waved them at her.

He told Elyse he'd see her later.

Duty beckoned, and Gamba was ready to serve.

Elyse had realized something. She'd been doing all this work to be grown and strong. Maybe going back to Burgundy's, bravely facing all her demons, would be the thing she needed to really believe in the changes. Alita had packed up all their things so they could move. Good thing it was the midsummer. Leno was sent to stay with his dad, and he got offered an internship at the car dealership so he could do something decent with his free time. Life was about to change for them all.

Alita had driven Elyse to the house one Sunday morning in early July. The minute Elyse said goodbye to Alita, she brought her things inside and placed them on the floor of the family room. Burgundy promptly laid out the ground rules.

"You are to walk around my house fully clothed, meaning no skimpy pajamas, no gym shorts, no wife-beater tanks, no thongs left in any of the bathrooms, no leaving your bras in the laundry room, no miniskirts are to be worn in this house as long as you are living in this house, no wearing of bikinis when you go swimming, and no being in the same room with him for any reason."

Elyse stared straight ahead as Burgundy barked orders.

"Him," aka Nate, was standing by and resembled a whimpering puppy. Burgundy insisted her husband be there when Elyse arrived so he too could know her rules.

Feeling insulted for being treated like a child, Nate refused to give either his wife or Elyse any eye contact. In fact, his jaw was rigid with anger. He didn't want the girl under his roof any more than Elyse wanted to be there. This was all Burgundy's idea. But he also wanted to prove to his wife that to him, Elyse was a nonfactor. What they used to have was over, and furthermore, he did not think of himself as a pervert or a rapist. One wrong action shouldn't eternally define a man, and he felt very misjudged.

Burgundy continued, "When I get up, you get up."

"What time do you get up?" Elyse asked.

"Six, sometimes seven."

"That's too early."

"And too early is exactly when you'll be waking up, so get used to it."

She continued. "When you want to eat breakfast or dinner, you and I can eat together in the kitchen. He can have the dining room. All his clothes are in a hall closet, so there is no reason on earth for him to be coming into the master bedroom for anything. You got that, Nate?"

He stared straight ahead and contemplated all kinds of troublesome thoughts.

Once Burgundy was done reading aloud her typewritten list of do's and don'ts, she asked Elyse sign and date at the bottom of the last sheet.

"Why?"

"It's for protection."

"What?"

"It protects both you and him. And me."

"Fine," Elyse said. "But I want a copy."

This time Burgundy was offended. "Why do you need a copy?"

"Gamba told me never to sign anything I don't agree with or understand. He said to always get a copy. And I do it every time Lita takes me to see the psychotherapists and family doctor."

"Do you always do what Gamba says?"

"Always."

"I see," Burgundy said, then shrugged. She mulled over the decision for a couple of minutes, then went and made a copy of the signed document and handed it to Elyse.

With the rules now spoken and understood, from then on, even though it was a typically hot July for Houston, inside that house the forecast turned into a bitter winter storm. Chilly, icy, with forcible winds threatening to tear down everything within sight.

The first week she lived there, nothing out of the ordinary happened. And by the third week, Elyse was resigned to settle in. She did not want to, but she had to. Gamba completed his Florida duties but immediately got sent on another military assignment, this time in California. She had no idea when she'd see him again. So Elyse adjusted to her new life: riding to work with Burgundy, fulfilling her job duties, working extra hours if she could get them, and going back to survive inside the big house.

Elyse complied. But she had questions every step of the way.

Supposedly, rules were designed to protect. But many rules were riddled with confusion . . . their origin always a mystery.

"Why can't I go get something to eat after ten o'clock at night? What if I'm hungry late at night?" This was what she asked Burgundy the fourth week that she'd been living there.

"House rules, Elyse."

"But dat don't answer my question."

Every time Elyse said "dat" instead of "that," Burgundy knew she had the upper hand.

"Elyse, I don't care what you say. As long as you stay under my roof, you will comply. If you do not, you're out the door. And there's nothing out there for you, so you're actually better off being right here. I do what I do because I care about you. We're family. Stop acting so hard."

"I'll stop acting hard when you do."

"Elyse, please!" Burgundy noticed how much feistier the girl had become. And she did not like it. "Anyway, haven't you talked to Alita?"

"We talk every day, many times a day."

"Then you should know that she's still looking for a job and hasn't gotten a single callback for any applications that she put in."

"Why don't you hire her to work for you, then? You have a bunch of businesses, and you could have hired your own sister."

Burgundy simply shook her head at Elyse. "I've noticed you've been feeling yourself lately. Dressing and talking like you're some type of Beyoncé clone. But let me tell you something, you have a lot to learn, young lady."

Elyse cast a sharp look at Burgundy. The sister who always knew what to do had become overbearing with all her insistent demands. It was difficult and unnatural for Elyse to walk around trying to remember what she could and could not do. For the first time in her life, Elyse wanted to be pretty and stylish. But Burgundy was against it.

With all the rules she had to follow, Elyse did not feel as if she were living. Having a roof over her head and food to eat did not seem worth it.

The weeks had flown by. And one Sunday in early August, Elyse grew restless. She decided to throw some fun in the mix.

She waited until Burgundy was in the kitchen preparing dinner. Elyse rummaged through her suitcase and quickly changed clothes. She strolled into the kitchen and waited.

"Elyse, what's wrong with you?" Burgundy asked, enraged. "Look at you, dressed like Kim Kardashian or like you're Lil' Kim."

"What you mean?" Elyse asked. She was wearing a sheer blouse with a matching bra that was the same color as her skin. It looked as if she were naked. And Elyse felt very liberated. She did not want to obtain her sister's approval for what she could wear around the house or at the workplace either.

She thought about all the things that Gamba had taught her. The important things Dru had shared with her to keep her strong. And right then Elyse decided fear would not keep her imprisoned.

"You're dressed like a whore, Elyse. Now I finally understand. No wonder my husband noticed you and sensual thoughts went through his mind. The way you dress, you were just asking for it."

Elyse wanted to slap Burgundy hard across her face.

"You're stupid," she yelled, unable to use eloquent words to express the way she really felt. "You know nothing. You're not me. And when dat man raped me, I wasn't even dressing like this."

Burgundy's stoic face crumbled, she was

so livid. But at Elyse's revelation she still couldn't calm down.

"If you don't want that type of attention, then you need to dress differently. Whores dress likes whores. Whores like to get half-naked."

"I am not a whore. I'm *not*. I don't care how I dress, he had no right to touch me. He forced himself on me, B, don't you understand."

"No, ma'am. I understand that you provoked him. You might not have done it on purpose, Elyse, but you did it."

"But I never dressed like this till now."

"Elyse, it doesn't matter. A modestly dressed woman can still seduce a man. Happens all the time. You try to play that innocent, stupid role, but look at you now. You're nothing like you used to be. That means you were putting on an act all along."

"I'm not fake," Elyse quietly told her. "I have to adjust to my surroundings. I do what I have to do to keep from going nuts."

"So you have to dress like a slut? Is that what you call adjusting, Elyse? That doesn't make any sense."

"You don't understand me. And now I know you don't really value me. And just because you don't value me don't mean I don't have value."

Burgundy could only stare at Elyse, pondering the most revealing thing she'd ever said to her. But her pride still could not allow her to accept this new Elyse.

"Bullshit. It sounds like something Dru would train you to say. We all know that Dru has been taking you to the side and teaching you all kinds of things. I don't trust any of the sisters. There is no loyalty in this family."

"You one to talk? Who you loyal to? A rapist? Why ain't he in jail?"

"Hey, I could ask you the same question. If you really felt violated, you could have called 911 and filed a complaint when it supposedly first happened. But you didn't. And it's because you enticed my husband. You wanted him to fuck you and that's why he did it!"

Feeling vindicated by her own reasoning, Burgundy immediately shut down any further rebuttal from Elyse. She was done. No one in the family would ever believe it, but she felt victimized herself. After she and Nate got married she still couldn't forget the petty comments they endured as the Taylors grew their businesses into successes. She still remembered the snide remarks she got from Alita about their McMansion, several expensive cars, the way her daughters acted and dressed like little princesses, and the additional petty scrutiny about everything she bought.

Burgundy felt that all of her sisters were envious of her and her family.

And jealous people act jealous. And maybe that's what all of this meant. And this probably was the reason why someone, who she did not know, had recently taken measures to formally file a complaint against Nate on behalf of Elyse.

Burgundy felt that everything she had was at stake. Her family, home, businesses, marriage. Everything. And she planned on doing something about it.

Chapter 14
Side Deals

The very next day Burgundy decided to take a different course of action. That morning she traveled to downtown Houston. She requested a meeting with Randall Burkett, the district attorney. They knew each other well. She stepped inside of his suite and got comfortable.

After they chatted for a few minutes, the door opened and an African American woman walked in.

Burkett stood up, "Burgundy, like I told you before, ordinarily this scenario wouldn't happen until the plea hearing, but I've asked my good friend to join us."

"Hello. I'm Judge Juanita Mallow." She was petite, confident, and no-nonsense. But she also was a member of Delta Sigma Theta just like Burgundy, and she hoped that would work in her favor.

"Nice to meet you, Judge. And fellow sorer," Burgundy said with a smile.

"I've heard a lot about you, Mrs. Taylor. And that latest is that you want to strike a deal with the DA. Why is that?"

"As you know, Judge Mallow, my husband and I do a lot to support the community. Between all of our businesses, we employ well over fifty-some people, mostly full-time. We support several local charities and give out free food to the hungry every year between Thanksgiving and Christmas. We've reached out and assisted in all types of initiatives and partnered with organizations that are about building the local infrastructure. We've helped a lot of citizens get back on their feet after they've gone through hard times." She continued. "Some of our employees used to serve time in your prisons. We took them in, dusted them off, and trained them how to be chefs, taught them how to properly cut hair, schooled them on how to become responsible. We gave them a chance and watched them become productive members of society. I'm very happy to report that none of the people we hired got turned back into the prison system. The DA already knows this. And I could go on and on."

"No need. I'm quite impressed. It says that you're a true risk taker. Not many people would welcome felons to work in their place of business," Judge Mallow said.

"Well, everyone deserves a second chance."

"And I'm glad you think that. But what's the true reason why you're here? What's going on with this case regarding Mr. Taylor? I recently learned that a sexual assault complaint was filed by a woman named Alita Washington?"

Burgundy grew silent. It was Alita who betrayed her. And it infuriated her.

"In the State of Texas, that's a serious allegation, Mrs. Taylor," the judge continued. "The Penal Code states that if the defendant has had sex with a 'child,' and a child is anyone under the age of seventeen —"

"She's twenty."

"But when did the act begin?"

"She was over seventeen."

"Do you know that for sure?"

Burgundy was tempted to lie, but in reality, she had no idea when the incidents began. She didn't want to hear, didn't want to know, nor could she imagine her husband conducting any deviant predatory behavior with an underage female. She knew what Elyse claimed, and fear made her hope that it wasn't completely true.

"I don't know the exact dates or anything like that."

"Like I was saying," the judge told her, "if your husband had sex with the victim without consent, if he threatened her in any way, through physical violence or otherwise, or if the victim is powerless against the defendant in that he was in charge of taking care of the victim such as being a health care provider, clergyman, public assistant, or as an employee of a facility in which the victim resides —"

"Okay, getting back to the reason that I'm here." Burgundy coughed and cleared her throat. "In light of the complaint of sexual assault with a minor, I also think the accusations are very serious. They'd have very terrible consequences for both parties involved. And because of this —"

Burgundy looked at the DA and the judge. "Is this conversation being taped?"

The judge held up her cell phone. "Take a look, my dear."

Burgundy boldly grabbed the woman's phone and was satisfied to see that they weren't being recorded. The DA performed the same gesture. Feeling relieved, Burgundy resumed her speech.

"How about we strike a plea deal? We would not want this type of thing to go before a jury. The courts are already very backed up. This thing could be dragged out for another year to two years. Honestly, I don't want to endure a long trial, and I'd never want to waste the taxpayer's time and money. And of course, since you're up for reelection I'd be happy to give a sizeable donation for your campaign. If we could simply put our heads together . . .

Burgundy hoped they wouldn't think she was bribing them. No! In her heart she was saving her husband, her livelihood. Besides, supporting an elected official wasn't anything new for Nate and Burgundy. They'd already done so twice before, and in her mind this offer wasn't anything different.

"May I interrupt, Burgundy?" the DA said. "You and I go back a long way; we've bumped into each other at different charity events, our kids have played together, etc., but of course, we've never had to deal with anything like this before."

"I know, Randall. It's weird and it's very frustrating the way life can suddenly change."

"That's true. Yet I still have to do my job, right?" he asked. "I still have to make sure I'm not getting messed up by trying to help you out, right?"

"Of course, sir," Burgundy insisted. She assumed Randall wanted to assist her the best way that he could, but she felt afraid on the inside. Things that did not go her way made her feel uneasy, and she wished she could change the circumstances.

"I want to ask a couple of questions," he said to her. "Think you can handle it?"

"I'll try my best."

"Do you know if a weapon was ever used in any instances of the sexual assault?"

"Absolutely not. I've never heard at any time that my husband pulled out a gun on her. He'd never do anything like that."

"How about if a date rape drug was used?"

"Are you serious, Randall? We don't have things like that sitting around the house. That's crazy."

"All right." The DA continued to probe by asking several more questions. When Burgundy emphatically responded no to each of them, he wanted to know, "Is the victim insane?"

Burgundy's eyes widened, and immediately she wished that they hadn't. Body language revealed everything that speech would not. She calmed down and allowed her eyes to flutter as if in deep thought.

"That one I don't know." She was afraid that once they found out Elyse went to therapists, then they'd request recorded evidence about anything the girl might have revealed to them. What if she contradicted everything Burgundy had just stated during their meeting?

"I'm sorry, Randall, I'll have to get back to you on that one."

"You don't know if Elyse is crazy or not?"

"Ha! Sometimes I think my entire family is nuts. You've met a few of them. Quite frankly, a lot of unsettling things happen within the family, but that doesn't mean that —"

"Fine, Burgundy. One last question. Do you believe that your husband is a threat to the general public? Or would you say that what happened with him was an isolated, domestic type of sexually inappropriate behavior?"

"Randall, I swear to you, no other employee, no customer, no family member has ever filed a complaint against Nate. About *anything.* And this incident only began after she came to live with us when she was fourteen. Prior to that we never had any issues between her and my husband. They got along very well from what I can recall. So this is definitely an isolated case, and he is not a threat to any other woman."

"I see." The DA nodded. "Again, what precisely do you want out of this, Burgundy?"

"If it ends up being very serious," she said

in a shaky voice, "I want him to get probation or no jail time."

"None?"

"Or at least very little jail time as possible." Burgundy imagined her husband chained up, him wearing an orange jumpsuit, him being locked up, isolated, and treated like a worthless individual . . . like he'd sunk to the bottom of a totem pole. And suddenly her heart began to panic. She felt like she could not breathe.

No! She couldn't bear to let it happen.

She grabbed her purse and tried to sound strong. "I'm prepared to write out a c-c-check to *any* institution that you wish. I-I-um, of course, this money would be looked upon as the payment of a fine, which I'm very willing to do."

"How much are we talking?" the judge asked just to see what she'd say.

"I can get my hands on three million, but no more than that."

Judge Mallow smirked, but the DA didn't.

"That's the highest I can go, DA. And please keep in mind, I can't afford for any of this information to be leaked. The publicity would kill our businesses, and in order for me to recoup the losses I will need to keep them all open. As you know, we give free barber cuts to all the underprivileged boys and girls right before they return to school every fall semester. So once this is all over with, I'll need you to seal the court documents."

"Mrs. Taylor," the judge said.

"Please, call me Burgundy."

"All right, Burgundy. The DA has gotten your thoughts about this. He's heard your suggestion. It's going to be up to him to make a decision. But I must say no matter how things end up, I recommend that Mr. Taylor seek psychological counseling. All the payments in the world won't help whatever is going on inside of his head. And you, you yourself need to be careful. You're putting yourself out over a man whom you don't really know."

"Excuse me," Burgundy said in a chilly voice. "Judge Mallow, if I heard you correctly, you are assuming that I don't know my own husband?"

"With all due respect, if you didn't believe these accusations against him, I can't see how you in good conscience would hit us up for such a deal."

"What? It happens all the time. Payment doesn't mean admission of guilt. It's something people do to get rid of the case, to make it go away. To keep it from going to trial, you know this."

"I know it, but somehow, ma'am, I think you know more than what you're telling. And, like I said before, you just don't know the man."

"Well, um, not only do I know Nate, see, I-I care about him. I know his good side. More importantly, this whole thing impacts our girls. And a lot is weighing on my shoulders right now. I have to make sure they are well taken care of." Burgundy could not believe she was in the DA's office having this type of conversation. If she had to choose between her own drama and Alita's, for the first time ever, she'd trade places with her.

"I-I don't know what the future holds," Burgundy continued. "And that makes me very afraid, if you want to know the truth. If we can come to an agreement together, this way I will have some sort of idea of how things can play out. I've always considered myself a decent negotiator and an even better gambler. And I always know when to hold 'em. I know when to fold 'em too. It's not time for me to walk away or run just yet."

"It sounds like you want to hold onto and protect your investments. Plural." Judge Mallow had a wry smile on her face. She was used to the Burgundy Taylors of the world: those who believed that their money, power, and influence could buy their way out of anything. Burgundy figured Randall had the judge attend the meeting to keep her honest. But she honestly did not care. She desperately needed all the help she could get from whomever could give it to her. And before the meeting concluded, the DA and Burgundy verbally struck a deal. But it would take a while to work out the details. Burgundy thanked them for their time and left the office with much on her mind.

She arrived home and got dressed so she could prepare to greet the nanny that she'd recently hired. Burgundy was no fool. She always planned ahead. And her most recent legal issues required her to make sure the girls were taken care of in all kinds of ways.

The woman's name was Elizabeth. Everyone called her Liz. She'd been working for them for a couple of weeks, and the girls loved her. Liz was fifty-five, old enough to be Natalia and Sid's grandmother. And she was fifty pounds overweight. She was short, round, and jolly. Burgundy made sure that the woman she hired would not be much to look at. Plus she could recall when her husband claimed that "fat" women weren't his type.

Burgundy was trying to survive in an increasingly difficult world. What was true? What was safe?

She still recalled the day when she first interviewed Liz at the house.

"Liz, I have a strict protocol that I need you to follow regarding the girls. Here it is," she said and handed her a two-page document.

Liz glanced over it and shrugged. "Everything seems doable."

"Good. I also need you to sign this paper."

"What is it?"

"It's a confidentiality and nondisclosure agreement."

"Why do you want me to sign that?"

"Well, there are things such as family medical histories and other private information that we don't want to be disclosed. To anybody. For any reason. We will give you passwords to computers, etc., that have to do with the girls. There are other things you might hear or see while working here. I need you to understand that what goes on in this house stays in this house."

Elizabeth looked confused.

"Let me explain. In times past, we've had encounters with the media, and some of our competitors were caught sniffing around in our garbage trying to steal trade secrets."

Burgundy made up that explanation on the spot. "You are not allowed to speak to the press."

Although it spooked her, Liz gave a casual shrug.

"I'm just here to do my job, ma'am."

"The first order of business is signing this agreement, all right, Liz?"

Liz signed and dated it.

"Great job! Welcome aboard."

A week after her meeting with Randall Burkett, she received a phone call from his office. He asked if she could meet with him and the judge in her chambers. Burgundy canceled all her other appointments and drove downtown.

"Hi," Burgundy said and greeted Randall and Judge Mallow. "I hope you have good news for me."

"Well, depends on how you look at it," replied the judge. She studied some notes and gazed thoughtfully at Burgundy. "We have reviewed your proposal in great detail, Burgundy. But we want to make a counter-offer," she said. "D.A Burkett and I have thought long and hard about this case and we understand your concerns and agree that you've made wonderful contributions to the community. But quite frankly, unwanted sexual attention is like an incurable disease that if untreated, it may grow into a cancer, a cataclysmic situation that will undoubtedly impact far too many people."

"Is that a metaphor for something? I'm not quite understanding —"

"A young woman's life has just about been ruined."

Burgundy frowned. "What are you trying to say?"

The DA stepped in. "Elyse Reeves is going to need support. All kinds of support. From long-term counseling designed to making sure she doesn't suffer from PTSD to watching out for her so that she doesn't exhibit the signs of deep depression and suicide, to trying to make sure she doesn't succumb to drug and alcohol dependency as a way to cope. She may seem fine now, but one doesn't know what her future holds."

"Okay, you are thinking of long-term psychological and emotional help. That's no problem. What's your counter-offer?"

"We are advising you to set up an interest-bearing trust fund for Elyse. The amount will be three million five, plus a total of one million dollars that you will give to our favorite charities."

"What? Are you serious?"

"We've very serious," the judge replied.

"But why won't you accept my original offer?" Burgundy asked. "And why are you trying to force me to pay my sister that kind of money? That's a lot of money!"

"Because you swore to us about how much you believed in and love your husband . . . because you let us know that you have so much at stake, a lot to lose, way more than four point five million dollars. Because you insisted in no uncertain terms that this case should not go to a jury trial, and so on, that you're willing to give us three million dollars to keep all of that from happening."

"This is ridiculous. It's insane."

"What's so insane about it?" the DA asked.

"Right," Judge Mallow cut in. "Because as I see it, you want your financial offer to help everyone except the true victim. Your sister. Your flesh and blood."

"That's not true."

"Oh, but the facts suggest that it is true. Did you for one second offer to do anything on the girl's behalf? Pay for her college tuition? Provide her her own housing or transportation? Isn't she struggling to make ends meet working at your restaurant, earning not even ten bucks an hour? Isn't she living with you and has become subjected to involuntary servitude or something to that effect?"

"That's a total lie. She's not a slave. Who have you been talking to? And why would you believe them over me?"

"*You* came to *us* about this situation," the judge replied. "A situation that you are inclined to manipulate and work out for your benefit. And there's nothing wrong with people wanting things to work out for their good. It's just that I believe other people that are involved should also get something out of the deal. Primarily the one that's hurting the most and who actually has more to lose than you do."

"Elyse?"

"Bingo." The judge's voice was sympathetic, and she stared at Burgundy as if to ask, *Why don't you feel the same way that I do?*

"I hear what you're saying," Burgundy said. "But we still haven't totally investigated what happened. What if she's lying about anything? Or about everything? Women lie."

"Do they?"

"W-why, of course women lie. There are plenty of so-called victims who make up stories because their sole objective is to get paid. They're willing to play a role for that

278

check. And actually, I can see Alita behind the scenes putting Elyse up to this. My sister is very hard up for cash and I wouldn't put it past her. Plus a lot of people that point fingers at others tend to be just as guilty as the one that they're accusing."

"Is that what you really think is going on, Mrs. Taylor?" The judge continued to stare Burgundy down until she could no longer look her in the eye.

"Let's just wrap this up since you're in such a hurry. The first thing you should do is convince your husband to sign a confession."

"What?"

"Yes, that's what will be needed to avoid the jury trial that you say you don't want."

"What would it all entail?"

"Get your husband to confess to his crimes in writing. Make sure that you speak with your attorneys about this and that Mr. Taylor understands everything that he is stating. If he pleads guilty in writing we will accept it. Plus we'll need evidence that the money for Elyse has been set up in that trust fund. Can you get this done as soon as possible?"

"Oh, my," Burgundy said. "This is getting to be too much for me to think about."

"That's how it goes, Mrs. Taylor. We deal

with this type of thing day in and day out," Randall explained. "Anyway, the next important thing to do is to get the girl into an adequate living situation. No way should she be residing in the same house as him. And get him into counseling. Think about the worst-case scenarios because when the public finds out about this, you need to plan on how to handle it from a PR standpoint. That's what we, what *I*, feel is the best course of action . . . for now."

It felt like she'd been backed in a corner and surrounded by a gang of enemies.

As she pondered the turn of events, Burgundy hated that someone else got to call the shots about her life. She resented that how she felt did not seem to matter. And the more she thought about Alita, the more Burgundy couldn't stand her.

"I thought my initial deal was fine. Now this. How did you come to this conclusion?" she asked.

The judge smiled. "Well, to be honest, your DA buddy had to do a little investigating. He had a little talk with the victim and the woman who has been caring for her. Randall got their statements."

"Alita?"

"Yeah, her," Randall spoke up. "Burgundy, she let me in on all the things she's had to go through in dealing with the entire situation. We discussed a possible trust fund. And right now I think that it's only fair that the victim gets a big financial settlement for what she's put up with. All kinds of sexual abuse since the age of fourteen."

Burgundy thought about the checks she'd written out to help save Alita from financial ruin.

"Please listen, Randall. I'm telling you. You can't trust family. Family will do anything to stab you in the back. I help out my family, and they act like they hate me."

"Why would they hate you if you help them, Mrs. Taylor?" That was the judge. She wasn't smiling. There was nothing to smile about.

The DA continued. "Alita told me that your husband is a Jekyll-and-Hyde type of man. That he seduced the girl and would never listen to her when she told him outright that he was hurting her."

"She's lying."

"Really, Mrs. Taylor?" The judge spoke up. "Why would the girl lie about something like that?"

"I don't think that she is," the DA said. "Elyse seemed very forthright. Well-spoken considering the circumstances. I'd say that we get down to business and strike a real deal."

"Well, I have to think about it." Burgundy had been blindsided. Why would Alita do this to her? None of it made any sense.

"You mean to tell me that you'd rather see this case progress to the point of a jury trial?" the DA asked. "You yourself said that the case could be tied up for a year or two. We'll have to assemble a jury. They may not be sympathetic to your husband regardless of his standing in the community. Only rich people protect other rich people. His philanthropic efforts do not give him a pass when it comes to sexual harassment and improper behavior with a minor. That's a first-degree felony."

Burgundy stared into space. Her hands balled into tight fists. "Nate is not a felon."

"Burgundy, dear." The DA tried to be gentle but firm. "You need to face the reality of this situation. "In the end, he could get fined. And when you do the math, you would lose a whole lot more than four million. You'd lose your husband, probably all of your businesses. You have the girls to think about. What's going to happen to them if their daddy is sent to prison for two decades? How will you pay the mortgage for a house, plus the expenses for your restaurant and barbershops? And I recall that you and Nate own a lake house somewhere in the Hill Country. I know you won't want to lose that property either. Because, truthfully, there could be other victims out there, Burgundy."

"No," she cried. "No, there aren't. This is a big mistake."

"The other victims could feel the courage to come forward. They may have all types of evidence against your husband that you didn't even know about. Are you prepared to fight them or offer them a settlement?"

"You're overexaggerating, Randall. You know him. You know the good he's done for Houston."

"I know," the DA said in a sober tone. "People love a community hero, but some love to see a hero's downfall too. So please consider what I'm saying. Think the best but prepare for the worst, okay my friend?"

Burgundy nervously rubbed the back of her neck. She certainly did not expect a turn of events such as this.

"My goodness, I have to think about it, all of it. I can't make a good decision upon such short notice."

"You go ahead and sleep on it," the judge told her. "And put yourself in that girl's shoes. She's a sweetheart. She deserves a fair chance at life. Forget about that man you got."

The words cut so deep that Burgundy left the chambers without saying goodbye. She cried all the way to The Woodlands.

She hated Alita. "She's such a snake."

She hated Nate. "Why couldn't he keep his weak-ass penis in his slacks?"

And she hated herself. "Why do all the bad things end up happening to me?" She had no answer. Only more questions.

CHAPTER 15
NO ONE WANTS TO SWIM IN THE RAIN

Burgundy was on a mission. She was in her car trembling with anger when she decided to place a phone call.

The phone rang three times then went into voice mail.

"Alita is avoiding me," Burgundy said. She placed another call, this time to Dru.

"Hey, Dru. What are you up to?"

"Nothing much. Doing some research regarding my thesis."

"Good girl. I know you'll earn that master's anytime now." Burgundy continued to make small talk then changed the subject. "Um, did you plan on picking up Elyse today from work?"

"Yes."

"You don't have to do that," Burgundy told her. "In fact, Alita volunteered to come get her."

"Really? Because I've already talked to Lita. She never told me she'd be going to get Elyse."

"Well, she must have forgotten. She's been doing a lot of that lately."

"What do you mean? Like how?"

"Like she will tell me she's going to do something. Of course, it will involve Elyse, but then she'll forget. Like our big sister has a lot on her mind." Burgundy paused. "Do you know what's going on with Lita? Has she discussed anything that she's involved with these days?"

"Not really. I know she's been applying for jobs and going on interviews. Other than that, nothing."

"Hmm, well, anyway, Dru Boo, you keep studying. I'll contact Lita and remind her to come pick up Elyse."

"All right. Thanks. Bye."

Burgundy sent a text telling her that Dru was studying so she shouldn't forget to come and get Elyse.

A few seconds after Burgundy sent the text, her phone rang. It was Alita.

"Hello. I knew you'd call me after I texted you. Why are you playing games?"

"B, I was busy when you called. And now I'm not."

"Good, because we need to talk. Why did you file against Nate?"

"W-what?"

"You filed a complaint against my husband. Why?"

"I did not do anything like that, B. I don't know what the hell you talkin' 'bout. You got me confused with someone else."

"Alita, don't even try it. I talked to the DA and he told me what happened. He even got a statement from you."

"DAs lie."

"Oh, c'mon, Sis. You need to do better than that. Just go on and admit you filed on him."

Alita wanted to tell her that she did and why she did it. She wished she could explain how Jerrod Dawson was still shaking her down for money. But she couldn't.

"I ain't admitting shit. Ain't that how Nate does things. He won't admit to anything."

"Okay, it's clear you're being petty and you want payback." Burgundy felt so betrayed that she found it difficult to think clearly. All she could do was feel angry . . . and disillusioned.

"Lita, you know when you do things like that, you aren't just hurting my husband. You're hurting me . . . your nieces . . . the family."

"Did he think about my . . ." She wanted to claim her daughter so bad but couldn't. Not yet. "He hurt Elyse. And he hurt me.

287

So what about us, or are you and your daughters the only ones that really count?"

"We're hurting too, Lita, don't you get it? But this thing goes way even beyond the family. Nate is an icon in the city. You had to know that filing on him would harm his reputation."

"I'm not thinking about his stupid-ass rep, B. Don't you get it?"

"No, I don't."

"Look I'm not trying to start any trouble, but you gotta hear me out." Alita paused, trying to find the words that she'd been holding in for weeks. "When we went to NYC it was the first time in a long time that I felt good, that I felt free. I needed that, B. I needed to get away and to find a little bit of happiness and to know that my heart could do something besides feel hurt, and stress, and regret and anger."

Burgundy listened to Alita, but it was hard.

"And I wanted those happy feelings to stay with me long after we got back to H-town. At first things were cool. But then I lost one of my jobs."

"I hope you aren't blaming that on my husband."

"No, it ain't like that. But it reminded me that shit will happen even when you're feeling the best you've ever felt." She paused. "Even though I was good and Baby Sis seemed like she was improving her life too, I was still scared, B. She has a man now. A solid man that she's really feeling. I haven't seen Elyse this happy in I don't know when. And I wanted *her* to stay happy. And I knew that as long as Nate is walking around acting like nothing ever happened, then her healing won't be complete. See, it's like this. One day when you stepped away from Morning Glory for a bank run or wherever you went, I showed up because Elyse will text me every time you pull that shit. Every time you leave her at that restaurant with him, hey, I'm dropping everything to come swing by and check on things. And I got there. I saw your iconic husband laughing and talking to the customers like he did not have a care on this earth. And it made me angry, B. And I pulled him to the side. And I said to him, I said 'You think you gone ever give Elyse an apology for touching her without her permission?' Now, of course I cleaned it up for him. I could have said 'for raping her' but I didn't. And this man acted like he didn't know what the hell I was talkin' 'bout. And for him to not even have it in his heart to tell the girl he was sorry. That he overstepped his boundaries and made a mistake. Well, I knew right then that this would be a matter for the courts. I thought about how he did not want to give that girl a Christmas bonus last year. He gave his other employees a financial gift but not *her*? And I thought about how he has gone on with his life and he's still making millions."

"Alita, shut up. I've heard enough. The fact that you brought up how much money he earns tells me everything I need to know. You are a fucking extortionist. That's what you are. You are willing to ruin my husband's reputation and possibly make us lose our jobs, our income, so we can stoop to your level."

"Really? Is that what you think, B?"

In reality Burgundy did not believe every single thing she was saying. But pride has an ugly habit of lying to anyone who's in denial.

"Yeah, I do think that. Because Nate is looked up to by young entrepreneurs, others in the restaurant industry. They see how he's managing multiple businesses and they are inspired. But his entire reputation will get ruined if you continue pursuing the complaint."

"Well, Jiminy Cricket. God knows I don't want to hurt his pearly white rep. I want to . . ." Alita wanted to reach through the phone and shake some sense into her sister. "If everything that Elyse has said about him is true, that on many days he stuck his dick into that girl's vagina when she did not want him to, then icon or not, you're married to a rapist. And I figured to let him get off with no punishment, no nothing, is to say his behavior is okay. And it's not okay. I don't care if he's black, white, purple, young or old, family or an alien from outer space. Nobody should be molesting anybody. It's sick. It's demonic. There is no excuse."

"Wow, Alita." Even though Burgundy felt her sister was entitled to some of her feelings, the words she spoke still stung like she'd been pinched. That was still her husband, and it was difficult to accept all that was happening to them.

"Remember how you used to praise my husband just last year? And the year before that?"

"That's because I didn't really *know* him, B. I only knew his reputation."

"Okay. Fine. We could have talked about this, though, Alita. But it seems like there is no forgiveness for him. Like you want to take him completely down," Burgundy bitterly complained. "If it's not a white person trying to take a black man down, it's his own family. Why is that?"

"If that isn't calling the kettle black. B, you need to be throwing these serious questions at your own husband. Stop putting the blame on your sisters. But to be honest, some people don't give a damn about family."

"Does that include you?"

"This ain't about me and you know it. It's about other people. People that don't even respect their own selves so how the hell they about to respect anyone else? That's why folks getting killed out here on these streets every single day. Because people don't respect themselves enough to do the right thing. B, you just don't understand. I have sat back and let the wrong thing happen over and over again. Well, I'm tired. I just am. And you may not like it but —" Unexpectedly Alita started sniffling. The sniffles turned into squiggly lines of water that soon rolled across her cheeks. She tried to keep herself from wailing. God knows she never wanted to break down like this. She wished that she hadn't gotten Dru to help her file the paperwork. But due to a clerical error, Alita was named as the person initiating the complaint instead of Dru. It was too late now. And she was no longer willing to act like everything would return to normal. But she believed that black people were notorious for sweeping family secrets under a rug. You'd be considered a traitor, or a snitch, if you aired your family's dirty laundry.

"I'm damned if I do, damned if I don't. Someone is going to hurt and it might as well be the perpetrator and not the victim."

In reality Burgundy could understand how Alita felt. But her first obligation was to support her husband. Yet part of her was terrified that what Elyse claimed she had gone through had actually happened, and she felt bad about it all. But there had to be another solution.

"Tell you what, why can't we dismiss this and just get everybody involved the help they need? We could seek intense counseling. We could do that. It'll be a lot cheaper."

"Ahh, you don't want to set up the trust fund?"

"I think this is just your way of getting money from somewhere else since your former bread and butter didn't pan out. Leno got kicked off the high school team over something stupid. Cheating on his exams with his buddies was so unnecessary. A scandal that was so embarrassing for his coach and the high school. And I guess he's now screwed up his chances to make it to the NBA. And it makes sense that you had to come up with a new game plan to score some cash. I swear, Alita, with you, it never seems to be enough. No matter how much you're given, you want more, more, more."

Alita was stunned. How dare she bring her son into this matter! And Burgundy had never been this blunt before when it came to her money problems. She felt dizzy and angry with surprise. Would a settlement help to put this entire tragedy behind them? Alita wasn't sure how much the trust fund would be, but the amount had to be better than nothing, which is the perfect description of what Elyse had gotten so far.

"Look, B. Let me fess up. I filed."

"Why, Alita?"

"Remember at our last Sister Day? The assignment was and I quote: 'Make a decision to do something you've been putting off.' Boom! Blame yourself for coming up with these wack-ass assignments that you want us to do."

Burgundy gasped in horror.

"Look, B. I'm not gonna totally blame Sister Day for what I did. But it had to be done. I'm sorry, all right?"

"No, you are not sorry or else you'd drop the whole thing. I mean, this is very awkward. I feel like I've been stabbed —"

"You feel stabbed?"

"It's just that you've put me in an uncomfortable position. That's my husband we're talking about. What affects him affects me. And besides, I doubt you have all the facts. Elyse isn't the best communicator in the world. She has trouble expressing herself, and maybe you've misinterpreted her."

"Nice try, B. I won't side with you on this one. My gut feeling tells me she is not lying. So I'm riding with Elyse."

Burgundy never liked being blindsided. She was the type of woman who was a meticulous planner and not one for surprises. Especially ones that had adverse effects that she could not control.

Burgundy said in a calm voice, "You do remember that the girl still lives under our roof?" She felt as if her stability, her entire world as she'd known it, was collapsing.

"Of course, I know she lives there. I'm not stupid. And I am working on finding another living place for Elyse. But it's gonna have to be rent-free 'cause I have no money right now to pay anybody. You think you can help a sista out?"

"You are really screwed up, you know that, don't you?" Burgundy said.

"B, quiet as it's kept, we are all screwed up in one way or another."

They hung up on each other. And instead

of Alita coming to pick up Elyse from work, Burgundy informed her that she'd be driving her back to her house.

Burgundy telephoned Nate with clear instructions.

"Don't come home."

"Why not?"

"Go and check into a nearby hotel. At least for the time being."

"Why? What for?"

"It's for your own good. Things are way too tense around the house. And it might just get worse."

"But I don't bother anybody. I stay out of the way —"

"You have no option, you hear me? People like you don't get a choice."

He was silent, then said, "Okay, I will make a reservation. For how long, though?"

She thought about it and how tense life was becoming. "For as long as possible, Nate. Grab as much of your personal belongings as you can so you won't have to come back soon."

"I'm not welcome in my own house anymore?"

"We have to fix things first. We must wait for things to calm down then we'll see what happens."

"I don't like how this sounds," Nate protested.

"This is critical. And I need to handle some important business regarding the family. It'll really help all of us out if you stay low-key for a minute."

"All right."

Burgundy got off work and drove Elyse with her to The Woodlands. Liz was at the house with Natalia and Sid. The girls screamed in delight when they saw Elyse.

"C'mon, Elyse, let's go swimming."

"Okay, let me go and change. I'll be out in a bit." Elyse actually didn't mind hanging out with the kids. And she wanted to practice her swimming.

Burgundy fiddled around the house working on some chores. But after a while, she received an unexpected call from a Baller Cutz employee. He informed her that she needed to handle a problem they were having with a distributor.

"This is a bad time. Can you get Nate to help?"

"His phone is off. That's why I called you, Mrs. Taylor."

Burgundy thought about it. Her husband must have gone to his hotel room and fallen asleep. Since Liz was there with the kids, it should be no problem to rush out and handle that little bit of business.

"If it's not one thing, it's another. Tell you what. I'm on the way."

Burgundy always loved when she could get away from everybody. She told Liz to watch the girls and that she'd return as soon as she could.

It was late afternoon. One half of the sky was clear, the other filled with slow-moving, dark clouds. The clouds threatened to release some rain so the girls had to hurry if they wanted to get in a good swim.

Elyse reclined on a cushioned chair and watched her beautiful nieces. The Taylors had an in-ground pool, but they also had space enough for an aboveground kiddie pool. Sidnee and Natalia laughed and played as they splashed water on each other. Then they jumped up and ran to leap into the larger, in-ground pool.

Elyse thoughtfully observed the girls. She wondered how it felt to be carefree and joyous without any worries.

"C'mon, Elyse. Get in." Natalia encouraged Elyse to join them.

She stood up and held her arms as she shivered.

"I can't swim that well. Gamba is supposed to give me some lessons. But I don't know when he's coming back."

"Don't wait on him. Swim!"

Natalia splashed around some more.

Elyse thought about it. How long could she wait for someone else in order to have fun, feel good, get some loving? She removed her cover-up and was wearing a bikini.

She knew she looked good and wished Gamba could see her.

Elyse walked over to the edge of the pool and dipped her toe in the water.

"Cold, too cold."

"No, it's not. C'mon."

"Okay, Nat. Hold on a sec." Elyse decided to muster up some courage. She walked backward, stopped, then raced toward the pool. She closed her eyes, pinched her nose, and hurled herself into the water. A loud splash could be heard.

Soon her entire body was covered in wetness. The sound of water rushed over her head. Elyse violently kicked her legs until she rose to the top. She let out a breath and an exhilarating shout.

"Woo, baby," she said with a laugh.

"Yay. You did it."

"I can't believe it, but yes. I did it," Elyse said to Natalia.

She awkwardly moved her arms about in the water but it felt like she was drowning.

As if the water was pulling and holding her down; like she was fighting to get free. Elyse did not like how that felt. Plus, it had just started to sprinkle. Gamba always warned her to get out of the water if it should ever begin to rain.

"Lightning is unpredictable," he had told her. "And you never know when a bolt of lightning will flash down from the sky. You don't know where it may strike."

It was as if her mentor were there with her, a guardian angel who never left her side. Elyse felt his presence and began to miss him.

Elyse hung around a bit longer as she felt raindrops fall on her head. She waded through the water and lifted herself out of the pool.

"I can't swim in the rain," she told the girls, who whined when they saw her get out.

"Why not?" Sid asked.

"Too dangerous. And both of you need to get out."

Liz was busy talking on her cell phone and wasn't completely aware of what the girls were doing. So they ignored Elyse and continued to play.

Elyse dried herself off and went to sit in a lounge chair that was inside the covered patio. Once she was done, she sat there with her mind on Gamba. Suddenly, she felt a hand touch her shoulder. She jumped. The girls were so busy playing that they never noticed their dad enter the backyard.

Elyse looked into his eyes, which loudly spoke to her. She shook her head. Nate bobbed his head and pointed to the door that led to the house.

Suddenly all the lessons that Dru and Gamba taught her rapidly disappeared. She couldn't think of one thing to say to him.

"Let's go," he said.

"Can't."

"Why?"

"Sick."

"I'll help you feel better."

Elyse quietly moaned as if her stomach was aching. She was glad Natalia and Sidnee were too preoccupied to see what was going on. Nate gave her an impatient look. She slowly got up. She glanced back at the girls, then quietly followed her brother-in-law into the house.

"Where is Liz?" he asked.

"She was there before. I dunno."

"It doesn't matter."

Elyse shrugged, but then she saw through the kitchen window when Liz emerged from the pool house. She must have briefly gone to the bathroom to talk on the phone.

Nate told Elyse, "Wait here."

When he returned he had a body camera attached to his shirt. He turned it on.

He asked her, "Elyse, so you say you don't feel well? What on you hurts?"

"Stomach."

He told her, "We have medicine for that. Follow me."

He walked to the powder room and opened up a medicine cabinet. He found something to relieve acid indigestion and belly aches. He ripped off two sheets of chewable tablets.

"Here you go. Eat a couple of these. It'll make you feel better."

She did as she was told and noticed that the camera was rolling.

He also gave her some other pills that had to be taken with water.

As he stood and watched Elyse, large dots of sweat covered his forehead, and his armpits were damp.

"Do you see what I'm doing?" he said.

She gave him a blank look.

"I'm being good to you. I'm watching out for you, for your well-being. That's what I do."

"That's what you do *now*."

Nate got Elyse a cold bottle of water to

wash down all the drugs then he went to put the medicine back in the powder room. When he returned, he heard voices coming from the kitchen area.

A voice was saying, "Where's Elyse?"

He strained his ears to listen.

"I dunno. We looked up and she was gone," Natalia said.

Then Sidnee asked, "Aunt Coco, can you make us a cheeseburger and some Kool-Aid? And some baked 'tato wedges?"

Coco laughed. "Y'all love my cooking, huh? Okay, baby girl. I need to find my sister first. Go upstairs and change into some play clothes. And don't get the carpet wet. Put on your flip-flops."

The girls said okay. The pitter-patter of their little feet could be heard as they pounded up the back stairs. Nate quickly escaped to the master bedroom before his daughters could see him. He locked his door and his mind began to race.

What's Coco doing here all of a sudden? Did she notice my car in the driveway? Shit, why didn't I pull the car into the garage?

His cell phone began to ring. It was Coco. But he did not answer. He decided to ignore his nosy sister-in-law and head for the shower. To try and clean himself off with lots of water.

CHAPTER 16
REINVENTION

The following day, Burgundy was seated in a restaurant booth across from a male companion. A hearty sandwich, a steaming bowl of soup, and a fresh salad were nicely arranged on the table in front of her. But she wasn't very hungry.

"How are you doing, Burgundy?" the man asked.

"I'm good."

"You sure?"

"I am."

"C'mon, it's me you're talking to."

Burgundy smiled. Her lunch partner could see right through her lies. Edmund Langston Murray was a recently divorced thirty-two-year-old who owned several catfish restaurants in the Houston area.

She took a sip of her ice water then set it down.

"Look at me," he commanded.

She did. It was difficult yet wonderfully

easy to lock eyes with Edmund. He possessed very strong, handsome features. A neat mustache, smooth, thick lips, penetrating eyes that could see right through her. Ed had that effect. And that's what made Burgundy happy yet afraid.

"You are going through a lot, Burgundy, probably way more than you've already told me."

"Hmm. You're right. It's just that I don't want to —"

"For the millionth time, you are not bothering me. We're buddies. We talk. That's what we do. We get things off our chest. God knows you were there for me when I needed somebody."

Burgundy shifted in her seat and crossed her legs. She was wearing a sleeveless belted dress with a pair of sandals that showed off her fresh pedicure. Ed liked a woman who knew how to take care of herself.

He admired that this woman had gone through hell with her no-good husband but she still knew how to keep her hair and nail salon appointments.

"Did you hear what I said?" he asked. "We can talk about whatever you want to talk about. No topic is off topic."

"That's easy for you to say. People claim they want to listen to you, but they're not always telling the truth. They say that just to be polite."

He reached over and caressed her hand.

"Please don't do that."

"Why not?"

She nervously glanced around the deli that they'd been patronizing for lunch dates during the past few weeks.

"You never know who is around. Or who's watching. Or who's taping you with their phone." She winced in anguish. "And you never know who you'll run into. How can I explain having lunch with you?" She laughed almost hysterically. "None of this makes a bit of sense."

"What? Why can't we be friends? We can't do lunch? Discuss business? Which, by the way, is what we do eighty percent of the time anyway. We discuss the restaurant business, am I right?"

"Yes, you are. You're just nice enough to listen to me gripe now and then, which is something I promised myself never to do again. Yet I find myself opening up to you in ways I never imagined."

Her voice was soft, gentle. Ed made her feel jittery. She surmised that her heart was now more involved than she ever wanted it to be.

I'm married, she told herself.

Then, *I'm horny and angry. I'm uptight and ruder than I've ever been. A nice piece of dick just might do the trick.*

She instantly pushed those thoughts far, far from her mind.

"If you want to stick to business, we can do that, Burgundy. I don't want to pressure you. I'll let you decide what we do, when we do it, where we do it —"

"Stop, stop, stop," she said as she toyed with her silverware. "Edmund, why do you do that? You always make me laugh even when you're not trying to."

"Hey, laughing feels good. Way better than crying."

"You're right."

"And it's good to laugh and let go sometimes. To chill and not worry about the industry, the trends, the whatevers that we tend to let bother us."

"The current spouses."

"And the ex-ones. Hey, if I could move on from a bad relationship anyone can." He winked at her and leaned back in his chair. Edmund was cool like that. That's why she enjoyed being around him.

"You're a free spirit, Elm." Elm was the nickname she'd recently given him, and he liked it.

"Oh, is that what you call it? I've been

called a lot of things, but the word 'free' has never been part of the description."

"You're something else."

"You ain't seen nothing yet, Burgundy."

She loved the way he pronounced her name. The syllables rolled off his tongue as if he were a soul singer.

Ed took a sip of his own drink and then waved over the server.

"This water here. It's good, man, but it just isn't doing it for us. Please bring us two mai tais."

"Elm —"

"C'mon, woman. You need to loosen up. You look so stiff that it's embarrassing. Lookin' like a statue in a wax museum."

"It's that bad?"

"Worse."

Her eyes twinkled. She laughed in spite of herself.

"What the hell?" she said. "Tell you what, skip the mai tai. Make that a hurricane for me."

"Whoa. You sure?" Ed asked.

"Positive."

"This I gotta see."

"Elm, you ain't seen nothing yet."

The couple continued to chat with ease, sipping slowly on their cocktails and nibbling on their Reuben sandwiches and chef salads.

If anybody had needed her during the lunch hour, she would have had no way of knowing. She had locked away her phone in a secret compartment in her SUV, a rarity for Burgundy, who was accustomed to always staying connected. She enjoyed how she was now purposely trying to calm down and ease back from the pressures of her life.

"If you knew what I knew about myself, you might not even want to be my buddy," she told him.

"It can't be that bad."

"It's worse." She thought about how bitchy she'd been with Elyse and with Alita. It wasn't in her nature to be that mean-spirited. And she felt awful inside.

But since early summer Burgundy had had Ed to help take her mind off her troubles.

Right then the restaurant atmosphere was relaxed and happy and filled with patrons enjoying their lunch breaks with easy conversation and good food.

"You know what? I adore this place, Elm. It reminds me of New York. Dammit, I had so much fun while there. It's sad that I rarely take a vacation. All I do is work and solve other people's problems. And it'll be good when I can find time to get away again."

"That's why I'm glad that we're attending the upcoming conference. It's not a real vacation, but it'll give you a little bit of a break."

She said nothing.

"You *are* still going, aren't you?"

"I guess so," she replied. "I mean, with everything else going on. Hiring the attorneys. Figuring out legal troubles. And making sure the nanny works out."

"Is Liz giving you problems?"

"She's working out okay, but I'm very picky. She seems to be devoted, but sometimes I sense that she is distracted. She is from Jamaica, you know, and she's always on her phone dealing with quite a few calls from her people. She told me she has relatives who live all over the world. And I understand she wants to hear from them, yet the whole thing irritates me. She acts like I don't notice how much she's on that damned phone."

"Families are always dealing with issues, Burgundy."

"Yes, they are."

"If you want to get away from it all even for a nice weekend trip, you need to commit to going to that trade show. It'll be nice to go mingle, gamble, and do other things as required."

"You just won't stop, will you?"

"Can't stop. Won't stop."

Later that evening, after Burgundy came home, she pondered the state of her affairs. And the more she thought about it, the more she felt that she should continue on her quest to keep her family strong and intact. It's just that trying to do it alone was draining. She needed some help.

And when she went to Nate, of all people, that's when she knew she was desperate.

They were seated outside on the covered patio. The bubbling of water could be heard from the swimming pool. It was late evening, twilight, and from outward appearances everything looked tranquil and perfect within their small world.

Nate was wearing his reading glasses and was studying a sheaf of documents.

"What are you up to?" Burgundy asked.

"These contracts. I'm going over the fine print. To see if every detail is right regarding the launch of the fourth Morning Glory. You know the one we want to set up in Clear Lake?" Clear Lake was a Houston suburb located on the southeast side of the city, and Nate had a goal of owning restaurants in the four corners of the metropolitan area.

"You know what, Nate? I've been thinking. I have a feeling we shouldn't open a fourth restaurant. The timing isn't good. And quite frankly, we're already spread too thin with the current three."

"Are you serious? A few weeks ago, you were getting on me to set things up."

"Many things have changed. So I've changed my mind."

"Seriously? But why, Burg?"

"I'm feeling overwhelmed. About a lot of things. These legal issues, these business ventures. Life isn't feeling right these days."

Burgundy bit her bottom lip, which threatened to start trembling. She could feel seeds of resentment building up inside of her. That was one of her faults. Some issues she could freely speak about. Others lodged deep inside of her and threatened to explode with no warning.

"I just feel that there is no need to add extra burdens to my life, Nate. I feel like I'm doing these very important things all on my own."

"But now we have Liz. You begged me to hire a nanny to help out."

"I know. I know, but it's still not enough." Burgundy knew she was skirting the issue.

Domestic help wasn't the problem that vexed her during the night.

"The girls are doing great," she continued. "They are happy and healthy. I'm not exactly worried about them."

"Then what are you worried about?"

"You."

"Me?"

"Yes." She felt exasperated. "You bother me, Nate. A lot. I just don't understand."

"What are you talking about this time?"

She stood up and started pacing on the cobblestone flooring that felt slippery underneath her feet.

"This time, Nate, I'm talking about how you seem to just blow off the Elyse thing like nothing ever happened. You expect me and our attorneys to clean up your messes for you. It's like you've washed your hands of anything that's happened. You duck, hide, and bury yourself in your work. It's an avoidance move that doesn't deal with the issues."

"Issues? What issues?"

"See, that's exactly what I'm talking about." She stopped talking. It was so hard to talk about "it," the awful "thing" that had apparently happened between her husband and Elyse. She hated him for it. And she felt caught in the middle.

What should she believe, what could she ignore?

"Nate, I am going to ask you something and I want you to be honest."

"All right."

"Did you ever . . . do you recall ever forcing yourself upon . . ."

"No. Never. It was always consensual."

Burgundy sighed. This wasn't going to be easy. "If it was consensual, why are people trying to put you in jail, huh?"

"Because they are either money hungry or they are ignorant and prone to exaggerate. I know that Alita is behind all this. She is the most foolish family member you've got. Nothing she does stems from a place of logic. She is emotional, judgmental, thinks that only what she says is the truth. She's a nut job. C'mon, Burg. You know this."

"I know, but still . . . Elyse has told Alita a few things. Very detailed incidents. Is Elyse a nut job too?" She thought a second about the girl who spent a lot of time going to see therapists.

"Never mind," Burgundy said out loud.

"There you go. You already know neither of them is wrapped too tight."

"But still. I don't know what the truth is. What's a lie . . . ?" She paused. "I want to believe you, Nate, but some of things I've heard simply don't add up."

"Such as?"

"I was told that you were parading around our house wearing only your sleeping pants. And Elyse was wearing your matching top. No bra on at all."

"*She* wanted to do that. It was all her idea. She thought it was funny, but I just ignored her." Nate's penis was getting harder and harder as he thought about Elyse. She was getting sexier and sexier these days. He'd noticed it. It was almost as if she was teasing him. Like she was throwing her newfound sexual liberation in his face. He wondered if she was screwing that Gamba guy.

"So there," he said. "No more questions, okay? I've done nothing. In fact, if I'm guilty of anything, it's being a man."

"What do you mean by that?"

"You don't understand, Burg. Men get horny. And when a woman walks around half naked, when she does things with her lips . . ."

"Elyse did that?"

"Yes! And since she did, in my head she was asking for it."

"Seriously? I don't know what she was doing, but no woman asks to be raped."

"It wasn't rape."

"No? Someone is lying then."

"Who?"

"Alita told me —"

"Here we go. Your sister is an unreliable witness or whatever you want to call it."

"Nate, you need to take things seriously. Because if you catch a case that goes to trial, a jury will decide your fate. The judge will decide the punishment. And if he doesn't think you're remorseful, it won't help you."

Nate's jaw remained rigid with stubbornness.

"This is not a game, and the casual way you've gone about it is very disheartening. This is a very serious issue — almost more than I can bear."

"What do you want me to do, Burg?"

"Apologize. Confess. Act sorry."

"For what?"

"Nate, even though you deny it, I believe you share some of the blame for the events that happened. Okay? For example, you went out of your way to lock her door when you entered Elyse's room. That act was totally unnecessary, yet you did it."

His face whitened when his wife said that.

"Locking a door sounds so shady. Like you didn't want her to escape. And don't tell me that she locked the fucking door because I won't believe it."

He fell silent.

"And, Nate, if you did that even one time, you *owe* Elyse an apology, because you trapped her in her room. You violated her body and thought nothing of it. You forced her to kiss you when she did not want you to. You stuck your —" Burgundy's cheeks got splashed with sudden tears. She closed her eyes and tried to block out the horrible mental picture of her husband's penis entering the girl.

"Your actions hurt Elyse . . . they hurt me. You haven't even apologized to me after all the stress this entire situation has put me through." She opened her eyes and stared at her husband. But he still seemed emotionless. She had one more weapon in her arsenal that needed to be used.

"I'm saying all this to tell you that if you won't apologize then you're going to pay. Believe me, you will pay in one way or another." She began to tell him what the DA suggested about setting up the trust fund for Elyse.

"That's millions of dollars, Nate, don't you get it?"

This time he stood up and paced around the patio, swearing and cursing and throwing up his hands.

"That's insane. Why I gotta give that . . .

that chick millions? For what? If you ask me, this whole thing is a setup. Your money-hungry sister put Elyse up to this."

"Not only that, Nate. In order to avoid jail time, you need to go to counseling."

"Me? See a psychiatrist? That's crazy."

"But that's part of the deal presented by the judge and Randall Burkett. And I have to agree with them."

"You trying to say I'm crazy?"

"I'm saying that you need help. You do. We all do. If something doesn't give, who knows what the fallout will be. And I've been doing some research, Nate. I don't want to pay, believe me, I don't."

"Paying means you're guilty. Like I said before, I'm guilty of nothing except being a man."

"Wait. I'm not done. You are my husband, and I care about you, but I do not agree with any perverse behavior toward any woman. *Any* woman, you hear me? It's disgusting and wrong. You ought to know better, Nate. You of all people ought to know."

Her grief ripped a wide hole deep inside of her heart. Her soul felt like an endless pit of sorrow. The reality finally caught up to her. In her mind, Nate could possibly be a rapist. He could be hauled off to jail. He could be registered as a sexual predator. And if that were to happen, their marriage would be in jeopardy. And perhaps paying the money was an important step that must be taken to get past this situation.

But what if it happened again? What if Nate served his sentence, was released, and next time became involved with a "new" Elyse?

Now, after talking with her husband and getting nowhere, Burgundy had an awakening, a reinvention of sorts that would change her attitude.

"You know what, Nate? Never mind. Do whatever you want to do. 'Do you' when it comes to not apologizing and thinking that all you were doing was just being a man. And 'do you' regarding that new restaurant venture. Because I've decided that I'm about to 'do me.' You can believe that."

"What are you saying?" he asked.

"Since we are now into only doing whatever pleases us with no remorse, I'm about to take a break."

"Meaning?"

"I'd been debating about whether or not to attend that restaurant convention that's coming up next weekend in Seattle. I registered for it a while ago but was going to cancel. But no, I'm going. I need to get away. Need to de-stress. Need to be alone."

"Alone?"

"Yes. I need to take some time out for myself . . . go on a retreat of sorts. The pressures of life have finally spoken to Burgundy Taylor. And she is listening for the first time in a long time."

CHAPTER 17
THE WEARY BLUES

The next day, Dru and Alita were hanging out. Alita needed to sort through some recent developments.

"I don't know what to do right now," she said. "And poor Shade. I know I'm 'bout to drive him crazy, and that's the last thing I want to do."

"What do you mean?"

"Thank God he let me shack up with him. Anyway, when we lie in bed at night, I know he wants to make love but all I can do is talk about my problems. And he is listening at first. But after a while, I'll look over and Shade is snoring."

Dru laughed out loud. "Whoa. Not a good sign."

"Who you telling? I feel damned if I do, damned if I don't. He's been so good to me, Dru. And I don't want anything to mess up what I have right now."

"It sounds like if you keep holding on and

staying strong, things will get better."

"Not so fast." Alita paused.

"What do you mean?"

"Sis, first of all I'm glad you getting back to talking to me and putting up with me after what happened. But I need you to know, it's still happening."

"Jerrod?"

"Yes."

"I wonder if there's anything I can do."

"No! The only thing you can do is avoid him at this point. Unfriend him and block him, Dru. Please."

"Okay, I will. But I don't quite understand why my ex started to harass you, Alita. It doesn't add up."

Alita told Dru that Jerrod was still harassing her, but she did not disclose the true reason.

"I dunno, Sis. Some men are strange like that. And some of 'em love the fantasy about smashing their ex's sister."

"That doesn't sound like him. I never would have believed it."

"I can't half believe it myself."

"What does he say exactly? And how?" Dru asked. "Do you still have any of his threatening texts?"

"Um, no. I deleted them."

"Oh."

"Yeah. So." Alita paused. Lying to Dru felt terrible. The woman had been so forgiving to her after she knew Alita withheld information from her. Was Alita's attempt to further protect Dru going to make things worse?

Alita took a deep breath. "Look, Sis," Alita told her. "I feel I need to come clean with you about something."

"What?

"The baby that I gave birth to . . . is Elyse."

At first Dru was silent. She stared at everything except Alita.

"I-I-I don't blame you if you're mad at me. I should have told you a long time ago, but it was so complicated. Our mother wanted it to be that way. I was young. I didn't know what else to do except go along with it. And it's the secret I've been keeping all her life."

"Look, don't blame yourself for what happened."

"Really, Dru?"

"No, because I don't."

"You don't?"

"No. Because logic suggests that I ought to hate you, but I don't. I envy you, Lita."

Alita was stunned. She blew out a big sigh of relief. Her mind whirled with thoughts.

Dru didn't look or seem angry. But she did resemble something that Alita couldn't describe.

"Anyway, all of this shit hopefully explains why I am the way I am. I've been holding all this in for a long time." Alita laughed. "My 'sister' is my daughter. Any woman would go crazy behind that. Plus all the other things that have happened lately. Everything feels so fucked up."

Dru nodded. She really did not hold anything against Alita. In fact, it felt good to finally put together the missing pieces of a complex puzzle.

"I'm sorry to hear what you're going through, Lita."

"This year hasn't been the best year, I don't think, for any of us."

Dru allowed herself to gaze upon the troubled face of her sister. She did not want Alita to be overly worried about anything. She wanted to see her the way she was when they were in New York: happy and smiling and loving her life.

"Hang in there, Lita. We are all going through something that we wish would just go away. I mean, it's good that those legal papers were filed against Nate. But the next step is to physically get Elyse, get your daughter, from that terrible situation."

"I'm already ahead of you. I've been checking out job openings for her," Alita replied.

"You have?"

"Yeah, Dru. I thought you were so busy and all with your work, plus you're studying for your master's, but if you're not as busy anymore . . ."

"I am very busy, Sis. That hasn't changed. And if you're trying to ask me if Elyse can come stay with me, sorry, but the answer is still no."

"You don't trust men at all, do you? My attitude must have rubbed off on you. Damn. I'm sorry, Dru. But if you think that —"

"No, Alita. Nice try. My concern has nothing to do with the fact that I live with my man. But maybe that's also why *you* haven't let her stay with you and Shade."

"Huh?"

"I did not stutter, Alita. You seem to care very much about Elyse and I'm glad that you do. You're doing certain things to help her out, but still it's not enough."

"Not enough? I've gone to the ends of the earth to help that girl. I think about her day and night. I drive all the way to the restaurant and will eat that food and sit up in that cold-ass restaurant to watch over her just in case *he* comes around. I think I've done a lot."

Dru just frowned at Alita. "I suppose you're doing your best. But I just think more could be done."

"That's it. I've had it. Only so much I can take. And on many days, I get tired. I am exhausted. Do you understand all the shit I've been through this year, last year, the past few years?"

"Here it comes," Dru murmured.

"You damn straight it's coming. And if I have to keep reminding you and every other person in our family what I have to deal with, then I will. Do you know that when I take Elyse to those psychotherapists, that they encourage me to seek therapy too? Me?" She laughed out loud. "That's a damn shame when a professional can spot a crazy person just that fast."

"You're not crazy, Alita. You're passionate and maybe a little bit overwhelmed. And when I really think about it, I apologize for even judging you. My life isn't like your life."

"Gee, thanks."

"No, I didn't mean that in a derogatory way. It's easy for me to sit on the sidelines and be the armchair coach that tells others what to do." Dru's eyes blazed with a fiery look. "In fact, the more I think about it, the more I know that I owe *you* an apology. I'm sorry for everything, Lita. I am."

"Oh, stop. It's no big deal." Dru's contrite attitude made Alita feel uncomfortable.

"No, you need to hear me out, Lita. I was on a break at my job the other day. And you know we only get so much time to eat or take care of personal business. And I decided to walk around to the food concourse. And when I got there, a long line had started to form. No big deal, right? But I heard the murmurs, the sighs, the impatience of the people who were standing behind me."

"Girl, what in the hell are you talking about?"

"Hold on. There's a point if you would just shut up and listen."

"All right. Go on."

"And there at the front of the line was a patient in a wheelchair that the salesclerk was waiting on. Only one salesclerk to help customers during the height of the lunch hour, right? But still. The person that was mostly complaining in line behind me was dressed in a nurse's uniform. The woman was able-bodied. Her wrists were adorned with nice jewelry. She had a Mercedes medallion on her key chain. Maybe she was married to a doctor. You could tell she had a good life from all outward appearances. But the crude remarks, the evil looks she was giving because she was forced to wait in a long line? Oooh, I wanted to tell her off."

"Don't tell me. I'm the patient in the wheelchair, right? Or am I the one married to the doctor?"

Dru began to snicker at her sister's silliness; then she grew serious.

"I'm saying that everything is a matter of perspective, depending on where you are standing. And so, I offered to let the impatient lady get in front of me."

"No!"

"Yes, because I was sick of her griping about how bad customer service is, etc."

"You're too much, Dru."

"But you know me, Alita. I tried to engage the lady in conversation so she could see that the person in the wheelchair needed extra assistance. But it was like she did not get it. And I got disgusted with that well-to-do person that had the smug, proud look on her face. Because some of us are so insulated from the feelings of others that we cannot imagine how it feels to walk in their shoes. Walk in, live in, and breathe through someone else's nostrils. I'm saying all that to say that no matter who we are or how good we have it, we *are* our brother's keeper. And if we aren't our brother's keeper, then why are we on this planet?"

"I don't know about you, but I'm here to pay a ton of bills I can't afford."

"Lita, be serious for a change."

"How? And for what?"

"Because then you can gain a new perspective, Alita. An important one. One that goes beyond your believing that the only purpose you have in life is to pay some bills." Dru's voice sounded incredulous.

"See, Sis," Dru continued, "there has to be more to life than worrying about our own situations. And even though it is hard, my dear sister, that's why I endeavor to try and understand. To walk in your shoes. To feel what you're feeling, to love you as if you never hurt me. Because one thing I know for sure. You got hurt and it spread to two families. And for that I really cannot blame you."

"You are a saint, Dru. A pure angel, Dru."

"I wouldn't say all of that."

"That's 'cause I can say it for you. You're amazing. And you missed out on the crazy DNA that the rest of us got cursed with."

"I wouldn't say all that either," Dru said, not wanting to joke around with her sister.

"You, Alita, did something that came natural. Being raped. That's not natural. But being able to give birth? That's God's doing. And if he did not want that child to be on this earth, she simply would not have even taken her first breath. That child was meant to be here and she came through you. She wasn't conceived in love, but at least she has love now. And at least you got to know how it felt to carry out God's plan."

"Oh, Dru, I'm so sorry." Alita hugged her sister tightly, more tightly than she'd ever done. She knew that Dru suffered with her infertility. She and Tyrique had had two miscarriages. And Alita wished that she could empower her sister to do something that so many other women took for granted. Giving birth was an honorable thing, but just because a woman could not hold a pregnancy should not mean that her life was worthless.

"I'm sorry about your physical situation, Dru, but let me tell you, you are more woman than a lot of chicks that can have five and ten babies but still haven't made anything of themselves. Hell, to me you're Oprah. Look at all the good things she has given to the world. She's smart, generous, she helps others, and she is not stuck on herself like some rich folk." Alita thought of

Burgundy and wanted to roll her eyes but fell short of doing so. "Some rich folk need a reality check. Like Jay-Z. He spends so much time trying to make money on top of money. For what? Does he really think when he takes his last breath that he's taking that money with him? Think he gone roll up in the afterlife with his eight-million-dollar car? Because he won't. So why waste time buying a car that costs more than a small town's budget?"

"You're entitled to your opinion, but I think it's great that we have wealthy black folks. And what they do with their money is their business," Dru said. "Because many of them buy what they want, but they also are committed to giving lots of money to charity. They build all kinds of schools or academies and provide water or solar power to African villages. Some rich black people will do what poor black people can't, such as build medical facilities. You can't ask for more than that."

"Hell, I can. I can ask P. Diddy, or whatever the hell he's calling himself these days, to do something unique. Instead of paying a million dollars to throw himself a sixtieth birthday party, why not give those dollars to me? I can make better use of it than he can. Because once you have millions to blow on stupid shit, like paying thirty-four thousand dollars for a luxury computer mouse, you know you've officially lost touch with reality. I hate those stupid-ass rappers that waste money like it's nothing but a game. Funny looking Jay-Z with his big-ass chicken-wing-eating lips. Lips so big he can whisper in his own ear. Hell, I'm glad Solange whipped that ass."

"Really, Lita? How do you know that really happened? Were you in that elevator?"

"Hello? The video put us in that elevator! Plus if he hadn't done anything wrong Solange wouldn't have swung at him. I'm glad he didn't hit her back, though. We wouldn't be calling him Jay-Z anymore. He'd be called Cray-Z."

Dru laughed, then asked, "How'd we get on this topic?"

"Because *I'm* crazy!"

Dru shook her head at Alita. "Don't change, Alita. I mean that. Never change."

"Don't worry, I won't. I don't even know how to do that anyway."

Elyse was at the house in The Woodlands. She was on the phone happy to squeeze in a few minutes of conversation with Gamba.

"I miss you," she told him.

"And I miss you. I think we'll be released

from this place in less than a week."

"Good. I can't wait to see you again."

Gamba felt his heart stirring. Absence made his heart grow fonder. Elyse was all he could think about while he was away serving the military.

"We'll do something special when I get back to town."

"Oh, yeah. Something special like what?"

"We'll spend the entire night together."

Her heart began racing. This is what she'd been dying to hear from him.

"Really? You serious, Gamba?"

"Yeah. I am. I care about you . . . I might even . . ."

"You might what?"

"I am so very crazy about you, Elyse, and I am sorry for not telling you. I just didn't want to hurt you."

"Oh, Gamba. That's all I ever wanted to know."

"But how could you not know? How do I treat you?"

"You treat me like I matter," she gushed. "Like I'm important. Like I'm a queen."

"And the way I treat you tells you how I feel about you, sweetie."

As she pressed the phone closer to her ear, Elyse felt warm and gooey on the inside.

"I know, but sometimes I want to hear it,"

she said in a stubborn voice. "I don't want to guess. I don't want to make a fool of myself and think you love me when really you don't."

He threw back his head and laughed. "That's understandable. But I was afraid to rush you. I would never want to hurt you, my dear. You've been through enough as it is." He paused. "And it sounds as if you're still going through it."

She had kept Gamba updated on everything that had been happening with Nate and Burgundy. It only made him want to rush back to Houston to coach her and be present while she went through all her troubles.

"I don't have much more time to be talking on the phone," he told her. "And before I hang up . . . I just want you to know that . . . I think about you every second of the day and I can't wait to kiss your sweet lips again, Elyse. Did you hear me?"

She beamed from ear to ear. She nodded her head. But he could not see her. She wanted to answer him, but she couldn't. She was too busy crying. Tears of joy wet her cheeks. She had waited so long for happiness that when she finally received it, she did not know how to react.

"I have to go now," Gamba said. "It

sounds like we're losing the connection because the reception here is bad. But I hope that you heard what I said. And I can't wait for us to be together again."

He paused. *"Ndinokuda."*

"What?"

"Oh, good, you're still there. It means 'I love you' in the Shona language. So long, my —" The call dropped. But it did not matter.

Elyse continued to hold the phone, trembling at Gamba's last words. She replayed his voice over and over, eager to savor the beauty of his lovely sentiments for as long as she could.

"Ndinokuda," she said to herself, and laughed.

Elyse knew nothing about his language. But she knew love when she felt it.

Being loved felt wonderful. Felt right. And it was starting to seem as if all Elyse's troubles were about to go away, hopefully for good.

CHAPTER 18
COCO IS LOCO

For the past few days, Coco had been lamenting about her dreadful love life. Alita knew all about it and thought she'd pay her a visit to check on her mental state. When Alita arrived at her house, she was happy to see the woman doing what made her happy: cooking for her kids.

"How you doing, Sis? I just wanted to see what's popping."

"Same old, same ole." Coco had one hand placed against her hip. The other hand held a spoon. She was stirring a fresh pot of collard greens. Alita sniffed and smelled pinto beans. A batch of cornbread batter sat in a mixing bowl.

"Hey, you got it smelling real good up in here."

"Okay, besides sniffing my food go and make yourself useful, Lita." Coco pointed to the dining room table. There was a bowl filled with freshly boiled potatoes. Right next to it were some onions, bell peppers, hard-boiled eggs, and stalks of celery.

"If you can stir up the potato salad that'll help me a lot. But wash your hands first. You know I don't play that nasty hands shit."

"My hands ain't nasty," Alita protested.

"Oh, but you and that man you got are nasty so —"

"Girl, please."

"Like I said, go and clean those hands, and wash 'em good."

Alita did as she was told, and soon she was seated at the table, dicing the last bit of vegetables and peeling the shells from the eggs. She stuck a big spoon in the jar of mayo and began to stir the ingredients together and seasoned everything until it tasted just right.

Alita looked at all the food. "What's the special occasion?"

"Nothing special. This is how we do up in here. My kids will always eat well. Just because there's no man in the house don't mean I gotta stop cooking and stop being a good mom, a good woman."

"Now that's what I'm talking about," Alita told her. "I was worried about you for a minute the way you've been crying the blues."

"I was just having a moment, that's all. I-I was on my period."

"Yeah, right." Alita loaded a piece of celery into her mouth and thoughtfully chewed on it. "I honestly was worried that you were going to lose your mind after you got dumped at the altar."

"Lita, please."

"No, Sis, I'm serious. I was wondering if you was *Waiting to Exhale* like that movie. Like, were you waiting to go and burn up Calhoun's clothes and then set him on fire?"

"Ha-ha, funny. I'm waiting all right, but it's on something else better than tearing up his shit," Coco said cryptically.

"Really? Like what? Do you really think Calhoun will do a three-sixty, change his mind, and then love is going to make him find his way back home?"

Coco laughed. "I wish. But I plan to have something even better than that. Something I've been needing and wanting for the longest."

Later that day Coco went over to Samira's to drop off the kids. This time Calhoun wasn't home, but Coco made nice with his wife and chitchatted.

"Do you two plan on having any babies?"

"Excuse me?" Samira asked. "You're talking to me?"

Coco laughed. "I know you usually see the back of my head as I'm coming and going, but I got a little time today. I am running errands for my big sis Burgundy, but I can wait a minute."

"Oh, I see. My husband and I haven't discussed children just yet."

"Word?" Coco said. "Me and him talked about all kinds of things . . . back when we were together. But now, we really speak a lot now. We keep things on a totally professional level. If it ain't about the kids, we ain't talking about it."

Samira smiled and nodded. "He is trying to stay focused on what's most important. Settling in concerning our marriage and being the best father to his adorable daughters. He's doing well, I must admit."

"Right. You really brought a change over this man, something I failed to do after five years."

Coco engaged Samira in more idle conversation, said goodbye and left. She drove over to the post office where Burgundy rented a huge box. She inserted the tiny key into the hole and was disgusted. There was lots of junk mail, some bills, and quite a few packages and boxes that had to be carried out to her car.

But it was cool, because finally she was getting paid to work for the Taylors.

"Another day. Another way to earn a dollar," she said to herself.

Things were looking up, but Coco still wasn't satisfied. In an effort to pull herself out of a foggy mood, Coco decided to pump up her radio. She tuned it to the twenty-four-hour hip-hop station and found herself caught up. Closing her eyes, she softly sang the lyrics to an SZA song.

This new artist was on fire. And Coco thought that SZA was the only female artist who perfectly described the way some women felt when it came to relationships. Coco sang the words like she lived that life and knew it perfectly.

As soon as the song was over, she went online and searched for the video. She watched the video for "The Weekend" thirty times in a row. And when she was done, she listened to another good song, "Broken Clocks," over and over. Every nuance seeped into Coco's soul.

Her conscience absorbed the words until they became life. They floated inside her until she allowed the concepts to shape her thinking and adjust her attitude.

■ ■ ■ ■

Another few days had passed. And by that Friday, Coco was ready to try something different. With the exception of Chance, in the early evening she dropped her kids off at Henrietta Humphries's house and explained there'd been a family emergency that she must attend to.

Henrietta looked skeptical. "Why can't any of your sisters take care of the kids?"

"Because they can't, all right? They're all tied up with something. I really appreciate their only living grandmamma helping me out, please, ma'am."

Henrietta's dark eyes bored a hole through Coco that made her feel like a thief, but she quickly thanked the woman and ran off anyway.

"I'll be back in a few hours, Ms. Henrietta."

"You do that."

Coco returned to her car and slammed the door shut. "What the hell? She thinks I'm supposed to be bogged down with the kids for the rest of my damned life like I can't ever catch a break? Hell to the fucking naw."

Chance, who was strapped up behind her

in the back seat, mimicked her. "Hell to the fucking naw."

"Boy, be quiet. Don't say that. Those are bad words, and only mommies can say them."

Chance just giggled. Every time his mother got mad and started to fuss at him, all he could do was crack up laughing. Soon Coco was laughing too. And she felt much better after she drove away.

She and Q were no longer kicking it. A few weeks ago, she had finally broken down and admitted that he wasn't Chance's father. Coco hadn't heard from him ever since.

And, Ricky, a man she recently met, agreed to meet her at a movie theater. She hated to bring her toddler with her on a date, but she didn't have enough nerve to ask Henrietta for more than what she did.

"It's me and you tonight, little homie. And Mommy's got a date, so you be on your best behavior, you hear me? Don't be cussing and shit."

Coco found Ricky waiting on her in the lobby. He was casually dressed but looked nice and smelled even nicer. Coco was all smiles when he paid for everything including their snacks. Ricky told her he did not mind that Chance had joined them.

The evening was starting out well, and that made Coco feel good and hopeful.

They all sat in the last row at the top section of the theater. They stretched back in their big lounge chairs and enjoyed the two-hour film. Coco covered her son's eyes during the sex scenes. And when she felt Ricky squeeze her hand while the couple made love on the screen, she already predicted where the night was headed.

"Let's go hang out at your crib," he suggested after the film was over. They were standing outside in the parking lot.

She hesitated but told him, "All right. We can go chill at my spot for a minute." Coco got in the car and drove toward her house with Ricky following behind in his vehicle.

"What the hell," she told herself. "I just met him, but I have needs. It'll be all right." Coco made up her mind, even though she was nervous about inviting a strange man inside her house. She'd met him at Burger King eight days earlier. They had exchanged phone numbers and talked every day for hours ever since.

"He's cool," she said again, but it bothered her that he never offered to disclose exactly where he lived. And when Coco had asked Ricky if he had a woman, he shrugged and told her, "It's complicated. But you good."

So there they were, inside her home. It was cold as ice because the AC had been cranked up all day. When she went to turn down the thermostat Ricky told her, "Don't even worry about that. I'm about to heat you up real good, Miss Lady."

"Oh, all righty then." She laughed, then went to place Chance down in his bed. She prayed he'd stay put for the next few hours. Even though she'd promised Henrietta she'd return to get her kids by a certain time, Coco knew it would not happen and she did not care.

"God knows I need this," she said once she got back to the living room. Ricky looked at her in admiration. She had quickly changed into another outfit and was modeling it for him.

Coco had lost more weight. She was looking good with her hair pinned up in braids. Her hair was still coarse and thick, and she resembled a queen, though she hardly felt like one. She wore a short-sleeved leopard print dress with her favorite pair of five-inch red leather pumps.

She sashayed over to Ricky, threw her arms about his neck, and kissed him. His lips were cold, chapped, and hard as brass. The texture of his lips was a turnoff, but she kept going.

He reached inside her dress, which was a V-neck style, and squeezed both her breasts.

"Woo, these are some jumbo-ass tits. You got implants?"

"No, they're real. Can't help it. It's always been that way."

"Don't apologize, baby. Be proud of what God gave you."

"Oh, don't worry. I am."

"I'ma start calling you Nicki Minaj."

She laughed and enjoyed the feeling of his hands flicking her nipples.

Ricky closed his eyes and tried to kiss her. She squeezed her mouth shut but he managed to force his tongue inside.

Oh, great, she thought. *It feels like I'm being kissed by a washer and dryer.*

Her eyes remained open. She glanced at his forehead. It was big, round, thick, and greasy looking. She took a sniff of him, and he didn't smell so good by then. Ricky was the type who easily sweated through his clothes, and his shirt felt damp as he pressed himself against her.

Ricky came up for air and gave her "the look." Although her heart felt sad, she backed away from him and began walking toward her bedroom. She knew they'd end up in the bed that she'd slept in many times with the love of her life. It had been a few months since Calhoun had ditched her, but Coco often thought of him.

With each step she took, Coco heard a voice in her head.

"Wait. Wait. Wait. Wait."

The voice sounded exactly like the talking crosswalk that pedestrians hear when standing at an intersection before they cross the street.

"Wait. Wait. Wait. Wait."

Five minutes later, Coco was naked and lying on her back, both her legs spread wide. Her red pumps were still attached to her feet. She was moaning and groaning. And Ricky's fat penis was tearing up her vagina as he shoved his torso against hers over and over.

"Ugh," she grunted. "Ugh, ugh." She gritted her teeth while the man with the sweaty back, sweaty chest, and hairy arms huffed and puffed and said nothing.

Ricky's breath smelled like Doritos and a Hershey bar with almonds, movie theater food that was now resting deep in her nostrils. Coco felt like throwing up all over the bed.

"Okay, that's enough," she told Ricky and gently pressed her hands against him.

"What?" His legs and hips were still wildly pumping like he was riding a bicycle.

"Get up off me, nigga."

"What?"

"Are you deaf? Get the fuck off. Now."

"Nah, nah, nah, baby, we ain't 'bout to do this. I'm 'bout to bust this nut. Like a whole gallon full. You can't stop now. Aren't I doing a good job?"

"I'll clap when I'm impressed."

Ricky ignored her sarcasm and kept going.

She yelled and slammed her fist against his back.

"Stop it, please. Get off me." Tears had now formed in Coco's eyes. But he kept going.

"Ricky. I'm warning you."

But he kept going, this time moaning and shaking like he was coming hard.

She stretched her neck, reached up, and bit him hard on his shoulder.

He yelled, smacked her across her face, then laughed.

"You're a biter, huh? I like that."

Afraid of getting hit, Coco let Ricky have his way. She wondered if Chance was still sleep and prayed he wouldn't wake up and sneak into her room. She cried as loud as she could, but she knew it meant nothing to a man like Ricky. To his ears, she was reaching her climax. But Coco wasn't having a good time. She was having regrets. But to a man like Ricky, the way Coco felt just did not matter.

Coco had been there before.

And she couldn't believe that she was in that stinking place again.

Thirty minutes later, Ricky finally left. Woozy from his orgasm, he staggered out the door talking about he'd hit her up later.

Coco watched him till he got inside his car. She immediately locked and bolted the door. She blocked his number from ever calling her again. She went and checked on Chance. He was sound asleep.

She showered, got dressed, and put on that leopard print dress. She went into the closet and found her red-and-white polka-dot raincoat. She secured the belt around her waist then grabbed her purse, keys, and cell phone and went out to her car.

It was midnight by now.

"It won't take long," she told herself. "Chance will be just fine. He's knocked out and I'll be right back."

Her conscience screamed, "No, no. no." But she blotted out its voice.

Coco cranked up the engine. Then she dialed Calhoun.

He answered after two rings.

"What up, Ma? The kids all right? You

back from that emergency?"

"Hmm, I guess your mama must have called you and told you I had some family issues to deal with."

"Something like that." He sounded very drowsy, but she was happy that he answered in spite of being sleepy. Maybe he still had feelings for her.

"Calhoun, we need to talk. Is this an okay time?"

She already knew he was alone. Samira had told Coco a couple of days ago that she was flying back to East Africa. Tanzania, to be exact. And she'd be gone for fourteen days total. Thirty-six hours to get there, and when she flew back out it would take thirty-six hours of connecting flights to reach her husband.

"We good," Calhoun said. "What's up?"

"It's been real tough out here. I don't know how to deal with it all, and I just needed someone to talk to."

He was silent.

"I take care of the kids and hardly ever get a break. I love them to death, but a mother needs a life too, you feel me?"

Calhoun said nothing.

"And I-I know you've moved on, but from time to time, I get to thinking, see? I think about the life I used to have with you. Sure, we'd fight and fuss, but we'd make up too. We'd work things out. I'd cook a good meal for you that I know you loved, am I right?"

He finally answered. "Yeah. You right."

"And we'd just do simple shit like hang out with the kids. Don't you miss that?"

"Coco —"

"Um, I'm just saying how I kind of miss the good times. I miss it when you'd come home after a long day at work and I'd watch the kids, our beautiful kids, scream and yell, 'Daddy.' They'd be fighting trying to see who got to you first." Coco laughed. "And it's a shame that Cypress won't have that experience. You aren't there to see her when she first opens her eyes after taking a nap. Did you know she rolls over now? I gotta keep my eyes on that one. She's feisty and nosy as hell. Always into something. She'll be walking before you know it, and after that, oh Lord."

Coco wanted to keep talking because Calhoun had stopped talking. The silence was so loud it was driving her crazy. Was he reflecting on the kids and how things used to be? Did he miss those times? Or was his mind on Samira? Did he really plan to be a good man to his wife, and if so, why? Why hadn't he devoted himself to Coco like he seemed to be doing for this woman?

The more Coco thought about how unfair things were, the madder she got. But she forced herself to sound sweet.

"All I'm saying, Calhoun, is sometimes I need someone to talk to. Y-you were my best friend. I thought I was yours."

Shit. Why'd she say that?

"Naw, my so-called best friend stabbed me in the fucking back when he fucked around and fucked you."

"Calhoun, don't be mad."

"Do you know how stupid you sound?"

"Baby, please. I didn't mean to say that."

"It ain't about the stupid thing you just said. It's about the stupid thing you did years ago. That you knew all along that that nigga was your baby daddy but you tried to play me and tell me you didn't know."

"But Calhoun, that's the thing. Um, Q ain't the daddy."

"What?"

"I said he is not the father of Chance."

"You lying."

"No, I'm not. I swear to God."

"Then who is?"

Coco had been driving, and now she was parked outside of Calhoun's house. It was after midnight. She got out of her car and hoped to God that he was there. It seemed like he was home; his vehicle was sitting in

351

the driveway. The lights were on in the house. Maybe her phone call disturbed him and he got out of bed, went to the living room, and turned on the TV.

Coco knew she looked good and hoped Calhoun would agree.

I'm about to do some side-chicking, some dick-licking, and some home-wrecking.

She went up the door and rang his doorbell.

"What the hell?" Calhoun said. "Someone at my damned door. I'm 'bout to grab my piece."

"Don't do that," Coco yelled from outside the door. "It's me, baby."

"What? Who is me?"

"Stop playing and open the door and see."

She put her hands on her hip and got ready to greet her ex.

Calhoun opened the door and blinked. She smiled and slowly untied the belt of her raincoat.

His eyes widened when he saw her big breasts and vagina exposed just for his pleasure. She pouted then closed the coat back up and rushed inside his house.

Calhoun quietly closed his door and followed her into the living room.

"What are you doing?" he asked.

"I couldn't sleep. And I wanted to talk to

someone. Talk to you."

"Coco, I know that's not why you're here."

"Okay, I'm busted. I want you too. I miss you. I need you. Love you."

Ten minutes later they were on the floor. Calhoun was hard as a brick. Good. That's exactly what she wanted. Coco giggled as Calhoun growled and planted kisses all on her neck, her lips, her thighs, her body.

"Mmm, baby," she told him. She let him do all sorts of wonderful things to her nipples, her butt hole, her vagina, and her ears.

"You eating those groceries, baby. Eat up," she told him.

She allowed herself to relax as Calhoun stroked her nice and good on his living room floor. He had gotten a blanket from the hall closet and a bunch of throw pillows surrounded them.

She let him do his thing, playing with and licking her vagina. She loved how he grabbed her pussy between his lips and dug down into it with his tongue like he was searching for treasure. He pressed his tongue against her clitoris then lifted it. Teasing her until she cried out. Her body lapsed into one amazing spasm after another. Coco shivered and shook and laughed and yelled. Even though she was sleepy, she made herself stay awake so she could climb on top and make love to her ex. That's what Coco was used to.

Being on top.

She grabbed her breasts and arched her neck as she rode Calhoun. Grinding like there was no tomorrow. Making him say her name.

Doing him felt great, yet strange.

Coco closed her eyes and recalled the recent conversation she had had with Samira when she came to pick up her kids from their home.

"You had a good thing," Samira had told her. "But it sounds like you messed it up."

"What did you say?"

Looking composed and elegant, Samira had calmly repeated herself.

"I was saying that if you would have been wiser, you would have told Calhoun the truth about Chance from the beginning. About the paternity of Chance."

"He told you that?"

"Of course. We talk about everything. He's passionate and a great listener."

With each lovely word that Samira spoke about the wonderfulness of their relationship, a dagger got plunged and twisted into Coco's heart.

So she did not feel an ounce of regret as

she fucked the hell out of Calhoun while Samira was almost nine thousand miles away being elegant, sophisticated, and happily married.

Coco enjoyed Calhoun's dick getting shoved deep inside of her. It was hot and hard and it felt damned good. They were making love without a condom. Coco wanted to laugh. She remembered how angry he was when he found out that she fucked Q and thought she got pregnant by him. If Calhoun didn't wear a condom with her, why would he expect Q to do it?

Coco knew that most men don't care about safe sex. They just want that raw feeling. They were willing to take the risk, so many risks. And right then Coco felt like a man. She was making love to Calhoun Humphries — something she never thought would happen again. Coco felt like a rock star.

"Whose pussy is this?" Calhoun asked.

"It's yours," she said. She knew their sex talk sounded stupid considering the circumstances, but if any woman knew that lust made men and women do foolish things, Coco knew.

CHAPTER 19
SLEEPING WITH MARRIED MEN

Coco's Bad Deed was done. She raced to get home and went to check on her child. Chance had stayed asleep all that time. She was happy yet miserable.

"That was some stupid shit right there, real stupid. I gotta do better." Coco took a shower and went to lie down for a quick nap. She woke up a few hours later. It was now Saturday morning, the third weekend in August. The sun blazed across the sky, making Houston feel hotter than hell.

Coco fixed herself and her son some breakfast. When they were done, she drove over to Henrietta's to pick up her other kids.

"Have you lost your damned mind?" the old woman asked upon answering the doorbell.

Coco stood before her looking despondent. "I'm sorry. So sorry. My emergency lasted all night."

Henrietta frowned at the girl. She kissed

356

her grandbabies goodbye and wagged her finger.

"I heard your car was outside my son's house last night. Something bad is going to happen to you if you keep up all this foolishness."

Henrietta slammed the door in Coco's face.

After Coco got home she played with her kids and tried to forget about everything that had happened during the past twenty-four hours. But she couldn't forget. She had had a good time with her ex and was glad that Calhoun had rocked her again for old time's sake, but she also realized that even though the woman was in Africa, Samira had her ex's last name and his wedding ring.

The realization that she was alone was unsettling. The notion that the dreams she had for her and Calhoun were gone made her feel hollow inside. Coco needed closure. She decided to give him a call.

When he did not answer, she called back. Calhoun finally picked up after she called him seven times.

"What?" he said. His voice was cold and unfriendly.

"Oh, excuse me," she replied in shock. "I thought you'd be in a happier mood after last night."

"No, Coco. I'm not in a good mood."

"Oh, baby, what's wrong? You want me to come over there and make you feel better?"

"No, you stupid-ass bitch. What I wish I could do is take my babies from you."

"What did you say?"

"You heard. My mama told me that you dumped off the girls last night talkin' 'bout you had an emergency. But she did a drive-by and saw your car parked over here."

"Well, I told you that I needed to talk to you. To me that *was* an emergency."

"You wanted to fuck me. That's what you wanted to do. Shit!"

It sounded like Calhoun was angry at himself. Like he realized what he'd done and was now sorry about their time together.

"Okay, maybe I was wrong for calling it an e*mer*gen—"

"You were wrong for leaving Chance home alone . . . again."

She grew silent.

"Yeah, me and my former neighbor Sylvie are tight, you know, your next-door neighbor? And I'm just now seeing that she texted me last night while I was dipping with you. Sylvie told me how you leave Chance alone at the crib like you some kind of fool. And she feels you did it again last night because she saw you when you left the house without him. What type of mother does that, Coco, huh? You could go to jail for that."

"Calhoun, please don't be mad at me. I don't know what I was thinking. I will never do it again, I promise you."

"You don't have to promise me shit. I am filing for full custody for those kids. And I might even take Chance from you too. Hell, I practically raised him anyway."

"What? No! Don't talk crazy like this!"

"You *know* I *could* get the kids. My life is stable now. I got a good wife. We both working —"

"You have a good wife that you're cheating on. And I have a good mind to tell that bitch how your mouth was all on my coochie last night —"

"Coco, if you ever tell her anything about this, I will personally see that you never breathe again, that you never walk again, that you never do *anything* ever again, you hear me?"

"Calhoun! You don't mean that. Don't say things like that."

"Don't come over here ever again with your nonsense, Coco. I've had it with you. Learn to grow the fuck up. I'm not your man anymore. I'm married. Leave me out of your fucked-up games."

He hung up. Coco screamed in frustration and threw her cell phone on the floor. Chance took one look at his mother and began to whine.

She shook uncontrollably, finally realizing that what she used to have with her ex was now history. And now he hated her, something that she could not imagine.

"I fucked up, Lord, I know I did. I'm sorry. I'm sorry." She went to grab Chance and apologized to her son as she wept.

Coco was so depressed that all she could do was lie around in bed, clutching her pillows and wiping her eyes with pieces of tissue. She managed to cook the kids some lunch then decided to drop all of them off at a twenty-four-hour day care. She knew she'd come pick up her kids the next day. Coco couldn't deal and she needed some alone time, one complete day of peace for trying to get herself together, then she felt she'd be all right.

After she drove away from the day care, Coco went home and spent a couple of hours sipping on a few glasses of Courvoisier Rosé and listening to more music by SZA.

By seven o'clock that evening her feelings of regret turned to fury.

"I hate Calhoun's cheating ass. 'Cause

bottom line he did me wrong. He did not respect me enough to tell me the truth. That he did not love me enough to marry me. If he had been straight with me, I could have gone on with my life. But he took the coward way out." She lifted a bottle of cold water to her mouth trying to get rid of the alcohol in her system. "Not only did Calhoun do me dirty, but so did Q, Ricky, and a few other men too. All of 'em did me wrong."

After a while, Coco's angry outbursts got interrupted.

Her doorbell rang. When she went to answer, Coco found Elyse standing outside her door. The young woman had caught an Uber and was dressed in her work uniform.

"Hey, girl," Coco said in a hoarse voice. "What's going on?"

"I had to leave," she told her. They walked into the house and stood around talking.

Elyse explained how she had tried her best to live with Burgundy and Nate, but it became too suffocating. "Today I went to work but I was so mad I ended up leaving. So I took an Uber over here. I needed someone to talk to."

"Okay, no problem, Sis. Where is Nate?"

"Don't know and I don't care. I'm 'bout

to quit that job. I can be homeless for all I care."

"Don't ever let a man keep you from making your paper. You have a right to keep making money till you find something better, Elyse. Just avoid him like you've been doing."

"I do my best to ignore that man, but I just couldn't take it anymore, Coco. May I stay with you? Please? I promise I won't be any trouble."

"Of course, you can. I have plenty of room. I mean, you might have to buy a cot and share the nursery with Cypress, but it's not a problem. I don't know why you never asked me in the first place."

"Lita told me I couldn't. 'Cause you have too many problems. You too depressed. You too mad."

"She don't know what the hell she talkin' about. I ain't mad. Seriously, I'm over Calhoun. Fuck that Negro. Fuck all men. I'ma bout to go lesbian on y'all."

Elyse laughed and rushed into Coco's arms. The big girl squeezed her tight. This was what love felt like. Elyse felt protected and cared for. She treasured that feeling and was glad Coco was so welcoming. But there was some unfinished business.

Elyse asked Coco for a huge favor. "I need

you to drive me back over to B's. I felt like I wanted to move out when I was at work. But I want to go back to that house and pick up my things. I don't want to stay with them one day longer. B is crazy and he is too."

Coco understood. "No problem. I don't mind taking you at all. But first I need to make a run to the post office."

"Why?"

"Because I don't agree with everything they do, but I still get paid by them to do some of their errands." Coco laughed. "So we can go and pick up their mail and drop that off at their house; let you get your stuff then we'll be on our way. You'll be my new roommate, and I could use the company."

Coco was wearing a taupe-colored top and some matching slacks. Her flip-flops were brand new and still had a price tag sticker stuck to the bottom of them. She located her purse, keys, and phone, then drove over to the post office. She went inside to the area where the boxes were located. Nate and Burgundy rented a large box. Coco had Elyse help her carry all of the packages, boxes, and first-class letters that had come in for Barber Cutz and Morning Glory. Then they drove out to The Woodlands, and she pulled up in front of the house. By that time, it was around nine. Coco had a gate card that granted her access into the wealthy subdivision. When they drove up, the property was well lit. She noticed that Burgundy's car was gone.

"Good thing, B's not around today. I think she went out of town to a business convention," Coco said.

"All right, I won't be but a minute."

They spotted an unfamiliar car in the driveway. But they didn't see Nate's vehicle, which was usually parked outside the house.

"That might be Liz's car," Coco said. She inserted her key in the door, and they walked into the foyer. "That's good. That means that the kids are here too."

While Coco remained downstairs she heard Elyse run up the back staircase. The Alexa speakers were on playing some music: a song by Mary J. Blige. Coco sang along as she looked in the refrigerator for a bottle of Vitamin Water.

She twisted off the cap and took a long swig of the drink.

Suddenly Natalia ran into the kitchen out of breath.

"Hey, niece," Coco said and gave her a hug.

Natalia went into the refrigerator and brought out a can of cookie dough. "Make me these," she demanded.

"Excuse me. Do I look like your personal chef?"

Natalia ignored Coco and went to turn on the oven.

"Girl, what's wrong with you? Where is your nanny?"

"She's not here right now. I think she will be back later, I think."

"Are you serious? Liz is gone? She left you girls home alone?"

"She took Sid with her, I think. But my daddy is here. He's upstairs."

Coco's heart missed a beat.

"Your father is here? I thought that was Liz's car."

"Liz got a phone call and had to leave. She said they'll be back soon. But all I want is some chocolate chip cookies and I need you to help me make 'em, Auntie Coco."

"I don't know about that. I won't have time for all that, but I promise to bake you my own cookies next time, all right Natalia?"

Natalia folded her arms and just stared at her aunt.

Coco decided to run upstairs to see what was taking Elyse so long. When she got outside the bedroom door, it was closed. She grabbed the handle and turned it. The door was locked. She heard voices.

"C'mon, Elyse, don't be this way. She has a yeast infection. I haven't had sex in I don't know how long."

That bastard.

Coco leaned in to listen.

"Help me out, okay?" he pleaded in a soft tone. "No one will ever know. You've been looking so damned good. And I've missed being with you. Our time together."

"Please leave me alone. I got to go."

"C'mon, give me five minutes." There was silence.

Then Coco heard, "Mmm mmm. No, Put that thing back. I don't want that."

"Then why are you dressed like that?" Nate's voice grew harsh.

Apparently, Elyse had taken off her work uniform and changed into another outfit.

"Because I want to dress like this. I love to look good, and it doesn't give you the right to try and make me do things I don't want to do."

Coco pumped the air with her fist, glad to hear Elyse taking up for herself.

It grew quiet. She heard kissing noises. A moan. Then a female voice. "You like that? Huh? Is that what you want?"

Stunned silence, then Nate answered. "Yeah, I like it. Give me more."

She heard him moan again. Coco wanted to throw up. What was going on in there? Furious, she ran downstairs to get a knife. She rushed back upstairs and jimmied the lock.

With her hand holding the doorknob, she heard more words: "I have the penis. You don't. *You* do what *I* say."

Coco twisted the knob and swung open the door. Nate was trying to pull Elyse's shirt down like he wanted to bare her shoulders or expose her breasts.

Coco asked, "Is this pervert trying to fuck you?"

"Yes," Elyse shouted.

"No, I wasn't. She was just trying to suck my dick."

Coco saw Nate's penis sticking out of the front of his pajamas. He wore a half-grin, had a dazed look in his eyes. The creepy sight of him made Coco so angry. Watching him reminded her of her own sordid experience with her brother-in-law. The fateful day that they had sex.

Coco and Calhoun had broken up weeks earlier. Feeling lonely and bored, she decided to call his boy Q to pick his brain. Q was sympathetic to Coco and acted so compassionate that she surprised herself by inviting him over.

They sat on her couch, drank a few beers, and talked about life and love. Before long Coco found herself leaning against Q, pretending like she was exhausted. He wrapped his arm around her shoulder. She closed her eyes, thought for a few minutes, and then lifted her face toward his. They begin to kiss each other. She moaned and felt herself getting turned on. Although it felt odd to be intimate with a man that Calhoun knew, Coco convinced herself it was no big deal. She and Calhoun were no longer a couple. All was fair in love and war.

But a few hours later after he'd left, when her brother-in-law Nate called, things grew bizarre. He was going to give her some furniture and told her that the U-Haul truck was there at his house. He'd rented the truck for Coco, and since she was getting the couch and two chairs, some floor lamps, plus a glass coffee table for free, all she needed to do was catch a cab to their house and drive the U-Haul back to her house.

"Why can't you just drive my furniture over to my house for me?" Coco asked.

"I'm tied up right now waiting on the cable company to stop by, and I don't want to take a chance and leave. Everything is ready. Just come over and pick up the stuff and bring the truck back after the furniture has been unloaded. Once you return the U-Haul, I can drive you home. Cable company work may be done by then."

Coco agreed. After all, they were giving her some nice, quality furniture that she wouldn't have to purchase. She took a cab to the house in The Woodlands and paid the driver.

The house seemed quiet and peaceful.

She rang the doorbell to get the key to the truck. When Nate opened the front door, she asked, "Where's my sister?"

"Hey there! Burg is busy as usual doing some running around. Hey, come on in for a minute," Nate told her.

Coco agreed. She was looking good that day. And after she sat down at the kitchen table, she accepted his offer of a cold soda and some hot wings that he'd just baked. She sat and ate and drank while they made a little small talk. After a while, however, she was shocked when Nate stood behind her and began to massage her shoulders.

"Just relax. You look very tense. Like you're stressed and haven't been taken care of."

Coco realized that she and Calhoun had broken up. It hurt. Bad. And she began to open up to Nate out of desperation. He nodded, and soon the hand that caressed her shoulders had moved to her upper back. She felt embarrassed about the rolls of skin. But

Nate did not seem to mind because he continued to press his fingers against her back, massaging her hard, like he was trying to relieve any stress she'd been feeling. She found herself beginning to relax.

"You're not wearing a bra, are you?" he asked.

"No. But why —"

Soon she felt Nate's hands grab her breasts from behind. He squeezed her nipples and flicked his fingers across them. It felt very erotic, and Coco closed her eyes. Soon she felt his lips on her neck, dotting kisses here and there and causing her to shiver and moan. And before she knew it she allowed him to lead her to a guest bedroom. Nate told her to sit on the bed. He quietly locked the door. He asked Coco to raise her hands. She did. He pulled her cotton shirt over her head. He gazed at her breasts then leaned over and kissed them. Then he pulled down her gym pants and slid her panties down to her ankles. He bent down and began to kiss her vagina while his hands gripped her fat ass. Oral sex was Coco's weakness. She closed her eyes and blocked out everything that hurt. Bottom line, she and Nate made love that day, just a few hours after she'd been intimate with Q.

And months later, when she confirmed that she was pregnant, Coco wanted to die.

Their consensual encounter produced a little boy named Chance. Coco still remembered how Nate said it wasn't his when she came to him and announced that she was pregnant.

"Nice try, Coco," he said. "Everyone in the family knows you love to sleep around. That you're a down-for-whatever type of woman. But you'd better blame that pregnancy on some other man, because I don't believe it's mine."

"What did you say? I don't get even a little bit of compassion and understanding from you?"

"Look, I'm sorry, Coco. We should not have done what we did. But I cannot help you out on this one, you realize that. Your sister would leave me. I don't want that. So please keep me out of this drama. I'm sorry, but I don't want to be involved."

Ever since that horrible encounter with Nate and the subsequent birth of Chance, she'd been tight-lipped about the identity of her son's father. And when she and Calhoun reconciled, none of the dirty past seemed to matter.

And right then, seeing her brother-in-law in that same house with Elyse only fueled her anger.

Nate undoubtedly was Chance's biological father, but she had never dealt with him

371

like that. To her he was just a man that she had accidentally had sex with.

Coco's cell phone was recording their conversation, and Nate had no idea it was happening.

"I can't believe you're doing this, Nate. Leave my sister alone."

"She came on to me."

"But it's true that you came on to me a few years ago too, so I don't put anything past you. I don't want you to get Elyse pregnant and do her like you did me."

"W-what are you talking about?" he asked.

"You never claimed Chance, yet he is your son. You deny him. You deny everything even when it's the truth."

"Why are you bringing that up now?" Nate seemed nervous.

"Because once and for all I want you to admit that we fucked. Here in this house."

"Why would I do that? Are you going to tell Burgundy?"

"No. I could never do that. But I just want to hear you claim Chance, even though you will never have a relationship with him. My boy deserves better than you."

"I don't care, I just don't believe that baby is mine, so I won't claim him."

"Do you remember making love to me?"

He said nothing. His eyes narrowed. Fists

balled up. "Just go on and get out of here. I'm terminating your employment effective immediately. You don't work for us anymore."

"What?"

"You heard me. You're trouble, Coco. You've always been bad news."

She disliked the man but felt like she still needed the extra paycheck, especially now that she did not have a man around to help foot some of the bills.

"Nate, please, I —"

"Just give me our PO box key right now. And find your way out of our house."

She was stunned and felt an incredible streak of pain race through her heart. She felt like she'd been stomped on with sharp-pointed heels. Like she didn't even have the worth of a stray animal, and that her value was nonexistent. In that moment, Coco hated Nate. She wished she'd never had slept with this man. With him or any other man who treated her like she was a game. An object of desire whose only purpose was to serve his carnal needs. But deep inside it wasn't how other people treated her, it was how she let them treat her.

She handed him the key but couldn't leave the house just yet.

"How could you be so cruel? You're treating me like I'm nothing."

"You slept with your sister's husband."

"And you slept with your sister-in-law, so what does that make you? Huh? I'm not taking all the blame for what we both did."

"Remember when you told me that Q took a blood test but turned out he wasn't the daddy."

She was silent.

"That proves that you like to sleep around, Coco, that you're a gutter snipe who'll sleep with anybody."

"You made a choice to be with me too, Nate. I did not make a decision all by myself. Yet you blame it all on me."

"I'm a man. I can't get pregnant. Your sexual decisions are way more critical than mine. Especially when you knowingly slept with two men in the same day. You had that info but I did not."

Coco hated to hear what he said; she wanted to argue but how could she? It was true that she'd made love to Q and Nate within hours of each other. And she had sex with her married ex like it was nothing. Could the men take all the blame for what happened, or would she finally rise up and admit her share of the problem?

All that time Coco forgot that Elyse was listening to her and Nate tell all their busi-

374

ness. She felt so bad. She was sick and tired of feeling so, so bad.

"Please get the hell out my house. And take Elyse with you."

On impulse Coco ran downstairs into Nate and Burgundy's bedroom. That's where she knew they kept a gun. It was placed underneath Burgundy's bed in case an intruder ever managed to break in.

Coco grabbed the weapon then ran back up the stairs. She heard Elyse yelling, "Leave me alone, you bastard. Before he let me leave he had the nerve to ask for a threesome."

"Are you serious?"

"She's lying, Coco. Don't believe her."

Coco withdrew the gun and pointed it at Nate. He raised his hands. "Don't do that, Coco. I'm sorry for everything."

"Are you, Nate, or are you just saying that?"

"Of course, I'm sorry. I take back everything I said to you."

"Are you my child's father?"

"Yes, yes. Yes. Now please put the gun down. We can talk about this if you put that gun away, please."

"Nothing would please me more than to blow your brains out."

Even Elyse was shocked. "No, Coco, don't

do that. Let's just get out of here."

"He's a sonofabitch, though. At the least he deserves to get his ass pistol-whipped."

Coco trembled as she stared at her brother-in-law. To her he represented every bad thing that had ever happened to her. She wanted him dead but knew he wasn't worth the trouble. She had to think of way more than how much she despised him.

She lowered the gun to her side.

Nate snatched the weapon right out of her hands. He pointed it at her. She yelled as loudly as she could and rushed toward him. They fought over the gun. Coco kneed him in his balls. The pain was unbearable and brought Nate to a standstill. She wrestled the gun out of his hands. Then she walloped him in his face several times, both with the gun and her long, manicured nails. Her nails cut into the underside of his cheeks. Nate yelled. The worst thing a woman can do is kick a man in his nuts. It made him want to kill her. He swung at Coco and aimed at her jaw. He caught the corner of her mouth. The impact broke the skin. She tasted blood then screamed.

Elyse begged, "C'mon, Coco, we need to leave. He isn't worth all dat."

Coco was furious. She wanted to harm him further, but she agreed with Elyse. Nate was still nursing the injury to his groin. This gave Coco more time. She fled downstairs and yelled back to Elyse, "Go ahead and finish getting the rest of your shit. We're out of here."

When she reached the kitchen, she laid the gun on the kitchen counter and instantly noticed how warm it felt in the room. She looked up and saw the troubled faced of her niece, Natalia. She felt ashamed. Surely the girl had heard their entire fight. Would she open up her mouth and tell her mother what she heard?

"Um, Natalia, we need to go. We have to get out of here right now. You come with me and Elyse. Turn off that oven. You ain't baking cookies today. And hurry up. I'll be in the car."

Coco was so nervous that she forgot about that gun. She ran back up the stairs to check on Elyse.

She saw Nate in an upstairs bathroom nursing the scratches on his face.

"C'mon, Elyse. Let's go."

She and Elyse finally raced down the stairs and ran out of the house with Natalia scrambling behind her.

"I want my daddy," she said.

"No, Nat. No," was all Coco could think of to tell her.

They piled into the car. She then remembered how she left the gun on the counter and ran back inside.

Seven minutes later she emerged from the house and jumped into her vehicle.

She started up her car and sped off. The culmination of the last few days took its toll. She drove and cried at the same time, blubbering away like she could not be consoled.

"Don't worry, Sis," Elyse told her. "I got your back. And you definitely showed me you got mines."

Coco managed to calm down as she continued to drive.

"What happened back there, Elyse?"

Elyse was silent for a while. She waited until she knew that Natalia had fallen asleep.

"I did what I had to do," she said.

"Meaning?"

"When I was in that room trying to pack my stuff, I heard him come through the door. And I was tired, Coco, so sick of him trying to take advantage of me. Thinking I was weak and a toy that he could play with. And I kind of lost it in there. I was like, 'If you want this come and get it.' "

"Are you serious?"

"Yes. I was trying to use reverse psychology. Dru told me about it. I thought that if I freely offered my body to him then he wouldn't want it anymore. So, I did kiss him and stuff. But nothing more than that happened. Because you walked in after that."

"Wow, Elyse." Coco was stunned. "But honestly, baby girl. Did you want him to fuck you?"

"No. Don't even ask me that question." Elyse was stubborn and angry. "I don't like him and I don't want him touching me."

"But did I hear y'all kissing, Elyse?"

She nodded. "Yes. I made him kiss me."

"You did?"

"Yes!"

"But why did you — ?"

"I was trying to survive, Coco. I had to do the first thing that came to my mind to make it out there alive." Elyse began to cry. "I wanted to let him know how it felt to be me. To feel powerless. And I thought if I acted like I really wanted him, it would turn him off."

"That's risky, though, Sis."

"I know, Coco." Elyse shuddered to think what might have happened if Coco hadn't interrupted. "I tried to do something I hoped would work. If I messed up, I'm sorry. I don't care about him. I don't want him at all. I want my man."

Coco nodded, understood. She knew that Elyse had been excited when Gamba told her that he'd be coming back to Houston soon. But then she got a second call from him informing her that plans had changed once more. Elyse was so frustrated. She missed Gamba. And now she again had no idea when he'd be back.

She felt like she was losing her strength.

And she sorely needed his presence to face the challenges she'd be forced to handle.

"It may have sounded and looked bad. But I swear to you that all I was trying to do was survive, Coco."

"I know, sweetie. Because I was trying to survive just like you."

CHAPTER 20
DEATH IS BETTER THAN LIFE

The big house in The Woodlands was silent all throughout the evening. And that's what Liz noticed when she first walked in the door early the next morning. She used her key to enter the house. And that's when the strong aroma hit her. She sniffed. Gas filled her nostrils. She covered her nose and immediately slammed the door shut. She'd had a key to the garage door that she'd go through in order to enter the house by way of the kitchen.

Liz's mind raced.

"What's going on with the gas? Why is it leaking?" Alarmed, she got her cell phone and dialed Mrs. Taylor.

It was six in the morning. And she'd never tried to contact her boss that early before.

The call went into voice mail.

"Mrs. Taylor. It's Liz. This is an emergency. You have a gas leak at your house. I'm going to call the gas company. I-I —

call me back."

Her mind whirled. Her heart pumped with fear. She thought about the girls. Liz had been working there since midsummer. Her normal procedure was to arrive at the house around six. Burgundy would already be up, but the girls would still be sleep. Liz would enter the house and, if needed, get breakfast started. She'd wake up the girls and get them ready for the day. Sometimes Natalia and Sidnee would have a schedule that included participating in planned activities created for children. Summer day camps, aquatic centers, and boat houses. Liz would play chauffeur and security guard. Basically, she'd do anything and everything that was asked of her — as long as she was with the girls.

Liz decided to turn around and take a few steps back down the walkway that led to the house.

"What on earth is going on here? Is the house about to explode?" She peered up to look at the windows of the second floor. Nothing seemed out of the ordinary. But looks could be deceiving.

When she first came to work for the Taylors, she was impressed, almost intimidated. This husband and wife were as close to a "power couple" as she'd ever been. Working for them was fascinating as well as stressful. She never wanted to make any mistakes while having the girls in her care.

While Liz stood there gazing at the house and fretting about what might happen, she realized she still had not hung up from the voice mail she'd left for Burgundy. Feeling anxious and embarrassed, Liz hung up and called Nate.

That call also went into voice mail. She left him the same message. Liz pulled up the Internet on her phone and located the number to CenterPoint Energy. She hung up and waited.

When a gas truck arrived, she identified herself and explained what was going on.

"Is there anyone in the house?" the gas company employee asked. Another uniformed male was also with him.

"Not that I know of. I called the owners of the house but got no answer."

"I see."

Liz used her to key to let them in. She waited outside, her heart wildly beating as she imagined what might have caused the leak.

The men were gone for about five minutes. She dialed Mrs. Taylor again while she waited but got no answer.

Soon the first guy came back outside. "It

was hot in the kitchen. And I noticed the oven had been left on. We shut off the gas and have opened all the windows. There's a smell. We know it as ethyl mercaptan. It's a pretty strong odor, but it's very strong on the first floor, and some has seeped up to the second. This is a huge house. It'll need to get it checked out. So I've called HFD too. We'll need an ambulance. There's a man lying down in a room. He's unconscious."

Liz let out a long wail. "Oh no. Please God. There are kids. Baby girls. Check their room. On the second floor. Hurry."

The man raced back upstairs. Liz paced outside the house, her mind racing as she waited.

The day before when she had had to go on her errand, she'd promised Sid that she could go with her. But the girl changed her mind at the last minute, and Liz left the house without thinking any more about it.

Soon the man came back downstairs. "There doesn't seem to be anyone else in the house. I checked all of the bedrooms."

Liz sighed in relief. "That's good, but I don't know where the girls could be. If their daddy was here, where are they? Why wouldn't anyone call me and tell me that the girls aren't here?" She explained that the lady of the house was out of town.

Soon an emergency vehicle siren could be heard wailing in the distance.

After a brief moment, a red Houston Fire Department vehicle pulled up in the driveway. Liz stood by in a daze and watched as two paramedics rolled a gurney into the house. A fireman was also with them. She wanted to run inside so bad. What if the girls had crawled into their parents' bed to go to sleep like they were known to do? That would explain why the men hadn't seen them in their own bedroom.

"Please check the master bedroom," she called out. Too afraid to enter the house herself, she wrestled with a foreboding that something bad had happened. So she began to pray.

When Nate was wheeled from the house his eyes were closed. He looked asleep.

"Do you know, can you tell, how long that gas was on?" she asked.

"No, ma'am. But if his brain didn't receive enough oxygen . . . anyway, we are taking him to Memorial Hermann The Woodlands. We need you to follow us. We'll need some information."

"Of course."

Liz stood to her feet. She could barely think. But as she drove, Liz recalled all the conversations she'd heard between her employers while she'd been in their presence. She knew they did not have a very happy marriage. She knew that Nate was forced to sleep in another room and not with his wife.

"Maybe he was very unhappy. Maybe his wife is trying to leave him. Oh God, why is this happening?" She prayed that everything would work out and wondered how much she could disclose since she'd signed that nondisclosure agreement.

"What if these people fire me for telling their personal business?"

A few minutes before she reached the hospital, her phone rang.

"Mrs. Taylor. Oh, my God. You have to come to the Woodlands hospital right now. Your husband —"

"Liz, what's going on?"

"The gas oven was left on at the house."

"What? Why? Where are you?"

Liz explained where she was and everything that had happened since she got to the house.

"My goodness. I'm in Seattle . . . at a convention. I'll have to catch the first flight out. How is my husband? Did you get to talk to him?"

"No, ma'am. H-he was unconscious."

"What? Is he going to be all right?"

"I-I don't know, ma'am. I just don't know."

Burgundy pressed her head into her chest with closed eyes. She hung up the phone and looked next to her. Ed was there in her hotel room. He was resting on the couch. They'd stayed up all night talking and didn't fall asleep until a couple hours ago. It was around six-forty in the morning in Houston. Four-forty in Seattle.

Suddenly a gust of freezing cold air blew in her direction. Her teeth started chattering. Burgundy regretted that she did not wear an extra layer of clothing that would provide protection from the brutal elements. But it was too late. And even though she was fully clothed, she felt naked. Vulnerable. Her husband was in trouble and she was in a hotel room with another man. They're weren't doing anything but talking. So why did she feel so guilty? How did she get here?

It's only after you're in a jam that you think about the things you've done to put yourself there.

"I'm scared, Elm, so afraid." She stood up and paced the floor with her bare feet and the perfect pedicure.

"What's wrong?"

"My husband has been in an accident. And they're taking him to the emergency room."

"What happened?"

Burgundy explained what she knew to Ed.

"Why are you still here? You should be on the phone trying to find the first flight out."

"I am. But I feel so frozen. Like my brain stopped functioning. I hate when I feel this way."

"I see. You want me to help you."

She nodded and closed her eyes.

Edmund took care of everything. He found a flight back to Houston for her. She rested on the bed as he placed phone calls. He knew she'd need to charter a private plane. Flying domestic out of Seattle that day would take hours.

"Burgundy, prices start at seventeen thousand."

She nodded, got her purse, and handed him a credit card.

While Edmund made the arrangements, Burgundy sat so stiffly that it was like she no longer had a heart.

Soon Edmund was talking to her again.

"Don't you want to pick up your cell?" he asked in between calls. "It's ringing off the hook."

She snapped to it and answered her phone.

"Hello?"

It was Liz.

"Mrs. Taylor. I'm sorry to tell you this, but . . . your husband died. They couldn't save him."

"What? Oh no!" She screamed and threw down the phone.

Burgundy did not hear as Liz went on. "And we can't find Sid. No one knows where she is."

When she finally landed in Houston, she took a car service that Edmund arranged to transport her so she wouldn't have to worry about driving herself. Soon they were on the way to a hospital in The Woodlands.

Burgundy got escorted to the room in which her husband's body lay. Burgundy slowly walked to his bedside. Nathaniel Taylor lay still. The room was so quiet it was eerie.

"I can't believe you're gone," she said. "I wish this wasn't happening. Talk to me, Nate. What happened?"

Before long the room began to fill up. Julianne, Nate's sister, stormed into the room with her hands shoved inside her jacket.

"That's two brothers I've lost," she said. "My parents are gone. Now it's just me."

Burgundy hugged her. "We're still family. That won't change."

They held each other up without saying another word.

Alita and Dru showed up. But Coco and Elyse were missing from the gathering. No one noticed at first.

"Damn, I feel bad now for every negative thing I spoke about the man. I wouldn't wish this on anybody," Alita mumbled. She could barely stand it and left to go sit in the lobby.

"This is fucked up." Her niece Natalia came to be with her.

"Where is Sid?" Alita asked.

Little Natalia hunched her shoulders.

"What do you mean, you don't know?"

"I don't know."

"When did you last see your sister? You're supposed to watch her at all times. That's what big sisters do."

"I dunno. I dunno," Natalia cried.

"Think. Try to remember. What were y'all doing yesterday?"

"We got up. Took our bath. Ate our breakfast. We played with Liz. She got a phone call. And . . . and."

"Think harder."

"I can't." Natalia burst into tears. Alita realized she shouldn't be pressuring a seven-year-old. Especially one that was usually accustomed to having things go her way.

Alita stood up. She walked back into Nate's room.

"B, where is Sid at? Why isn't she here with us?"

Burgundy looked confused. "Sid? I don't know. Liz should know. Find Liz."

The next few moments resulted in confusion, shouts, accusations, and threats. Burgundy decided to leave the hospital. She signed the necessary papers regarding Nate's body then had Alita drive her all the way to The Woodlands. Natalia was in the car with them. Liz followed behind in her own vehicle.

But before they reached Burgundy's house, she got a phone call.

"This is the Houston Fire Department," a man said. "And a child who appears to be around four years old was found —" The man continued talking. After a while Burgundy stopped listening. She stared into space. She reached over and gripped Alita's arm, pinching her skin until it was raw.

"They found Sid. They found her."

"What? What do you mean found her? Is she all right?"

"They told me she had a seizure in her sleep."

"But is she all right?"

"They found vomit in her mouth."

"B, is Sid all right?"

"My baby is unconscious."

There usually comes a moment in a person's life when they question God.

Why?

That's all I want to know. Why did you let this happen? Why didn't you stop it?

Why, God, why?

And Burgundy knew beyond a shadow of a doubt that she believed in God. In his existence. In his ability to provide, protect, and deliver people out of trouble. Moses was proof of that. And so was David. You can't forget Daniel, who was trapped in that lion's den. And there were many others.

But none resonated more than Job. The man who saw so much trouble that he despaired of life to the point of wishing himself dead.

And for a moment, Burgundy entertained morbid thoughts.

"Take me too, Lord. I don't want to live anymore. I can't imagine life beyond this. It hurts. God, it hurts."

How could she even think past the horrible things that she'd just found out. It was like a bad dream, a cruel trick that someone had played on her.

But why?

She managed to pull herself together enough to allow the fire marshal to tell her what happened.

"We searched the entire house from top to bottom and we wanted to make sure we covered all our bases. And we did a second very thorough search. One of my men went into the family room."

Burgundy nodded with a dazed look on her face.

"He pulled back furniture. That's when he found the little girl. She was curled up into a little ball. Behind the huge sofa. Like she'd simply fallen asleep. But we assumed it was the carbon monoxide."

"Hide and go seek," Burgundy whispered.

"What?" Alita said.

"Sidnee prided herself on being better than everyone else at that game. She wanted to find a hiding place that no one could guess."

"Oh, my baby," Alita said. "My baby."

No one could say anything.

All Burgundy could do at that point was deaden her emotions. She asked Alita to go to her medicine closet in her master bedroom.

"Bring me that bottle of sedatives. Get me a glass of water. I want to go to . . . go to sleep."

Alita gave her a sharp look.

"I don't know about that. We are driving right back to the hospital to see about your baby."

"Lita, please . . . yes. Just help me to think, to move, to breathe.."

"I got you, Sis."

Alita and Burgundy returned to the hospital. Sidnee Taylor was in a coma. There was no telling if or when she'd pull out of it.

More and more family members began to arrive, both at the hospital and at her house. Burgundy remained at her daughter's side, wishing so bad that she could fall asleep. But she was too afraid.

But as the hours dragged on, she knew she had to snap out of it, collect herself, and be the strong woman that she knew she was.

She was able to lie down on a couch located in Sid's room. She let Alita bring her some tea from the café. After she sipped from a cup, she allowed herself to feel again.

Aside from the comfort she received from

being surrounded by loved ones, Burgundy struggled with other emotions. Shock, for one. Because in all her years of being a mother and a wife, and through all the things her family had been through, she never imagined that her husband would die so young, in his early forties, and that her youngest child would lapse into a coma on the same day.

What happened? Why would our oven be left on, and by whom? How long was it on?

She needed some answers. As she sat on the couch in the room that was so cold that her teeth chattered, Burgundy began to search within her mind.

Nate was in a normal state of mind when I left the house to go to the airport. We said our goodbyes like normal. He seemed fine. I was the one who was nervous. I knew Edmund was traveling to the same airport that I was.

Her train of thought was interrupted. "Nate was found in the guest bedroom," she recalled Liz telling her.

She wondered about what might have happened during Nate's last few hours of life.

She immediately fought with guilt.

"He shouldn't have been banned from our bedroom. I just should have let him sleep with me every night. I should have —"

"B, give it up. I don't mean to sound harsh, but you did what you felt you had to do, sweetie," Alita told her. "You didn't know all this would happen."

"I know. But I still feel like it's all my fault."

"No, mm-mm. Noooo. We are not about to do that. I mean it. I won't allow you to blame yourself." Alita's voice was loud and clear. "That what us women have done so many times. We've taken the blame and pointed the fingers at ourselves and suffered over and over. Not this time. Please don't, B. I think we all have had a hard time dealing with truth." Alita laughed. "It's so damned ugly that we don't want to look truth in its face. And really, who could blame us? But we must learn to do better. Me, you, Coco, Dru, Elyse. All of us."

Alita knew firsthand about doing better. Because recently, when Elyse came home very upset and told Alita some of what happened between Nate, Coco, and herself and how she tried to fight back in her own way, that's the moment that Alita decided she could no longer hold it in. She had to reveal what needed to be known.

She took a deep breath and told Elyse that she indeed was her mother. Alita bravely told her the whole story. And Elyse felt shocked then ecstatic at the news. Her re-action caused Alita to feel humbled and thankful that the girl wasn't angry. The young lady felt relieved to learn the true story about her existence.

With that in mind, Alita felt that it was a start. And that's all that Burgundy needed. A new and better start for her present cir-cumstances.

"Lita," Burgundy finally replied. "I know we're supposed to do better. I clearly hear what you're saying and I agree with you, but it's too damned hard. I feel too . . . frustrated at how everything has played out. I feel so, so angry."

". . . And you have a right to feel that way . . . for a minute. But after a while you gotta make a decision. You can pout and have a temper tantrum, or you can choose to change your attitude. Being mad won't solve shit."

As much as Burgundy wanted to argue, how could she?

"Lita, I never knew you could be so wise."

"Oh, trust me, I got wise when I shut up and started to listen more."

"Listen?"

"Listen to that good man that I got to meet and know and learn from."

"Shade?"

"Yeah, your friend that you introduced me to last year is the wise one. He's my anchor. He lets me see things through eyes that aren't mine. And I've learned to listen to what my baby tells me, B."

"That's the smartest thing you've ever done," Burgundy told her with a grateful smile.

"I guess it is. Now don't get me wrong. Sometimes I don't listen, but most of the time I do. I'm glad when I do."

The two sisters embraced. She wanted to take back previous harsh words, but then wasn't the time to bring that up.

For now, Alita knew she had to be the stronger one of the two women. She'd never been through anything like this before in her life. Yet she couldn't worry. She just had to be strong . . . for her family . . . and for herself.

When her youngest daughter's eyes fluttered the next day, Burgundy felt like she wanted to collapse. The doctors examined Sidnee and cautiously predicted there'd be no long-term effects. After a while Sidnee could talk, eat, and move all her fingers and toes. Her vital signs looked good, and Burgundy felt more grateful than she'd ever felt in her entire life.

During the next day or so, Burgundy's

main focus was to plan a funeral. During the course of setting up the arrangements, she received a telephone call.

"I just want you to know that the coroner had recommended an autopsy on Nate."

"Nate? Why?"

"Because scratches were found on his body. DNA was discovered underneath his fingernails."

"Are you suggesting that there was a struggle or some type of fight before he died?"

"That's what we need to find out."

"But with whom?"

"We're trying to find out, ma'am."

"So is this an official investigation?"

"Yes, ma'am."

The police told her that he would need her whereabouts as well as other people who would have been inside the house that day.

"Even Natalia?"

"Yes."

"She's only seven."

"We need to talk to her. Don't worry. We'll be gentle."

"Oh, my God." Burgundy was aghast. She wanted to protect her daughter, not subject her to a police investigation.

"We want to get any security tape that may have been rolling either inside or outside your estate for the past few days."

Burgundy nearly lost her breath.

Did someone kill her husband? And if so, who?

Coco and Elyse were seated inside of her car. Coco had just gone to the post office. She always had a duplicate key to her sister's PO box, and she went there to pick up and drop off packages. Elyse had remained inside the car while Coco took care of business. And now that she was back behind the driver's seat, Coco's brain felt twisted and tired.

"Why are you still working for them?"

"Because I am," she stubbornly told Elyse. "No one knows that Nate fired me except you. And that's how we're going to keep things. No one has to know."

"All right."

With that matter settled, Coco tried to relax, but it was hard. The whole ordeal took a lot of out of her. Nate was dead. Burgundy was beyond distressed. And Sid would recover. But all Coco could think about was who would believe her story? Who would believe that the gas had been left on at the house and that Natalia was the one given the task to turn it off?

The truth was always hard to believe

anyway. But to know that she had nothing to do with her brother-in-law's death didn't seem good enough. Her track record was bad. She was known for lying, for harboring secrets, for doing one foolish thing after another.

"Elyse."

"What?"

"I'm trying to go on like normal, but I'm scared. I can't think straight. I just want to die."

"Don't say dat. Don't!"

"But he's dead. B said the police will do an investigation. And they gone think I had something to do with it."

"They might think I did it too, though."

Coco stopped crying. She'd forgotten about that. What if the police arrested Elyse instead of her? That would be remarkable. But it would feel wrong. But what if it happened anyway? Police were known for sloppy work at times, and it wouldn't be the first time they locked up the wrong person.

Coco thought hard. Her mind raced with all the possible ways this thing could end up. But the more she thought about it, the worse her breathing got. She was hyperventilating at one point, in great need of some oxygen.

"Breathe in, breathe out," Elyse instructed

her. "Take a deep breath. You know you got high blood pressure."

"I know."

"Then stop trying to make yourself sick."

"It's not like I'm doing this shit on purpose."

"Calm down. You say you did not kill him."

"I didn't kill him. And you know it."

"Then relax. If you tell the truth, then they'll let you go."

What Elyse said sounded good and logical, but Coco still wasn't convinced. Bad things seemed to constantly swirl around her like an autumn wind. You could never see it or predict which direction it was going to come. But you could always feel it and see its effects.

"Damn it." Coco took one hand and massaged her nostrils while she tried to control the gasps that threatened to take over. She looked out her car window. Her knees began to knock when she saw a police car drive by. It kept going, and Coco sighed in relief.

"I can't take this shit," she said.

"Calm down."

"I can't."

"The good thing is that he's gone. He can't bother me or you anymore. He can't hurt us ever again."

"Don't be so sure about that," Coco said and waited. She waited for what would happen next.

CHAPTER 21
SURVIVOR'S REMORSE

When it came to Nathaniel Taylor plenty of well-wishers came to pay their respects. The restaurant workers, barbers, neighbors, many of the vendors who had worked with Nate, and community leaders who'd known him for years. They felt that his tragic accident was so unexpected, and they had sympathy for him and his family.

Coco stayed in the back as long as she could, not knowing if her odd behavior suggested guilt or grief.

"I don't want to look at his face," she said to herself. "I just can't."

But when the family line was formed, Coco stood in it. And when they made a trail to view his body, she shut her eyes. She opened them. Then she shut them again.

Natalia had never laid eyes on a dead person before.

"Mommy, is Daddy asleep?"

"Yes."

"For how long?"

"A long time."

Natalia gave her daddy a curious look. She softly sang out loud, " 'So long, farewell, auf Wiedersehen, good night.' "

Attendants scurried about handing out obituaries. Others offered fresh tissues to mourners. Organ music played in the background.

Before they knew it, the two-hour ceremony concluded. Then the family gathered at Solomon's Temple, where a room had been dedicated for the repast.

Burgundy remained stoic and gave the appearance of being strong. Inside her nerves felt like twisted rags. She knew that her husband's body would not be placed into the ground that day. The inquest had to happen first.

When Burgundy came across Coco at the church, she gave her a puzzled look.

"Well, why weren't you at my husband's funeral, huh?"

"What are you talking about? I was there. You didn't see me?"

"I-I guess not. I don't remember."

Coco shrugged. "You may not have remembered, but trust me I was there." The words she did not say hung in the air. *I hope she doesn't think that I killed Nate.*

■ ■ ■ ■

In an odd way, death sometimes brought a family together. And when the family came together, sometimes much-needed conversations were held.

All that time Dru kept in her feelings about what happened to Nate. She was alone with Elyse helping to braid the young woman's hair the Sunday after the funeral.

"Are you excited?" Dru asked.

"Yes, I will finally get to see my man. It's been a long time since we were together. I'm gonna hug him and kiss him and probably scare him away I'll be so happy to see Gamba."

"Good," Dru said. "I'm glad for you." She paused. "You've been through a lot. We all have. Hopefully, in time, everything will be all right."

"Hope so."

"Elyse, I know that both of us were shocked at what Alita told us."

"About her being my real mommy?"

"Yes."

"Yeah." Elyse stared into space. "I did not know what to think or how to feel. But I am happy to know that my mother isn't dead. All this time I felt bad because I thought I lost my mother. And when times got tough, I really needed Greta Reeves, but she was gone."

"I know that's hard, because Greta was the only mom you really knew. But now you have a second chance, with crazy-ass Alita."

Elyse laughed. "It's okay. She understands me . . . most of the time. And she helps me a lot. And I'm okay with it all, really I am."

"But see, I have to adjust too," Dru told her. "Because all this time I thought you were the baby sis. But really, I'm her. And even though technically, I guess I am now the youngest Reeves sister, in my head and in my heart, you are still Baby Sis. That's all we've ever known. And in my heart, that's how it's always going to be."

"Seriously?"

"Yes."

"Good. Because I liked being Baby Sis. I love being spoiled and having all y'all look out for me. But I think I'm getting much better at looking out for myself."

The two hugged. They felt like sisters. They would always be sisters.

After the turmoil of the funeral died down, first chance Coco got, she met up with Alita. The two sisters may have butted heads at times, but it did not stop Coco from turning to her oldest sister when she was desperate. She knew that an autopsy had been ordered regarding Nate but wondered why, since it was apparent that he'd died from the effects of carbon monoxide poisoning. Yet and still, her conscience bothered her.

"Lita, I got something to tell you. Now I don't want you to judge me. Please don't judge me. But I want you to know that . . . Nate Taylor is Chance's daddy."

"Oh, shit, Coco, please tell me you lying or making this up. Please."

"See, that's why I never wanted you to know."

For a long time, Alita could not even speak. She was so angry. So disgusted. And felt so hurt for Coco. But then she grew sober and knew that her being angry would never change the facts.

"What happened? Tell me everything."

Coco did. She recounted the day that she allowed herself to be sexually intimate with two different men on the same day.

"Did you do it with him more than once?"

"No, Alita, I swear to God."

"Was it any good?"

Coco burst out laughing. "You wrong for that, Sis."

"I wish I could be wrong about this whole thing. But it is what it is." Alita thought about the terrible scandals that she and some of her other siblings, her daughter, had all endured.

"Are we cursed or something? Because nobody would believe that several women of the same family went through the same thing."

"It happens, Lita, that's the thing. More than you think. It's just not talked about. And that's what these sick-ass men are counting on. That we keep our secrets a secret. That way they can keep doing it over and over to other women. Other nieces and sisters and cousins and aunties."

Alita knew that what Coco disclosed could be perceived as truth, that as incredible as it sounded, the same type of abuse, physical, sexual, mental, verbal, and the like, could be a common experience within a family, a tragic secret that tied them together even more than blood ties do.

"Nobody should be forced to do something they don't want to do especially when it comes to their own bodies." Coco told her about her experiences with Ricky and how she wished things had turned out differently. "When bad things happen to me, it's like I end up making bad decisions. That's what I've noticed about myself. Like, when me and Calhoun broke up. I should have just focused on myself and getting my head straight. But instead I tried to bury the hurt I was feeling by hooking up with Q. And Nate."

"You needed love, girl. Nothing wrong with that."

"But how I went about getting it," Coco concluded in anguish. "I wish I would have done things different, and better."

"That's fine, but it still doesn't excuse what we got done to us. As far as I am concerned, we have nothing to be ashamed of," Alita concluded. "And it's a damn shame that we have gone around walking around on our tiptoes, our heads hung in shame as if we did something wrong. We're the victims. We were threatened and lived in fear year after year. Even though my brother-in-law is dead, I can't say I'm sorry."

"Lita!"

"Look, I misjudged him. I thought he was a cool dude at first. But after I learned about the real him, I could not respect him. But I'm torn. All I care about is you and my nephew. And in some ways, I still wish that Calhoun could be his daddy."

"You wish that? Wow! You really do hate Nate."

"You have no idea, Coco. I mean, hate is

a strong word. But I do hate that something made him act that way. Like, why did he have to mess over people? What happened to him that caused him to be that way? He's dead now, so it's not like we can ask him."

"It's not like he would have told you the truth either."

"Sicko! Okay, that's enough. We gotta get through this somehow, someway. We're Reeveses. I love you, Sis, and I don't blame you for what happened. I have to make up lost time with my daughter, Elyse."

"Huh?"

"Oh, that's another skeleton that I'm pulling out the closet."

"Lord Jesus, I sure hope there are no more secrets in this family."

"But Dark Skin, did you ever tell B about what happened? About Chance?" Alita said.

"No. I just can't. Why do that at this point?"

"Until you tell her what happened, there are more secrets in our family, Sis."

After Burgundy saw her daughter's health improve and that she'd gradually recover, one thing that helped her resume a sense of normalcy was going to work inside her church's bookstore. And that's what she did the two weeks following her husband's death.

It was almost the end of September. Shade was at Solomon's Temple that Sunday morning, helping to staff the store along with Burgundy.

"You need any help with the reshelving of these books?" he asked.

"No. I'm good. I'd rather handle the job myself. I need the distraction."

"I understand."

She stared into space, blindly removing books from one shelf and finding space on another one.

"It seems silly how we move things around as if it's going to make any difference. This is what I call busy work." Burgundy shrugged. "A year ago, this monotony would have driven me nuts. Now it's like a life-saver."

"It probably helps that you're in a place where you feel safe. Solomon's Temple is like a refuge from a storm."

"True. I need my church. I love Sundays."

She'd come to dread Saturdays. Saturday was the day that Nate passed away, and when her youngest daughter was found unresponsive. The events were so shocking that Burgundy felt she would never be the same again.

"I've always preferred an easy Sunday morning to a rough Saturday night."

"We all can relate to that," Shade told her. "But don't feel bad. Maybe one day you'll enjoy Saturdays again. That's my prayer for you."

She looked at him. "Thank you, Shade. You've been amazing throughout this whole ordeal." She paused. "My sister is one lucky woman."

He said nothing.

In the aftermath of the tragedies, life appeared bleak. So dark. But in a way it felt like morningtime darkness. This means that even though it was very black outside, you didn't have to really worry about it. Because you knew that once morning came back around, the sun would shine again. It was just a matter of time.

Burgundy, Shade, and Alita had worked hard the last Saturday morning in September. It was a sunny day filled with the brightest of sunshine. The sun hovered above them as they shoved the last of a few boxes into a moving van.

"Are you sure you're okay with this, Burgundy?" Alita asked.

"Of course, I'm sure. I don't need all of

Nate's clothes. He had a ton of them, you know."

"Hmm, I'll bet he did," Alita replied as she looked at a dozen boxes and bags of clothing items.

Burgundy laughed. "No, seriously. I think that donating some of his things to charity is a good thing to do. The more sentimental pieces, I will hold onto them. Except for the things he wore the last day or two of his life. The police came by and took away those items."

"Oh shit, are you okay with that?"

"I'm good, Lita. It's fine."

"Okay, B. Just let us know, because if you change your mind in the next few minutes we will haul all this heavy shit right back in the house," Alita remarked. "We'll walk up all the way up that big staircase. We'll break our backs and sacrifice our health to do whatever you need, Sis. And I won't tell you what I *really* want to say because I'm trying to live like a Christian."

"You're a fool." Burgundy appreciated a good laugh, and no one could bring the giggles better than Alita.

Her cell phone screen lit up.

It was Edmund. Should she answer?

No, she'd call him back later. He'd understand.

After the boxes were loaded in the truck and the door secured, the three headed back inside the house. Oh, how it felt so strange to Burgundy to exist inside the four walls of a home that just weeks ago was filled with the activities of her entire family.

But life had changed.

"Has anyone heard from Coco today?" Alita wanted to know.

"No," Burgundy said. "She's been acting very distant. I don't know what her problem is."

"She's loco, that's what's wrong with her," Alita said, not wanting to give away her sister's dark secrets.

"And you should know crazy when you see it, huh?" Burgundy said with a giggle.

"No, *I* am the one that knows crazy when I see it," Shade remarked and side-eyed Alita. They all broke out in laughter.

The trio managed to continue joking and trying to move on one day at a time. It wasn't that everything was rosy and great. Far from it. But Burgundy was resigned to do the best she could, with every breath, and with every step she could take.

The irony about life is that the thing designed to destroy a person could also be what's used to build people up and provide strength. And in the end, if you survived the heartbreak, if you bounced back from the tragedy, you won.

And as odd as it sounded the Reeves family was determined to find the good within the bad — they planned to win — no matter what.

ACKNOWLEDGMENTS

Many exciting things have happened in such a short time that there are more people to thank — and that's always a good thing.

First of all, to the Creator who keeps directing my paths and paving the way to new and forward-leaping opportunities, THANK YOU!

I'm grateful for the Houston Public Library who makes me feel welcome. Darryl Kiser is truly my brother in spirit. Thanks to the staff of the Young Neighborhood Branch — H-town, Third Ward. To all the beautiful kindred souls who have crossed my path last year. You're amazing.

And to those that came out to support me: Lisa Benford, Cynthia King, Davie John, et al., thank you for being there.

And I must give a huge shout out to Kim Roby; she's been in this publishing industry a long time and her success appears to shine brighter year by year, yet she remains humble, giving, kind, helpful . . . That's how I want to be. Thanks for all that you do to help others.

To my publisher, my extraordinary editor, Esi Sogah, the entire Kensington team, literary agent Claudia Menza, Claire Hill, each of you, I appreciate your efforts on my behalf. And to the original book cover designer. You knocked it out of the park. Great job!!

Thanks again, Officer Stanley, for info about the legal system. And thanks to UH Fire Marshal Christopher McDonald for the carbon monoxide info.

Special thanks to graphic novelist Jerry Craft. You rock! Salute!

Kudos to my first virtual assistant, Erica Watkins. You are a brilliant, talented lifesaver. Thanks for all of your hard work. Also, many thanks to the talented woman Tasha Aziz, my Caribbean lifesaver who knows just how to make things dazzle at special events. Thanks for help during FEMPIRE.

Much appreciation to the people that gave me early feedback on *A Sister's Secret*. Krissy Scarbrough Christian — your comments were so very helpful. Nessa Black, whoop, whoop, thanks for reading. And Pamela Wagner Bradsher, I'm so happy you enjoyed the novel. And thanks to T'Quila Smith, Michelle Sloan, and LaShan Davis-Carr for your support.

And to MonaLisa Lynconia McRae for a wonderful caged bird quote.

Now on to the readers: authors can't SURVIVE without you. Keep tweeting, continue to mention our books on social media, tote the books around to the bank, the grocery store, church (oops, never mind), and show it off to everyone you come across!!

Shout out to my mother (Margaret), sister (Adrienne), brother-in-law (Darryl), son (Brandon), and family members (Collins, Hamiltons, Barnetts) far and wide.

Also, I love to hear from people — industry folks, readers, prospective writers, people who have a dream but don't know how to make it come true — hit me up at booksbycyd@aol.com. Let's connect. Facebook Pages (plural), and Instagram (@cydneyrax).

Bookmark my links via www.cydneyrax .com

Forever grateful,
Cydney

Cydney Rax Social Media

Cydney Rax Facebook Page
https://www.facebook.com/Author
CydneyRax/

**Cydney Rax's Love and Revenge
Facebook Page**
https://www.facebook.com/CydneyRax
Novels/

**Cydney Rax's Sister Series Facebook
Page**
https://www.facebook.com/CydneyRax
SisterNovels/

Twitter
https://twitter.com/NeeCee48204

Instagram
https://www.instagram.com/cydneyrax/

ABOUT THE AUTHOR

Cydney Rax became obsessed with becoming a writer after reading Terry McMillan's *Disappearing Acts*. Her author dreams were realized through her eyebrow-raising debut novel, *My Daughter's Boyfriend*. Her novels include *My Husband's Girlfriend, Scandalous Betrayal, Brothers & Wives,* and *My Sister's Ex* (cited by *Essence®* as one of 2009's best reads). She has also contributed to the anthologies *Crush* and *Reckless.*

Born and raised in Detroit, Cydney graduated from Cass Technical High School and earned an undergraduate degree from Eastern Michigan University. She resides in Houston. Visit her online via Facebook, www.cydneyrax.com, or email her at booksbycyd@aol.com.